Annie Macmanus is an internationally renowned DJ and broadcaster. She was born in Dublin and attended Queen's University Belfast where she studied English Literature. She now lives in London. *Mother Mother* is her first book.

Praise for *Mother Mother*:

'I loved it. Annie Macmanus is writer whose understanding and capturing of human nature comes as easily to her as breathing'
Candice Carty-Williams

'Macmanus writes with flair and confidence rarely seen in a debut'
Sinéad Gleeson

'A brave and occasionally heartbreaking portrait of a family falling apart and the woman who's been holding them all together for far too long. Macmanus' debut novel is assured, evocative and, like her characters, full of gentle strength'
Jan Carson

'*Mother Mother* is a brilliant book … that explores the brutal legacy of addiction and the consequences of a deep grief left to stagnate'
Sara Cox

'Macmanus' immersive novel reminds us that the minutiae of daily struggles are always worth honing in on. . .This is a work of gilded melancholy that is going to take everyone by surprise'
Una Mullally

'I adored it. I loved the characters and stories, and I became completely immersed in that world. It's so beautifully written . . . Moving and brilliant'
Emily Eavis

MOTHER MOTHER

ANNIE MACMANUS

WILDFIRE

First published in 2021 by
WILDFIRE
an imprint of HEADLINE PUBLISHING GROUP

First published in paperback in 2022 by
WILDFIRE
an imprint of HEADLINE PUBLISHING GROUP

Epigraph: Heaney, S. (2001) Interviewed by Jim Dwyer for *The New York Times*, 2nd June.
Available at: https://www.nytimes.com/2001/06/02/books/rare-fuss-for-a-poet-of-the-
everyday.html (Accessed: 14th September 2020).

1

Cataloguing in Publication Data is available from the British Library

ISBN 978 1 4722 7592 9

Typeset in Dante MT by CC Book Production
Printed and bound in Great Britain by Clays Ltd, Elcograf S.p.A.

MIX
Paper from
responsible sources
FSC® C104740
www.fsc.org

Headline's policy is to use papers that are natural, renewable and
recyclable products and made from wood grown in well-managed forests
and other controlled sources. The logging and manufacturing processes are
expected to conform to the environmental regulations of the country of origin.

HEADLINE PUBLISHING GROUP
An Hachette UK Company
Carmelite House
50 Victoria Embankment
London EC4Y 0DZ

www.headline.co.uk
www.hachette.co.uk

For my mother, Rosetta Macmanus

'I'm not personally obsessed with death. At a certain age, the light that you live in is inhabited by the shades . . . I'm very conscious that people dear to me are alive in my imagination . . . These people are with me. It's just a stage of your life when the death of people doesn't banish them out of your consciousness. They're part of the light in your head.'

Seamus Heaney

PROLOGUE

MARY, PRESENT

She pulls up to the entrance and stops outside the gates. Leaning back as far as she can into her seat, she grips the wheel tightly, arms ruler-straight. Inside the small car, there is only her, and him, and the sound of her short breaths.

In the glare of her headlights, the ornate curls of wrought iron on the gates seem grotesque. She has never been to the cemetery so far into the night. Her head fills with memories: the slice of a shovel into soil, the growl of a mower starting up, the thick, stale air of the drying room . . .

She inhales deeply and slips out of the car, leaving the engine running, to unlock the gates with a large bunch of keys from her hoodie pocket. She rushes to the car, drives it inside, then stops again to close and lock the gates behind her before hurrying back to the car once more.

She drives slowly away from the formal flower beds at the main entrance and down the slight hill of the west road. The ground lights along the edges of the road are pathetic against the darkness, so she flicks her headlights on to full beam, and there are the rows and rows of stones, falling away into the black. She always felt calmed by the uniformity of this place. This spread of fields that holds the bones and ashes of tens of thousands of lives, all neatly arranged in their allotted spaces. She knows that every life ends with words. Every life – and the dreams that come with it. She thinks of the patterns of words now as she leans forwards into the wheel; how they are imprinted on her memory like street signs from childhood. How their repeated refrains echo all over this place, again and again: dearly beloved, sadly missed, in loving memory of.

She feels a tightness in her throat as the headlights fall on a copse of silver birches ahead. Their white bark gleams; they are ghosts, lying in wait. She quickly turns the knob to switch the lights off, and stares through the glass until the birch trunks appear as dark shapes in front of her again. She will carry on without light. She knows every corner and every turn, every stone and every word etched on to it.

Gone from our home but not from our hearts, good night and God bless, in our hearts you will always stay, loved and remembered every day, she danced into our hearts, to know her was to love her, together always, the Lord is my shepherd, gone but not forgotten, rest in peace. Peace, perfect peace.

She knows the pebbles, embedded with sparkles; the paper flags, the faded flowers in glass cases, the teddy bears and the fairy doors, the stone hearts and the angels, dead-eyed and staring right through you. You have to be careful on a windy day: the trinkets can blow away from the plots.

She sniffs and jolts her foot down on the accelerator so the car moves again. There is the glass surface of the lake on their right, reflecting the clouds as they jostle for front place. She pictures the moorhens curled up in their nests at the edges of the water, their heads twisted and tucked deep into their wings, their tiny feathered chests moving with their breaths. Is the heron that lived by the lake watching over them tonight? She always loved the heron, for her grace and her silence and her magisterial proportions as she took flight.

She slows the car to a stop where the road bends around to the right and allows the quiet to settle around her. A small handcrafted bumblebee air freshener sways slowly on its string from the rear-view mirror. She registers that her hands have stopped sweating now as she lifts him up from the passenger seat and draws him close to her chest. Her thoughts are fizzing and popping and she has to keep moving, she has to keep moving. She sniffs loudly to break the silence and, still clutching him, climbs out of the car.

They are at the very edge of the cemetery, where the paths are less worn. There are no designer pebbles here. The ground is uneven, and the rectangular grave plots tilt with it, like boats on gentle waves. She walks slowly and methodically, feeling out the ground with her feet, until they stop at a small marble stone. She stands over it, resting her chin on her chest, listening to the rustles and whispers of the branches of the ash tree a few metres away. She knows that the tree will be heavy with bunches of September seed – helicopters, they used to call them, for the way they spun through the air as they fell. She closes her eyes and hugs him close to her chest. She can feel her heart thumping frantically against him. After a few minutes, she steps up to the stone and sits down cross-legged directly in front of it, her knees wedged up against it. Carefully, she lays him on the grass beside her, and turns back to the stone.

It is a crude grey square with two roses etched on to the top right and left corners, flanking the calligraphy below. She traces the letters, allowing her fingers to move shakily through the grooves, and when she gets to the end of the final number, she wraps her arms around the top of the stone and pulls herself close. It is comforting in its cold, solid form. The air fills with misty rain and its light touch feels like a caress on her skin. The damp from the grass is seeping through her leggings to her legs and bottom. She allows her back to slump over into a hunch as she leans the full weight of her head against the stone. She starts to feel her breathing slow down into a regular rhythm. She is moored to this marble. Wet skin on wet stone. Soaking it all in.

CHAPTER 1

TJ, PRESENT

He lies still for a few seconds, blinking himself awake. There is a crack in the ceiling plaster and his eyes follow it to the window where the shadow of Black Mountain darkens the blind. His toes are hanging out of his Manchester United duvet and he pulls them in, rubbing his feet together to warm them. As he turns on his side to face the wardrobe, he squeezes his eyes shut and opens them wide again, as if to reset himself. He isn't used to waking up so abruptly at the weekend. Normally it is a long, slow sludge into the day, a repetitive pattern of dozing and yawning that ends with the inevitable phone scroll and hauling himself out of bed on account of her shouting at him from the bottom of the stairs. He strains his ears to listen for her. Normally her noise is filling up the house in some way. He pulls himself up to sitting, rubs his eyes and tilts back his head to shout.

Ma-aa.

There is no reply. There's a scratchiness in the air, as if it's charged with something. He glances down at his phone on the bedside table. It tells him that it is Saturday, 15 September and it is 11.30 a.m. He has a night off work tonight. This is all normal. It is not normal for her to be out on a Saturday morning. He briefly contemplates the lump of hash wrapped in tinfoil in a matchbox in his bedside drawer. Not on a weekend, he thinks. Not when she's going to be around. He climbs out of bed and pulls on a pair of green tracksuit bottoms lying in a heap on the floor. His movements are reflected in the mirror stuck to the wardrobe door and he stands still for a moment to inspect himself. His chest is concave and hairless. He inhales and pulls his shoulders back, trying to breathe some broadness into himself. His ma says he is growing in fast forward. He hopes that soon he can start growing out as well as up. He pulls open his bedroom door and shouts again.

Ma-aa.

He walks across the tiny landing space into her room and up to her bedroom window, and peers out from behind the net curtain. Slate roofs and satellite dishes stretch into the distance. No sign of her car. He pulls his phone out of his tracksuit bottoms pocket and unlocks it with his finger. She is at the top of his list of favourites.

Ma.

He presses the phone button and then the speaker button and stands with the phone held by his mouth, looking out the window. He rubs his eyes, which still feels puffy from sleep, and scratches at the light fluff above his top lip. The street is busy enough for a Saturday, he thinks. A new family has moved in up the road and the dad is out washing his car with a hose and a bucket. Every so often, he flicks the hose towards the twin girls who are hovering nearby and they screech with glee and run away. He can see the clothes dangling off the washing line in the Kavanaghs' back garden. Big granny knickers and the lot. Right below him, old Mrs McGuinness is gliding past. Her hand trembles on her walking stick. Her son was killed in a bomb on the Falls Road – he couldn't have been much older than TJ is now.

Hello, this is Mary, leave a message, please.

It's her formal voice, all clipped and flat. He opens his mouth to leave a message and then suddenly feels self-conscious and hangs up the phone. He takes the stairs two at a time. Four of his long lolloping strides and he's in the kitchen. The silhouettes of his ma's plants are casting their shadows over the black and white tiled floor. He stands in the middle of it now, looking for signs of her. The calendar hangs by the fridge, with her scrawled handwriting all over it.

Belfast Tech clearing day!! on Tuesday.

Aunt Bridget birthday, flanked by two shakily drawn stars, on Wednesday.

Today is left blank. He pictures her busying herself around the space, humming along to the radio, inspecting her plants in that intense way she does, holding the pot right up to her face and turning it around slowly in the light as if there are dark secrets hidden amongst the leaves. He opens the fridge. Maybe she's gone to get groceries. He sees bacon and eggs, tomatoes and yoghurts. He takes out the milk and fetches a box of cereal from the cupboard above. He gets a spoon and a bowl and flicks the switch on the electric kettle. The teapot sits clean and untouched by the radio. Has she not even had breakfast? He lowers himself down to sit on the bench and allows his face to drop into his hands.

A queasy feeling creeps into his stomach. Could she be upset with him? Because of last night? The kettle clicks in a cloud of steam and he sits up suddenly. He'll go and find her at the park.

CHAPTER 2

MARY, 1990

West Belfast had been softening under relentless sunshine for two solid weeks. The last days of August seemed to melt into each other, punctuated by the occasional sound of gunfire from the barracks and the tinny ring of the ice cream van. Mary lay on her stomach in the small patch of long grass at the back of the house. She was nine years old, with a small wash of freckles across her nose and hair the colour of fox fur. The garden was no bigger than a bus shelter and was bordered with stinging nettles, but she loved the feeling of being in the middle of it. Like she was part of somewhere else. She was crafting a daisy chain, using her nails to gently push holes through the stems and threading the flowers into a delicate line. She could hear Bryan Adams' cracked voice drifting through the late afternoon haze from a window in the distance.

There was the hammer of footsteps as a group of boys ran up the alleyway towards the main street. She flinched and ducked instinctively. The alleyway ran along the back of her street and in the holidays it was a busy by-way to the green. Now there came three soldiers, talking loudly, breathing heavily, taking off their helmets to shake away the sweat. The source of the boys' haste. She kept her head down, fixed the two end daisies on the line into each other and carefully pulled the circle over her head. With the soldiers out of sight, she pulled herself up and walked inside.

They were the second-last house on the street. The kitchen was tucked into the back corner; it was brown and beige chequered linoleum floor tiles, and walls grubby with the residue of years of grease and smoke. The bedrooms were upstairs and Sean's room was the biggest. It looked out over the front of the house. They used to share, but now Mary slept in the box room above the kitchen. It was normal for her to go a whole day without seeing Sean in the school holidays. She knew he was out there somewhere, in a pair of cut tracksuit bottoms and his T-shirt hanging off him, begging a soldier for a hold of his gun, shouting from a wall or a tree, presiding over a football match or a fight. He was always in the middle of a huddle of heads. He stayed out, eating at friends' houses, or not eating at all, coming home covered in dirt and sometimes blood to stuff pieces of bread and butter into his mouth before running out again. There were no half measures with Sean.

Her father's room was at the back of the house, looking out over the alley. They didn't go into his room. He was there now, sleeping off the night shift. He worked in the sorting office of the Belfast postal service. Mary understood the grave responsibility her father carried with his job. To be in charge of all those letters and packages going to the right places. One slip of his hand and a life could be changed forever. He'd be up and out to the Glen pub soon. Over the course of the summer, she had noticed that her father's drunkenness had overtaken his sobriety once and for all. She wasn't sure if he was drinking more, or if maybe the drink had just become part of him now, seeping through his veins into his brain, turning everything inside him the colour of cloudy stout. She knew when he had gone too far from the second he walked into the house, from the heaviness of a door slam or his footsteps stumbling on the stairs. She knew to move around him and behind him, to take shelter from him as if from a biting wind.

She walked up the hall and pulled the front door open and sat on the front step, wrapping her arms around her shins and resting her chin on her knees while she waited. Mrs Kavanagh was always first. Her front door opened and her head popped out, looking from side to side. She hesitated a few seconds and then she shuffled to the gate in her slippers and leaned against the post. Then she lifted her face and bellowed her children's names into the air.

Connor!

Cian!

Niamh!

Bronagh!

Dinner time!

NOW!

Mary watched her as she took a box of cigarettes out of her pocket and lit one and drew on it deeply, closing her eyes in the pleasure of it. She watched Mrs Kavanagh's face soften as she saw her kids run towards her, one by one. She was fascinated by these daily declarations, these names in the air, bouncing around the estate night after night. Fascinated by the mothers themselves. She thought of the photo of her mother by Sean's bed. Her back was turned, and her head looked over her shoulder at the camera: eyebrows raised, mouth set in a slight smile, like she had been caught in the act of thinking about something that pleased her. Mary practised that expression often in front of the bathroom mirror.

Three doors down, another mother was yelling at her children now, too. And another from the street next to theirs. Here was Connor running towards his mother, talking to himself.

Jesus Christ, Connor, look at the dirt of ye.

Then Cian.

Where are your shoes?

In Jonty's garden, Mammy.

Mrs Kavanagh flicked her fingers towards the end of the road, still squeezing the cigarette.

Well, go back and get them, right now!

Mary had observed the children of the estate becoming louder as the summer holidays drew to a close. She saw them out the window, running screeching and shoeless, skipping

12

behind the soldiers until they lost their sense of humour and ordered them away home.

Then the tiny twins, Niamh and Bronagh.

She watched Mrs Kavanagh herd her children up the path before stubbing her cigarette out on the wall and standing on it with her slipper. Before turning to go back into her house, Mrs Kavanagh saw Mary and lifted a hand in the air in greeting. Mary smiled and waved.

Y'all right, Mary McConnell?

Aye, Mrs Kavanagh.

She stood up, shy then, and went to the kitchen to put her sandals on, wondering how it would feel to have someone shout her name into the air with such conviction. The home phone clanged through from the hall and made her jump. She ran to pick it up.

Hello?

Mary, it's Bridget. I need to speak to your father.

Right. He's in bed . . .

You'll have to wake him up so.

Hokay.

Daddy!

She called up the stairs.

Aunt Bridget's on the phone!

She clutched the phone, unsure whether to make conversation with Bridget while they waited. A phonecall from her was rare these days. Bridget was their father's sister, and she had looked after them from when Mary was two until she

13

was five years old. She took up a lot of space in all Mary's early childhood memories. She was a big woman, with a small, beak-like mouth that rarely smiled. It was always very clear to them that Bridget was not a replacement mother, mainly due to her relentless insistence on this point.

I'm not your mother, you will not get away with that behaviour with me!

Bridget liked order. She cooked and cleaned and taught them how to do the same. She used to come to the house, about once a fortnight, to show Mary how to cook the meals her father and brother would want to eat.

Here was her father now, making his slow descent down the stairs. He could look like a desert islander after a sleep; the whites of his eyes a surprise in the mess of hair on his head and face. He would have been taller, but his neck folded into his shoulders, giving him a vulture-like stoop. He stood on the bottom step and stretched his arms up. She watched in silence as his mouth gaped open, suspended in a long yawn, and his T-shirt rode up to expose a rounded and rock-hard beer belly. When he flopped his arms back down, he took the phone from Mary.

Bridget.

She watched his brow furrow as Bridget talked, and she watched him pull the phone cable under the living room door and push it closed behind him. She pressed her cheek up to the wood of the door and strained to hear.

He was stood on top of the car? Was it still burning?

Where was it?

Jesus. He shouldn't be that far away.

There was a long pause. Then.

Right, Bridget. Well, thanks for letting me know.

Yes. Yes, I will, of course.

Mary raced back to the kitchen, then opened a tin of beans from the cupboard and tipped them into a saucepan. There was no movement from the living room. She pulled on a cardigan and closed the front door behind her, then set off down the road. She didn't dare look back into the living room window for fear of catching a glimpse of his expression. Across the road, she spied the Barry brothers marching towards their house. She shouted across at them.

Is Sean on the green?

They nodded in unison at her. The green was a small patch of grass and trees, stretching about half an acre at the top of their road. You could jump over the wall from the main road and walk straight through it to get to their street. It was empty of bodies this evening, apart from two older boys leaning against a wall on the other side, sharing something to smoke. She made her way towards the line of trees at the far end.

Sean?

She stood at the bottom of the tallest tree, staring up into the leaves, searching for the shape of him until she saw movement in the branches and bare legs clambering down. He landed deftly on the bare earth, flicked his hair out of his eyes and returned her smile with a half-smile. He was eleven years old now and stretching out of his clothes. He would be going to secondary school in two weeks, leaving her behind to finish her last two years at St John's Primary. They walked home side by side. The kerbs were painted in coloured sections, green, white and orange. Up ahead, some men sat in a row along the kerb, clutching cans of beer. Their naked backs were lobster-pink and shining with sweat. Mary spoke first.

Bridget called. She told Daddy something about you and a car.

What the fuck?

Sean turned to her. His face was grubby up close.

Shite, she must have seen me.

At the house, Mary opened the door using the key around her neck and immediately caught the thin, musky scent of her father's spray deodorant.

He's away out, she said, and Sean's shoulders relaxed. They ate their beans on toast on the sofa in front of the television as the helicopters started up outside.

As she took his plate, Mary asked, Don't you need to get a new uniform for school?

He sighed out and rolled his eyes. Sean hadn't talked about going to secondary school at all to Mary. She felt nervous for him. From when she was four years old, she had walked to school with her brother. She remembered her first morning because Bridget plaited her hair into two thick, neat plaits and tied white ribbons around the bottom of them. And she remembered Sean then taking her hand to walk her through the estate, and up the long hill to school. There was a wall up by the main road that Sean sometimes climbed over. He used to give Mary a leg up first and she would sit on top waiting while he pulled himself over, before helping her down the other side. When it rained, they squeezed on to the bus. The school was one building, split down the middle, each side a mirror image of the other, one for the boys and one for the girls. As he got taller, Sean sped up as they got closer to the school gates, walking just a few steps ahead of her so he wouldn't have to acknowledge her daily goodbye. She still whispered it to herself as she walked behind him.

See ye, Sean, have a lovely day.

She was comforted that his new school was in the same direction from the estate as her primary school. They could still travel together every morning. Sean shifted his weight on the sofa.

Yeah, I have to get a whole new one and books and everything.

You better tell Daddy.

His face darkened and he spoke to the TV screen.

He's gonna be raging with me after today.

She looked at him with a serious expression.

Do it in the morning. Sean, you can't help needing a new uniform! He can't say anything to that!

Mary slept deeply when the helicopters were up; their thick drone drowned out any dreams. But she woke with a start around midnight, to the sound of the door slamming.

She could hear the uneven footsteps of her father making his way down the hall. She prayed Sean had gone to his bedroom, but there was his voice directly below her, still high and unbroken, speaking short clusters of words she couldn't fathom. Her father's growl rose up through the ceiling and she covered her mouth with her hand. There was a loud crash and the sound of glass breaking and then the back door slamming as her father went out for a cigarette. She sat up in her bed, holding on to the edges of her matress as if it was moving and she needed the balance. She heard Sean's slow ascent of the stairs. She heard his bedroom door close. She waited until everything was completely still, and then she tiptoed out to the hall and across the landing.

The streetlights outside the window were the only light in the room. He lay on his bed with his hand over his eye. She saw tracks of tears on his face. He stayed looking up, not acknowledging her presence until she reached out to move his hand away from his eye. He flinched at her touch, but immediately softened and let his arm go limp. She held his hand firmly, squeezed it and slowly moved it down to lie on the mattress. Then she saw his eye. It was swollen shut, already crimson from the blow.

Oh, Sean!

She rushed to the bathroom and ran freezing cold water over a face cloth, then came back. Sean moaned in pain as she folded the cloth and laid it over his eye. She whispered, her voice wavering, I'll go and get ye some paracetamol.

Before she opened his door, she pulled her shoulders back and tightened the belt of her dressing gown. She clenched her fists tight, digging her nails into her palms as she quietly padded her way down the stairs, past the crooked framed photo of Granny Olive on the wall. The living room door was open and she saw her father's feet stretched out in front of the TV, his hand cradling a can of Heineken. She moved swiftly into the kitchen. The glass butter dish was smashed and lying in pieces all over the floor.

She quietly tut-tutted as she tiptoed over to the back door and slipped her pale feet into Sean's trainers, which were sitting on the doormat. She clumped around in his oversized shoes, cleaning up the mess with the dustpan and brush, then poured a glass of water and got the paracetamol from the first-aid box. She made a mental note to keep her own first-aid box in her room.

She turned around and then jumped at the sight of her father in the doorway. He was staring at her with a frightened look in his eyes. She could see his shirt straining under his buttons as he breathed. She saw him look to her hand.

For his eye, she said. She kicked off Sean's shoes and hurried past her father into the hall. As she turned to go up the stairs, she saw her father steady himself in the door frame and cover his face with his hands.

The following morning, Mary hummed nervously in the kitchen, cooking breakfast for her father and brother. Her voice sing-songed.

One egg or two, Daddy?

Two'll do.

Their father was bent over a newspaper, wearing the polyester trousers and short-sleeved shirt of his Royal Mail uniform. He leaned back to make room for Mary to put his plate down and immediately started stabbing at his food with a fork. Sean was just finishing his fry and quickly stood. He dropped his plate into the sink with such force that the plate cracked in two. Their father looked up.

Would ye fucking slow down.

He glared at his son.

Shit, muttered Sean now as he lifted the pieces of the plate out of the sink. His eye had flowered overnight into a deep purple colour.

Here.

Mary handed him a plastic bag to put the pieces in and he carried it out the door to put in the bin. When he returned, he sat down at the kitchen table next to their father, fidgeting.

Da, I start at St Michael's in two weeks and I need a new uniform. Here's the letter.

He unfolded a piece of paper on the table and laid it beside the newspaper. Their father stopped chewing his toast to glance at the letter. His face shone with a thin gleam of sweat. He stared at the amount on the bottom of the page for a long time.

Are these uniforms gold-plated or something?

He looked up at his son, then, and fixed his gaze on to his bruised eye. He closed his eyes for a few seconds before speaking.

I'll put it out for you on Friday. Remember what Bridget used to say. Buy big. And son.

Sean looked at him.

Your eye.

He looked down at his fist then, as if it was a foreign thing on his arm, and for a split second, Mary thought he might cry. Then he focused back on his son.

Sean, you have to stop this hooligan shite. You'll get community justice. You'll be beaten to a pulp.

Sean swallowed and looked at his feet.

Five days later, on a sunny Saturday afternoon, Sean walked in the back door with flushed cheeks and two plastic bags. He tried it all on for Mary in his room. A dark grey polyester jumper with the folds still in it. A white non-iron shirt and a clip-on navy tie. Grey flannel trousers with the crease set in down the front and black shoes, one size too big so he could grow into them. He bought a new blue backpack for all his books. Mary opened and closed the zip of the bag, slipping her hand into all the compartments to feel out the space of them. She hovered beside him as he carefully wrote his name on the labels inside the different parts of his uniform. She stood close to him, watching him impatiently flick his hair out of his eyes as he wrote.

Sean, you'll have to cut your hair. I can do it for you.

As if!

Honestly, Sean, let me try! I can use those thin scissors in the kitchen.

21

He sat on a stool in front of the mirror in their bathroom, with a pillowcase round his neck to catch the hair. It took her half an hour to do it, tongue curled around her lip in deep concentration, and when she was finished, he asked, Do you think it's okay?

His face was all there, every inch of it: crooked front teeth, freckles on his nose with dead skin peeling off the tip. The skin around his eye was a faded yellowy-green colour.

It looks proper. Like a proper haircut, she said.

He looked at himself in the mirror and touched the bruising around his eye softly, testing it for pain.

Is it sore?

Not any more, no.

He sighed.

Da is fucking miserable.

Maybe he misses Mammy, Mary said quietly, wiping the hair off his neck with a cloth.

Sean touched the palms of his hands to his cheeks and rested his face in his hands.

She always said my hands were warm as toast, he said. You know, when she held my hand.

Mary stared at her brother.

Let me feel them.

She wrapped her hand around his and the corners of her mouth turned upwards ever so slightly.

They *are* warm, Sean.

Sean stayed on the stool while she cleaned up around him.

CHAPTER 3

MARY, 1994

They walked up the hill together on a brutally cold October morning. The sky was a thicket of dark cloud. They passed the care home and a house with tricolour flags hanging limp out of every window. Sean wore his layers of grey, tie hanging loose around his neck. Mary wore her royal blue blazer and tartan skirt. Her hair was brushed back from her face and hanging over her shoulders. She pushed her hands under her arms to keep them warm. They said nothing until he stopped her at the corner of the Taylors' house.

Mary, you go on. I'm gonna call on Paddy and go with him, okay?

She squinted at him in sullen silence. It had never occurred to her that she would not walk to school with her brother. She already went home on her own, squeezing on to the bus to avoid the walk past the Suffolk estate. On a bad day, if you walked with your uniform on, you could get stones thrown at you, and the soldiers never helped. She had seen Sean from the bus the day before with Paddy McGrath from the estate and two other boys she didn't know. He was walking different, pushing himself higher on the soles of his feet, flailing his arms around. She watched as he shouted something in Paddy's ear and pushed him hard in the back. She saw Paddy jerk forwards and just manage to stay on his feet. Paddy laughed loudly, but didn't push back.

Sean was walking backwards away from her, his eyebrows raised in expectation.

You'll be grand, Mary! See you later, okay?

A magpie squawked nearby. She spoke quietly.

Okay, Sean.

She hurried up the main road, frantically humming a breathy repetition of a Take That song that she had heard on the radio that morning. Her blue canvas backpack bounced gently off her lower back with every stride. She tried to focus on the rhythm of it as she sped up her pace, humming herself all the way to the gates of St Tiarnan's School and drifting into the current of blue blazers.

The building was set back from the road, three stories of red brick and glass, with several extensions and prefabs stretching out behind and to the sides, trying to accommodate the eight hundred girls who went there from all over West Belfast. Mary was in her second year, and there were things about it that really suited her. She felt safe being part of a system of rules that didn't bend. She liked the purpose of homework, and the definitive nature of deadlines. But the formal distance between the teachers and the pupils at St Tiarnan's unsettled her.

In her first year, she had stayed out of the way of her schoolmates, quietly observing the ease of their chatter and the natural flow of their movements from the edges of the playground. This year, Louise O'Mara had joined her class and everything had changed.

Mary flinched as she felt a pair of hands cover her eyes from behind.

Guess whoooooo?

She turned around to see Louise's face grinning inanely about six inches from her own. Her skin was the colour of milk, her hair a wispy white blond. Her slight overbite gave her face a sweet goofiness that Mary loved. Mary burst into self-conscious giggles.

Jeez, Louise, you gave me a fright!

Louise took Mary's hand and marched her towards their classroom, merrily swinging their clasped hands back and forth. Mary rolled her eyes and smiled. Louise was so at ease in her own skin, it was like she had lived in her own body for a hundred lifetimes. It had taken a while for Mary to get her head around Louise's public displays of affection. There was something about the idea of handholding, of the sense of her belonging to someone that she was breathlessly attracted to. But she couldn't get used to the act of it.

Well? What's the story?

Louise looked down at her, still grinning.

Sean ditched me on the way to school. That'll be it now.

Louise turned to her, a look of concern sweeping over her face. She squeezed Mary's hand in hers.

Did ye get any hassle?

Naw, it was grand. I'll probably get the bus now, though, just to be safe.

At least it's warmer. Tell Sean he has to give you the money for it. Your hair is gorgeous down like that.

Louise was looking at her with genuine admiration. Mary immediately felt the colour rise in her cheeks and swallowed down the urge to tell her to shut up. There was heat and rage in her when she had to think about what she looked like. Lately she had been whiling away the lonely hours at home after school standing naked from the waist up in front of the big bathroom mirror. She studied herself carefully: green eyes, dull orange hair, two tiny lumps that you couldn't even call breasts yet. She felt that everything about her was embarrassingly plain. She wanted to fold herself up and slide into the smallest space in every room.

As they walked into class, Mary gently pulled her hand out of Louise's grip. Louise paraded through the rows of desks to the front left of the class and Mary followed.

Hey, Lanky Louise.

Niamh O'Mahony, a big-shouldered girl with a face full of acne shouted at her from the back of the class.

A wave of nervous laughter washed over the classroom.

Louise gave Niamh the finger as she swung her bag off her shoulder and slammed it down on to her desk. Monday morning was double Geography. Louise sat in the front row and Mary sat directly behind her. She liked being able to see her all the time.

As Louise took out her books, she leaned back and whispered in Mary's ear.

Hey, are you wearing your you-know-what?

Mary smiled and nodded. Last Friday after school, Louise and her mother Rita had taken Mary with them on a trip to buy a bra. They had gone to the Marks and Spencer on Donegall Place and stood side by side, listening solemnly as Rita explained how bras worked. The number and letter codes of the sizing was a whole new language to learn, and Mary felt overwhelming relief when Rita's mum bought them both a set of three T-shirt bras that didn't have any fasteners. As Rita drove them out of the city centre that evening, she sat in the back, fingering her new purchases, feeling nervous excitement. She looked at Rita in her driving mirror to say thank you before getting out of the car at the bus stop. It was hard to convey how she felt in words. Rita smiled at her and told her to hurry up and get out or they'd be in trouble.

Rita and Louise lived on Arndale Street. It was one of the many streets that fell away from the west side of the Falls Road, sloping down into the looming shadow of Black Mountain. Louise's house sat at the very end of the road.

After school, Mary and Louise walked the fifteen minutes down the length of Arndale, chattering and laughing the whole way. Mary had a bunch of flowers carefully packed into a shoe box inside her bag, picked from the park the day before, and put in water on her windowsill overnight to keep fresh. They were her way of saying thank you to Rita for buying her the bra. The girls skipped up the drive and knocked on the door, giggling as Rita opened it.

Ach, here they are, the clever twins!

Rita had a way of smiling without moving her mouth.

Get those shoes off and hang your coats up and youse can do your homework on the table down here.

Rita, I brought these for ye . . .

Mary stuck her arm out with the flowers, a little limp and now hovering under Rita's face.

Ach, Mary!

Rita took the flowers and bent down, giving Mary a hug with her spare arm. Mary held her breath. She was loosening up to the affection now and she looked forward to the sensations of it.

We'll put them right here on the table.

Mary took her coat off and hung it on the hook, then walked back into the kitchen to start her homework. Rita was pouring milk into a pan. A baby boy was sitting in the corner of the kitchen in his nappy, all fleshy folds and curly brown ringlets, warbling a continuous stream of noises and syllables. Rita was a childminder by day.

28

Ach, look at him all serious like he's having a proper conversation! Mary exclaimed.

Rita said, Connor makes perfect sense to himself, it's just a shame I haven't a holy clue what he's talking about.

Mary smiled.

Louise pulled her tie over her head and shuffled in beside Mary on the bench. She took a long drink of water from her glass and let out a performative belch for her friend and mother.

Beautiful, Louise. Just beautiful.

Rita shook her head.

What's homework today, then?

Mary opened her Geography textbook.

Tectonic plates.

Louise sat back against the wall of the kitchen.

Mammy, our Geography teacher Mr O'Connell actually snorts when he talks and now that we've noticed it, it's so hard not to laugh.

Rita looked perplexed.

He's like a human pig!

Louise stood up from the bench and threw her shoulders back and stretched her head towards the ceiling. She clasped her hands behind her back and strode around the linoleum.

Now class <snort> if you open your textbooks to page fifty-six <snort> you will see <snort> that the world is actually <snort> round and not flat <snort>.

Mary and Rita laughed.

How does he not notice? Rita asked.

29

It's like he honestly doesn't know, Mammy!

Louise sat back down.

Like, how could you live with that every day, like, sit at the dinner table with him, and not say anything, like? His poor fucking family!

Language, Louise. Jesus Christ, I'd better watch out for that snort at the parent teachers' meeting, Rita deadpanned, cup of tea hovering in front of her mouth as she leaned against the counter.

Mary giggled.

Three hours later, after oven pizza and ice cream, Mary went to the coat rack again. Connor had been collected and Rita was upstairs with with Louise's little brother Frank.

Louise hugged Mary goodbye tightly.

Bye bye, darlin'. Will you be all right getting home?

Of course.

If anyone comes near you, just . . .

Hyaaaaaaaa!

Louise clenched her teeth and karate-kicked the front door.

Mary laughed as she stepped out into the dark. A few weeks earlier, she and Louise had been stopped by a soldier, who asked them all sorts of creepy questions about their underwear and what they wore to bed at night. Louise managed to excuse them by saying they had to be home for their tea. Mary remembered walking away from the soldier shaking all over, bracing her back for the bullet, and the two of them, in perfect unison, breaking into a sprint as soon as they got round the corner out of his sight.

When she reached the bustle of the Falls Road, she saw a black taxi and stuck her hand out. It was always either a bus or a black hack home from Louise's, whatever came first. Both were the same price, but the black hacks meant closer proximity to strangers, breathing on to each other and asking questions. The taxi came to a stop and she climbed into the back, nodding shyly at the other passengers as she squeezed into the middle seat. A woman opposite her was holding a young girl on her lap. She stared at Mary with enormous eyes. Mary smiled briefly at the girl and her mother, and focused her eyes on the floor to replay the scenes from Louise's house in her head.

She considered Arndale Road her own private case study for how family life should be. Louise's father had left them when they were young and had moved away. Then Rita had met someone else and had Frank. Frank's dad worked in Africa, so was rarely around. Unlike her own single-parent family, Arndale Street was always filled with colour and noise. There was singing and screeching and chasing each other around the house. There were legs intertwined on the sofa and arms slung casually around shoulders. Louise moaned about her mammy a lot, but she didn't seem to live in constant yearning for her other parent like Mary did. Mary thought of Louise and Rita's arguments, of which she had seen a few. How they could rage wildly at each other, screaming insults and slamming doors, and be laughing again the next day. All these melodramatic theatrics, like trapeze artists at the circus with their safety net underneath. Rita was Louise's confidante. Her constant. Rita was home.

When she got out of the taxi just before the roundabout, she made herself forget Arndale Street and focus on where she was going. She thought about the contents of the food cupboards as she turned off the main road and into the estate. They had barley and carrots and an onion, she knew. She would make soup for tomorrow, she decided as she quickened her pace, trying not to allow the darkness to frighten her.

The air on the estate smelt of burning peat. She saw glimpses of faces lit up by TV screens through Venetian blinds and the odd front door hanging open with people smoking on front doorsteps. Number forty-two was always identifiable by its lack of light. In the front yard, the weeds grew tall and wiry up through the cracks in the paving stones. They blossomed yellow flowers, so Mary didn't pull them out. She knew very little about her own mother, but there were some concrete facts that she clung on to, and one of those was that she liked the garden and the flowers that grew in it. Her name was Mary, too. She died when Mary was two years old. Sean told her that her brain drowned in blood. When she was small, Mary spent a lot of her time wondering when her mother would come back, like Aunt Bridget told her Jesus did from the dead.

She opened the door tentatively and paused a second on the step to listen for telltale noises. She felt the wave of disappointment swell through her at the cold silence of the house. She knew there were places Sean went after school with his friends, patches of land he could occupy comfortably without being told to move away. The corners of the park, behind the church and, most recently, an alleyway down by their local shop. She knew her daddy would be at work or at the pub. She threw her bag on the kitchen table and ran upstairs to her room, pulling herself up by the bannisters. Humming loudly, she changed into some tracksuit bottoms and a knitted baggy jumper. On her way back to the kitchen, she went to Sean's room and pressed play on his stereo. Then she went to the living room and turned the telly up loud, and lastly she turned on the radio in the kitchen. She put on her old apron and began to peel the carrots.

CHAPTER 4

TJ, PRESENT

His mother's voice is loud in his head as the door slams behind him.

TJ, you don't know your own strength!

He walks at a quick pace up the road and out of the estate towards the bus stop. His hands are wedged deep into the pockets of his jacket and his hood is up. He's not in the mood for small talk. As he turns the corner on to the main road, he can see the bus nearing the stop, and he runs across the road, breaks into a jog and sticks his hand in the air in an awkward wave. The driver stops and TJ nods in gratitude as he swings himself into a seat at the back. He is breathing heavily. He has to get back into football again, he thinks as he leans his head against the window. At the sound of a muted beep, he pulls his phone out of his pocket. It's Aiden.

What you saying, big man?

His fingers hesitate over his phone. Aiden works as a

barman at Devaney's pub in town, and had taken on TJ as his 'fun apprentice' when TJ got a part-time job there at the start of the year. At twenty-two years old, and with his own flat, Aiden was a new type of friend. He made TJ's school friends look boring. They were all starting university, getting drunk on cider at freshers' week. Aiden was a professional: he got wrecked like other people ate dinner, with a much more sophisticated list of ingredients. He had been responsible for the majority of TJ's hangovers this summer, including the one that sparked the argument with his ma.

I have a job for you, Aiden had said as they pulled their coats on, on their way out the door of Devaney's on Thursday night.

Aye? TJ raised his eyebrows sceptically.

New skunk. I need someone to smoke it with.

Ha! Don't be springing that on me now!

Listen, big man. We've had four pints each. This can be our dessert. What's your favourite dessert?

Aiden cocked his head at TJ. His cheekbones jutted out sharply under his eyes.

Eh, I think, banoffee pie.

See yiz! shouted Aiden to no one in particular, and pulled the door closed behind them. He stopped and turned to TJ.

This is going to taste like banoffee pie from the fucking gods.

They walked up Ormeau Avenue to Aiden's rented flat. He lived on the ground floor of a terraced house on Cairo Street, in the heart of the Holylands, a cluster of shabby streets tucked in between Queen's University, the Botanic

Gardens and the River Lagan. The flat stank of un-emptied ashtrays, and the kitchen wall held a picture of Donald Trump that doubled up as a darts board. They ended up slouched into each other on Aiden's couch in a fog of skunk smoke with Aiden merrily leading them into a YouTube wormhole. Aiden had a little goatee, which he was particularly proud of, and when the skunk hit TJ's brain and Aiden stopped making sense to him, he had to focus really hard on Aiden's moustache moving up and down, watching it dance on his top lip with the rapid movement of his talking. At some point, TJ tipped into sleep and woke up with Aiden shouting his name and laughing maniacally in his face.

TJ sat in the back of a taxi that Aiden had called, trying to contain the overwhelming sense of spinning in his head until he realised they weren't moving any more, and the driver was politely waiting for him to get out of the car. He fell into bed in a haze and woke up at 2 p.m.

When his ma came home from work later that evening, TJ was lying horizontally across the sofa in his tracksuit bottoms, with a carton of milk in one hand and a tube of Pringles in the other, watching a quiz show. She walked into the room, looked at him, then turned around and walked straight out without missing a beat. After rolling his eyes and tipping the end of the tube of Pringles into his mouth, he followed her into the kitchen. When she turned to face him, he blocked her path. He was six inches taller than her last time they measured it.

Ma, I think you forgot to say hello?

TJ, have you seen the state of the house? Have you noticed that you are drinking milk from the carton? Have you smelt yourself?

His ma was staring up at him with her handbag still over her shoulder and her keys in her hand. Her nose was screwed up as if she was moving through a rotten stench. Her skin had a doll-like shine to it and was free of make-up. She wore zipped-up overalls to work, like you'd see a mechanic wear. And a big woolly hat that TJ had christened 'the mushroom'.

No, I have not smelt myself, Ma. Have you checked your hair for leaves recently?

The hat was off, but her hair was still flattened. She rolled her eyes as he reached over to pull out a small piece of brown leaf from behind her right ear. In one fluid movement, he put the leaf in the bin, turned to the sink and started rinsing off his dirty dishes. She stood in the middle of the kitchen, slowly unwinding her scarf from her neck, and walked out to the hall to hang up her coat and bag. When she walked back in, she went to the radio and flicked it on, then turned on the oven. He was at the dishwasher, unloading the plates and cutlery. He stepped back to make space for her to get the chopping board from behind the kettle. He saw her take out two white onions from the food cupboard and pulled the knife from the dishwasher, holding it aloft for her. For a while there was just the sound of the clinking of dishes and the blunt thud of her knife on the board. Until his mother spoke.

It's been three months, TJ. We're in September. At some point you have to take responsibility for this year.

Her head was down over the board. He had stopped unloading and was standing with a plate in his hand, his eyes pulled wide in exasperation.

I'm aware, Ma. I'm SO aware. I just need a bit of time to figure it all out . . .

TJ. You don't have the luxury of figuring things out. You apply for jobs. You get in there, to anyone who will take you, for a proper job.

Jesus Christ, Ma. Half-yelling, he turned around to face her.

She was ready for him, standing with the knife in one hand and half an onion in the other.

Don't bring him into it, son. You are collecting glasses in a pub. You have more to give to the world than this.

Ma, I'm eighteen. I can do what I want.

She didn't raise her voice to meet his.

TJ, I want to see you be the best you can be . . .

Says the woman who works in a fuckin' park.

There was a second of silence. She stood, staring at him, and then quickly swivelled round to the chopping board again.

Ma?

Ma.

She didn't turn around.

Ma, I . . . sorry, Ma . . . but maybe I want to GO somewhere. This is the time where you're supposed to do that stuff.

She was chopping the onions again. She didn't turn around when she spoke.

Go where?

I – I want to go to New York.

Right.

She sighed, and wiped her right eye with the back of her hand. Her voice was flat.

Is there a reason why you want to go to New York specifically?

It's just the coolest city, isn't it? He said it as if he had travelled the world three times over.

Her phone rang then, and made them both jump. It was comically loud.

Jesus, Ma.

He laughed as he picked up the phone from the table; he was trying to lighten the mood.

Are you gone deaf or something?

He looked at the screen.

Unknown number.

He handed it to her.

She took it from him and blinked at the glowing screen for a second, before hanging up the call.

He watched her closely.

Why didn't you answer it?

She spoke to the wall with glassy eyes. You have to empty the outside bin. It's almost overflowing.

He narrowed his eyes at her as he went to the large green

recycling box tucked behind the hall door. He walked outside and emptied it into the blue bin in the front drive, then came back inside. In the kitchen, he saw his mother standing over the kitchen counter, head bowed, pinching the bridge of her nose.

Ma?

She didn't turn around.

It's okay. It's just the onions. You go and chill. I'll leave the pie in the oven for you.

He did as he was told. When he came down a few hours later, she wasn't there, so he ate the pie in front of the TV. Later that night, he hesitated in front of her bedroom, his clenched fist suspended a few inches from the door, but he never knocked. Instead, he lay in the dark and went over the conversation again and again. He had been dreading telling her about New York. At least it was out there now. At least she knew where his head was at. Again and again, he saw the tension in her face collapsing as she turned away from him to face the counter. Lying there in the dark, he made silent promises to her. Promises of warm hugs, promises to make her laugh, even to take her for breakfast.

It was only last night, he thinks now, looking at his watch as he walks up the road towards Ballybawn Park. It's not too late to apologise. He sticks his chest out and pulls his shoulders back as he walks through the main gate. He pictures where she will be. She will look tiny under the trees, and she will be working tirelessly, probably moving piles of leaves into green garden sacks with her long-handled leaf grabber. Her hair will be poking out under the mushroom, and she will have her overalls on, and her canvas work boots and her old gardening gloves. There will be flashes of a frown on her face. He will yell her name and when she looks up and waves, he will walk to her and admonish her for not telling him where she was. Playfully pretend to take on the parental role. Then he will persuade her to come to the cafe with him for tea and toast. And he will make her laugh as she blows on her tea to cool it down.

The clouds are low. He feels a single raindrop on his nose and quickens his pace. He is searching now, scanning the green for her frame. A man stares into the distance as his dog urinates on the side of an oak tree. A squirrel is upside down on the trunk above. He walks up the main path, scanning from side to side, past the playground, which is heaving with the Saturday morning rush, past the group of oak trees where he thought she would be, and finally over to the outhouse where she keeps her equipment. The padlock is in place, holding the two aluminium doors locked. He pulls on it anyway, frowning. Could she be starting late? The fresh air is making him feel sick. He isn't even hungover. He kicks a stone back up the path, and slumps down on to a park bench to wait.

CHAPTER 5

MARY, 1995

A cold front moved in over the city at the start of November. On the first Saturday of the month, the rain came down slanted on the back windows, making a dull drumming sound. Mary watched her brother as he left the house to travel to his new job at Atlantic Homecare.

Cheerio, he said as the back door banged shut. She saw him pause at the alleyway and hunch to light up his cigarette. He inhaled deeply, pulling his shoulders back and tilting his chin up, as if opening himself up to allow the smoke to travel to the deepest corners of his body before exhalation. An exact imitation of their father's movements, she thought. They both loved smoking cigarettes, and seemed to take pleasure in ignoring the rain.

She went to the window above the kitchen sink and pushed it open and out, just a few inches, to let the air in but not the wet. Behind her, propped up against the wall in the corner, there was a canvas pull-along trolley. It was black, with a large tartan zipped lid and a tartan pocket on the front and on the inside. On the back was a metal frame with two shiny black wheels to pull it. She'd found it the day before, under her father's instruction, laid flat on the concrete in the back of the cupboard under the stairs, covered in dust and cobwebs.

It was your mother's, he said, mouth set in a flat line. It was to help her carry the shopping when she went to Curley's.

Mary had spent that evening gently cleaning it with warm water and soap and searching every compartment for evidence of her mother. She found nothing. She had practised pulling it across the room, enjoying the feeling of her hands in the same place as her mother's had been. She imagined her mother fifteen years ago, pregnant with her and pushing Sean in a pram. How would she have pulled the trolley when she had to push the pram? Did their father help or did she do the shopping on her own? What food did she buy? What did she cook? Mary had thousands of questions about her mother stored up in her head, in long, neat lists with title headings. Questions about the sound of her voice, the feel of her skin, the look of her. Questions about her love for their father, and her love for her children. She wanted to take the trolley to bed with her and hug it tight, like she imagined her mother did to her when she was a baby. She looked forward to using it for the shop later.

When her father came down for his lunch, the bacon was sizzling and she was cutting thick slices of bread from a loaf. He liked to spend more time in the pub at weekends. Instead of sleeping until the late afternoon after a Friday night shift, he set an alarm to wake him at lunchtime. He looked worn out, she thought, as he walked into the kitchen, straight to the high cupboard over the fridge to pull out a packet of paracetamol. His hair hung over his eyes and ears, lank and greasy, and she wished for a half second that she could cut it. Mary watched the back of him from the corner of her eye as she put a cup of steaming tea on the table, his three sugars already stirred in. He wore stained old jeans, a fisherman's old wool jumper and his work boots. He sighed out and sank into the chair, throwing two pills into his mouth and slurping his tea.

Well, Daddy . . . how was work?

She was behind him, leaning into the corner of the worktop, pouring sugar from the packet into the bowl. He turned his head over his shoulder, with some effort, to look at her. She looked up from her task with a shy smile. He stared at her for a few seconds, eyebrows raised, as if he had only now noticed her presence in the room.

Not bad . . .

This will be ready for you in a few minutes.

He nodded slowly and then took his hand out of his pocket to reveal a roll of bank notes.

Here. Before I forget.

He peeled off two twenty-pound notes and handed them to her. She noticed his gold wedding ring looked like it was cutting off the blood supply to his finger. She stepped forwards and stretched out her hand to take the notes, but he didn't release them. He was staring at her hand. Her nails were painted blood red.

I hope you're not spending my money on that crap.

No, Daddy, it was Louise. She did them for me. It was hers . . . I mean, it was her mum's. Rita, her name is.

Her father looked at her sharply and pulled himself up to standing. He opened the back door and stepped out, squinting towards the clouds. The rain had slowed to a lazy drizzle.

You'd like Rita, I think, Daddy.

She spoke to him out the open back door as she cut his sandwich on a plate. He lit his cigarette, his head crouched into his hands. His shoulders sank as he blew out a thick plume of smoke. He turned around to look back into the kitchen.

Would I now?

He nodded in approval at the cleaned trolley by the door.

Good as new.

She half smiled.

Aye.

She was very still. She felt the heat rise in her cheeks.

Daddy. Please could you tell me a bit about her?

His eyes narrowed as he took another long drag from his cigarette.

Something in her had held back from pushing her father for information on her mother up to now; a fear of something inside of him cracking like ice, and eventually giving way, until there was nothing to stop him drowning in his grief. He blew out again, this time upwards, and she saw the full patchy carpet of his beard.

Mary pushed on.

Why did she not have a family?

Suspended silence. Mary opened her mouth to say something more, but he was speaking now, low and gentle.

All she was told about her family was that her mother, your grandmother, got pregnant out of wedlock. She was sent to one of those homes – you know, for mothers and babies – and she died when your mother was very small. They gave your mother away for adoption. Or probably fucking sold her for cash. She ended up in foster care. She never wanted to talk about her childhood. She just said she moved around a lot. She came to Belfast when she was sixteen and looked after the house of an old Protestant woman over East, who she hated. I met her at the Royal Mail when she got a job there. She was . . .

He paused and frowned, trying to find the right word.

She was tough. Didn't take any shit from anyone.

Mary took a step closer to the door and held on to the handle of it.

And what happened next?

She could hear the small sizzle of his cigarette burning through as he took another deep drag.

What happened next?

He blew thick smoke into the air in front of his face.

Belfast was a war zone. There were bombs all over the place. I nearly got blown up by an IRA bomb walking past a shop downtown. That's what this here scar is from.

He pointed to a place under his chin, covered by his beard. Mary stared. He wiped his nose with the back of his shirt sleeve.

We got married soon after that.

He paused and his eyes went somewhere else.

She was twenty-three. But she knew a whole lot more about the world than I did.

He looked pained. As if the words hurt him on the way out of him. Mary's eyes tickled with the beginnings of tears. He looked at her now, with an intensity that made her knuckles turn white around the door handle.

She called you Mary because she wanted to have something to show for herself. You were her, trying to leave her mark on the world.

Mary stared at him as he dropped his cigarette on to the doorstep, crushed it with his boot and stepped into the room. He hovered in front of her now, and she felt the trail of a lone tear on her cheek. She saw his eyes were glistening.

Sometimes you're so like her . . . it's like she left a piece of herself behind. In you.

She looked up at him.

I'm sorry, Daddy. I'm sorry that you lost her.

He was staring into nothing again. She needed to get out of the room.

I will leave you in peace, she said, as she grabbed the trolley and hurried out the front door, gulping down big lungfuls of cold air. She concentrated on her steps, putting one foot in front of the other, counting them as far as the end of the road. She traced the steps of their conversation, the words and the order of them. Would he still be there now, staring at the wall, head full of thoughts of her mother? She walked around the corner to the main road and up the hill to the roundabout. She wanted to walk forever, but she forced herself to stop at the roundabout and craned her neck for a black taxi.

She yearned for Sean. There was so much to tell him. Did he know about their father and the bomb? She pictured her father in a pile of smouldering rubble, his hair white with ash, his chin spilling blood. She held her hand up to hail a black hack coming towards her. She pulled down the seat directly behind the driver and watched the Stewartstown Road fall away behind her.

She went over his words again and again, memorising the order of them and cursing herself for not asking about her mother and religion. It was the only lasting legacy her mother had left behind which had really affected Mary's life. Their father told them from a young age that their mother refused to have them baptised, and consequently there would be no Holy Communions or confessions, and no Confirmations. There was never any real explanation for this and Mary and Sean suffered Bridget's incredulous protestations for years.

How you couldn't even baptise your own babies? Something serious must have happened to your mother, for I couldn't think of a more evil thing to do to your own children.

Bridget took matters into her own hands in the end, and had them baptised in secret, without a congregation or even their father in attendance. After their father found out her visits stopped.

The taxi passed the entrance to the Forest Park and then the

Barracks, with its black caged porch, as if dangerous animals dwelled inside. Maybe something serious *did* happen to her mother because their father was very committed to following her wishes, and went to see the sisters of St Frances at Mary and Sean's schools and managed to persuade them to allow his children to be excused from Religious Education lessons. She and a girl called Nipar, who had Indian parents, used to sit and read their books in the library room every Monday and Friday while the other children learned about their sacraments. They didn't have to sit in on prayer groups or rosary groups and were exempt from all the excitement of Holy Communion. They didn't get to dress up in white frills like dolls, they didn't get money slipped into their purses from their relatives. Sean used to give out about missing out on all the money. Mary tolerated the isolation of it out of intrigue about her mother. It was a sign of something she didn't understand yet. And, of course, they were Catholic in all the other ways: their estate, their uniforms, just the general look of them.

Curley's sat in the heart of West Belfast, just where the Falls Road started its slow curve into the city centre. It was part of a bigger shopping complex called the Kennedy Centre, and when she saw the building in the distance, she knocked on the window behind her for the taxi to pull over. She gripped her trolley tight as she crossed the road.

Mary and Sean had done the food shop together since she was old enough to remember, and she missed the camaraderie of their old excursions, him commanding the shopping trolley and ordering her about the shop, with his carefully folded notes from their father zipped up in his pocket. The bickering over what to buy and the silent joy of a post-shopping ice lolly in the sunshine, their plastic bags circled around their feet. She talked herself slowly around the shop, her mother's old trolley wedged sideways into the shopping trolley, and at the cashier she took enormous satisfaction in packing up the groceries.

That'll be forty-two fifty, please, said the cashier.

Mary frowned and took a packet of lamb chops out of the top of the trolley.

Can you take these off?

She heard a disapproving sigh and turned to face the woman standing behind her in the queue. Her skin was pigmented and grey like marble. She was staring at Mary accusingly, holding her purse in her hand. Mary, thinking of her father's description of her mother, dared to give her a shade of a dirty look, and then glanced quickly back to the cashier. She took her change and pulled her trolley out of the shop. She would save the change for chips tonight.

They always had chips from the chippie on Saturday night. Mary walked there with her hands tucked into her sleeves, seeing her breath blow out in balloons that disappeared in front of her. She saw Sean immediately, outside the shop, leaning against the railings, looking sideways over at his friends. Another guy was shouting something and they were all laughing. She walked in past them and gave Sean a shy smile and a half wave. He raised his chin in acknowledgement of her. She queued with her back to him, self-conscious, and as she was just about to order, she heard his voice behind her.

Large chips with mushy peas, please. Loads of salt and vinegar, and a can of Coke.

She turned to him in surprise. He handed the woman behind the counter a crisp ten-pound note with affected indifference.

Thanks, Sean!

All good, sis!

He was jovial, two hands on her shoulders, rocking her back and forth affectionately. She felt the certainty of his grip, and smelt the sweet cider smell of his breath before breaking away to reach out for the brown paper bag the cashier offered. Mary opened her mouth to speak, but he had already turned and was walking out of the shop. She walked out behind him and stood awkwardly outside the shop door, looking at his group of friends. Paddy McGrath, Paul Connors and the short guy, Danny Donnelly. She saw Danny about from time to time, and he always said hello and asked how she was. They all looked at her.

Well, Mary, said Paddy, nodding solemnly.

Hello, Paddy, Paul, Danny.

She turned to each of them to greet them, and Danny said, Howya, Mary.

She felt her cheeks blushing and she quickly spoke. Well, I'm off, cheerio.

Enjoy your chips! shouted Sean as she hurried away into the darkness.

There were helicopters tonight, more than usual. Their noise ripped through the darkness around her, making the air shake. She kept her head down and quickened her pace. At the top of the road, she saw the blue and red flashing light of a police wagon. There were two armoured Saracens blocking her road, and soldiers patrolling the roundabout, stopping cars and leaning their camouflaged helmets into windows. She walked up to the edge of the road and waited to catch a soldier's eye to make sure it was okay to cross. She could feel the paper bag in her hand starting to disintegrate from the grease of her chips. The soldier saw her and shouted.

Where are you going?

Just down to Purves estate, she shouted back.

Go on. Hurry up.

He gesticulated with his rifle towards the other side of the road. She kept her head down and walked fast. Half an hour later she was curled up in the comfy chair, relishing her chips, listening to Louise chatter down the phone.

Which one do you like though, Mary? I think Graham Coxon is your type.

Louise was obsessed with boybands. Boyzone and Take That were in full attendance in her bedroom, pouting and posturing on every wall. More recently she had shifted her attentions to the band Blur. Mary recalled watching a Blur music video on Louise's TV the week before. Louise had crawled across the carpet to lay her hand flat on the TV screen as Damon Albarn sang about a big house in the country.

Look at him Mary. He is so gorgeous I can't handle it.

You could go out with Graham and I could go out with Damon, she was saying now. We could all hang out in London together.

Mary swallowed her chip and took a deep breath.

Louise, I found out something about my mother today. My daddy told me stuff.

What? Louise whispered.

Just that, well, she named me Mary because she had no family or anything, and calling me Mary was her way of leaving her mark on the world. Like having something to show for herself.

Oh my God, Mary! That is so cute. So you are your mammy's own mascot.

Yes, said Mary, smiling down the receiver while the hot chips warmed her from the inside out.

Later that night, she heard the sound of coughing outside, right below her window. She got out of her bed in her pyjamas and peered around her blind to see the figure of Sean, doubled over, hands on knees, leaning against the wall, vomiting. She heard the splatter of the liquid on the cement and then saw him stumble towards the back door. Then she heard her father's bass tone, muffled through the floor. He will have just got in from the pub, she thought, and pictured him heavy breathing himself around the kitchen, eating her stew straight from the pot on the hob. She wondered did part of him crack with all that talk of her mother. She heard him murmur some-thing to Sean and then Sean was shouting wildly.

Oh here we go, Da, you gonna be the big man again, are you? Come on then!

Then the dull smack sound of fist to cheek and scuffling and a chair knocked to the ground and glass smashing and more smacks and two big thuds as a body hit the door and then the floor. Sean ran up the stairs, three at a time, then slammed his door and locked it. She heard him thrash around his room, the unidentifiable thuds of things being knocked off shelves, and then a terrifying howl.

Fuuuuucking cuuuuunt!

And silence.

She stood with her back flat against the door, looking up at the ceiling with her eyes clenched shut and her fingernails digging into her palms. She waited for three long, icy min-utes until she heard the scrape of a chair on the linoleum downstairs. Her daddy wasn't dead, then. Her heart started to slow down and she could hear her breath fluttering, phasing in her ears, as she moved to sit down on the edge of her bed. She could hear him slowly heaving himself up the stairs. She held her breath, staring at the same patch of paint on her wall as her father's footsteps passed her door and went into the bathroom. She listened to his pee hitting the water in the bowl. Then the water was running, and then there were three heavy steps and the walls reverberated to the slam of his door.

CHAPTER 6

MARY, 1996

She was pulled out of her dreams by a wet sensation between her legs. When she felt it with her fingers, she jumped up and out of bed, quickly turning on the light. Louise had told her what it was like, but she had never imagined there could be so much. It was running down her thighs and on her hands, and there was a small, round puddle of it on her sheet. Her only bedsheet.

She felt light-headed and confused in her sleepiness. She ripped her bedsheet off and cursed at the blood stain on the mattress below. She went to her drawer and found fresh underpants and a nightie and ran to the bathroom. She stood in the bath and cleaned the blood off with warm water and dried herself carefully, avoiding between her legs so as not to get more blood on the towel. Then she found the toilet roll and fashioned a thick layer of padding that she wedged into her underpants.

It was 3 a.m. Everyone would be in their beds by now. She tiptoed downstairs in her nightie and filled a bucket with warm water and bleach. The first thing she did was scrub her mattress until her fingers were red raw. Then she pushed her sheet and underpants and nightie in the bucket to soak. She remembered Bridget. She loved to soak things. Fill the bucket, she would say to her, up to the top. And Mary would watch the water turn cloudy when Bridget sprinkled in the powder, and stick her hand in to feel the chalkiness of it. You can soak anything clean, Mary, she would say, pushing the clothes into the water.

She spent the rest of the night lying rigid on a towel on her mattress, listening to her heart beat loudly in her ears. She thought of Louise and of what she would tell her; of the expression on her face when she heard her news. Louise was sure to make a big, loud celebration of it. She was smiling, deep in thoughts of Louise, when she heard the first birds start to chirp outside her window. She made a run for the bathroom, feeling the blood rush out of her and on to the towel she held between her legs.

Fucking hell, she whispered to herself as she sat on the toilet, listening to the blood drop into the water. Afterwards, she wedged more tissues in her knickers and went back to her room. The water in the bucket was a dirty brown colour. She looked at her watch: 6.30 a.m. If she brought it downstairs now, she would have half an hour before the others appeared. In her school skirt, shirt and tights, she poured the water from the bucket down the drain by the back step.

Then she squeezed the sheet down into the plastic sieve-like structure at the top of the bucket. When it was squeezed as dry as her red hands could manage it, she brought the buckets back into the kitchen and washed them out and put them away. She shook out the sheet and held it up to the light of the window. There was still a brown outline of a circle on it. Fuck, she whispered, shaking her head. She turned to the cupboard by the fridge, took out some Vanish and rubbed the white powder around the brown circle. Then she ran quietly upstairs to her bedroom and hung the sheet across her chair and her bookshelf to dry.

She left the house before her father and brother had stirred and walked the long way to school along the edges of Ballybawn Park. Tiny green leaves were unfurling themselves on the branches above. The birds were louder today, she thought, or was it because it was earlier than normal? It was glorious. She sighed with relief into the morning air and tried to take in the importance of the day. Spring was here, and she had got her period and she was still fourteen. There was emergency money that her father left in the back of the cutlery drawer, and that is what she used to buy a packet of large sanitary towels from the big shop on the main road. Three pounds forty-nine. She thought about how she would repay the money over the next few weeks with the shopping. He wouldn't have to know.

She was first to school. She spent fifteen minutes in the toilet cubicle, wiping herself, fixing the towel in, staring at the red pool in the cistern beneath her.

At first breaktime, she sat on the ground with Louise, leaning against the wall of the main school building, surveying the playground packed with girls in front of them. Louise was wolfing down cold spaghetti bolognese from a Tupperware box while she talked.

Mr O'Connell is such a div. Like, I feel so sorry for Richard, because I can't imagine anything more embarrassing than your dad being a teacher in school and, like, the worst of the worst, your dad teaching the class that you are in . . .

Louise.

Wha?

I got my period.

Oh. My. God. Mary!

Louise held her arms out and wrapped herself around Mary, still chewing her mouthful of pasta.

Well? she asked.

It's like a horror film! There's so much of it.

Mary stuck her tongue out in an expression of disgust and Louise sat back against the wall, knowing and nodding.

Are you getting cramps?

Yeah, it's a proper weird pain, like the whole inside of my tummy is sore. And my thighs are all achey.

She rubbed her hands up and down her thighs. She looked especially pale today, like the blood was sucking all the colour from her skin.

Ach, Mary, you're a woman now, Louise said in mock motherly tones, and Mary giggled it off.

You've got to try a tampon. It's way less messy. I have one in my bag! We'll try it tonight.

Later, at Louise's house, Mary tried to insert a tampon, while Louise hovered outside the bathroom door. She hated the feeling of it stuck there, halfway. She hated the feeling of the string hanging out of her. She came out and shook her head sadly at Louise's hopeful face.

Pads it is then, baby.

Louise put her arm around her friend and guided her back downstairs.

Rita made them fish fingers and chips. Halfway through dinner, Louise leaned over the table and whispered theatrically to her mother.

Mammy?

Rita had her mouth full. She had the same fragile features as her daughter, but her angles were softer, more rounded. She focused on Louise, still chewing.

Mary got her period, Louise whispered again, using her hands to shield the words from Frank. Mary, feeling the weight of attention on her, immediately recoiled in embarrassment.

Jesus, Louise, she said.

Rita smiled. Oh, Mary love, big day for ye!

Later in the evening, as Mary was pulling her coat on in the hall, Rita walked down the stairs and paused at the bottom.

Have you got everything you need for your period?

Mary looked down at her feet. Hearing it spoken out loud like that, in such a matter-of-fact tone, felt like a relief.

Aye, I think so. It's just . . . there's . . . a lot of it. It's a bit . . . scary.

Well, it *is* scary, love. You're bleeding heavily from your insides for days. She sighed out and her face changed as she saw the fear in Mary's eyes.

Don't be scared, love. We're good at pain. You wait, it'll be just another day of the week.

On the bus home, Mary's dinner felt like a brick in her stomach, pulling her down to the ground. She wanted to curl up on the bus floor under the seat like a cat and fall asleep. When she saw the roundabout, she stood up to get off the bus and felt the blood rush out of her. She thought of Rita in her hallway and her look of weathered endurance, like a statue in the lashing rain. There was a strength to her that bolstered Mary. Rita would never blow away in the wind.

When she got home, the house was empty, and she went straight to the bathroom and sat on the toilet. She carefully ripped off the pad and rolled it up and wrapped it in tissue paper. She didn't want her father or brother to see her pads, so she would keep them in a rubbish bag in her bedroom. She fixed a new pad on to her underpants and stood to examine her reflection in the mirror. There were dark circles under her eyes. She looked exactly the same. She thought of Louise's angled cheekbones, her sharp fringe, of how she already seemed primed and ready for the world. Mary pulled her hair back from her face, twisting it into a tight bun and pulling a scrunchy three times around it. She used kirby grips to clip in the stray frizz around her hairline and took a lipstick from her pencil case of make-up, smearing it over her lips. It looked violent on her face, like a pantomime wound. She smiled, lowered her chin and looked straight into the mirror, holding her gaze. Suddenly self-conscious, she slid down on to the floor of the bathroom with her back resting against the bath.

There were mustard-coloured stains of dried urine around the bottom of the toilet bowl. She wondered whether she would see Sean tonight. She missed him. He had a girlfriend now, a girl from the shop, who pushed the buttons on the till and clicked barcodes with the electric wand. Her name was Julie. Sean had left her outside the house once or twice when he called in to pick things up or change his clothes. Mary had stared out the window at her, watching the smoke curling up from her cigarette. Her make up slid off the small mounds of her spots like sand on stones. Mary wanted to know everything and nothing about her at the same time.

She thought of the weekend before, when she had been in the kitchen with Sean and her father. Sean bowled around the kitchen in his Atlantic Homecare uniform, taking up all the space, banging cupboard doors open and shut. He went to the fridge and took out a can of cider and downed half of it standing in the middle of the room.

Their father sat at the table, eating his supper, studiously ignoring his son. He didn't look up from his newspaper once, even though he would have heard the click of the ring pull. The loud gulps. He finished his last bite and looked only at Mary as he said thanks and then took himself upstairs. They were repelling magnets. Mary sensed the relief from both of them, that they had broken apart for good.

She pulled herself up to standing and started to wipe off the lipstick with make-up remover. She would make cheese sandwiches and leave them out and then climb into bed. It was becoming hard to tell who owned the heavy footsteps on the stairs late at night.

CHAPTER 7

TJ, PRESENT

TJ turns the key in the door, pushes it open halfway, and then pauses to listen out for any sound of her.

Ma?

Nothing. He lasted half an hour on the park bench before his phone died and he came home to get warm. He runs upstairs, plugs his phone in by his bed and walks straight to his mother's bedroom. He sits down on her bed with his coat still on, leaning back on to the white patchwork blanket with his elbows. There is a cobweb floating in the air in the corner. Normally she wouldn't stand for that. He takes in the room. It is painted the softest yellow, the colour of a newly born baby chick. The window is open just an inch and the floor-length white net curtains swell with air. Over the fireplace, there is a silk scarf with vivid flowers on it, tacked on to a mount and framed. On one end of the mantelpiece is the old gold clock that has been there for as long as he remembers. He lets his ears tune into it now and he hears the muted clicks of the ticker, quietly occupying the room. He's never really listened to the clock before. It says it is ten past one. Something isn't right. It is not certain, but it *is* likely, that something isn't right. His queasiness remains. He breathes deeply and pushes himself up to standing.

Opposite her bed there is a neat wooden chest of drawers with framed photos on top. He walks over for a closer look. There is one of him as a baby, just a few months old, his eyes staring up at someone out of shot, giving them a big gummy smile. Beside it is a shot of his mother with her brother when they were children, one of those classic school photos with the mottled background. His ma is sitting on a wooden stool angled to the side, wearing white knee-socks, shined shoes and two plaits tied with perfect white bows. Her smile is so wide and fake it's nearly a grimace. Sean is standing beside her with the tail end of a grin and a crew cut, his hand placed awkwardly on her shoulder.

He opens the top drawer of the chest to reveal a box of sanitary towels and tampons, and some neatly folded underwear, and swiftly pushes it shut again.

He turns back around to survey the space. Her wardrobe is on the other side, filled with all her clothes, her best jumpers wrapped in plastic so the moths won't get them. He used to hide in there when he was a boy. He would sit with his arms wrapped round his knees, giggling as he listened to his ma pretending to not know where he was. She would always play along, wondering aloud, Where could he be? Until finally, theatrically, she would open the wardrobe to find him there.

TJ walks over to it now, opens the doors, pushes off each trainers with the opposite foot and steps inside, slowly inching down until he is sitting on the soft cushion of her slippers. His legs are folded up tight with his arms wrapped around them. His feet are pushed up against the wood.

Staring at his feet, he suddenly remembers a pair of trainers that his friend Timmy had in the first year of secondary school. They were fake Adidas, two stripes rather than three, and they were so obviously fake that TJ was incredulous that Timmy even agreed to let his mum buy them for him. Timmy lived on their road and TJ had known him since they were tiny, climbing trees and scooting around the estate together. He was the closest thing TJ had to a brother then, a default ally, and he was grateful that they had each other in that first year of big school.

They were walking back from PE to the changing rooms in their first week of school, and had slowed to watch some of the bigger lads play football on their lunch break. A tall, red-headed boy from the year above walked over to them, pointing at Timmy's trainers and laughing. Then he laughed some more big, overdone laughter. Timmy tried to shrug it off, looking away, but the boy walked up to him, and without looking him in the eye, grabbed his right leg with one hand and pulled the trainer off his foot with the other.

The red-headed boy started throwing the trainer around with his friends, up over their heads like an American football, while TJ watched from the sidelines in dismay. Timmy was chasing his shoe, hopping on the tarmac, trying to intercept it in the air while the boys laughed hysterically. TJ was furious at Timmy for looking so pathetic and, more in anger at Timmy than anything else, he ran in and caught the shoe while it was spinning through the air on its way to the red-headed boy. He handed it back to Timmy without saying a word. Timmy scrambled to put it on. He was crouching down, double knotting the laces as the boy walked over to TJ and squared his shoulders up to him. The boys had stopped playing football and were all watching as he leaned into TJ's face, so close that TJ smelt the acid vinegar stench of his breath.

You just fucked that one up big time.

TJ knew if he spoke his voice would give away his terror. He looked towards the block, hoping a teacher would intervene, and felt an explosion of pain on the right side of his face. It was his first ever punch and it was way more brutal and violent than it looked in the films. He had never experienced bare-knuckle cruelty like that before. He fell, more from the shock than the impact, and curled up in a ball on the ground. He remembered seeing the feet of the red-headed boy running away towards the classroom block.

When his ma had seen his black eye that evening, her face had lost all its colour. She made him sit down opposite her at the table and tell her everything. He had allowed himself to cry while she stroked his face and squeezed his hands. Afterwards he felt floppy and soft, emptied out of feelings. His eye was throbbing, and he knew from his mother's serious tone that he had been through something significant, even life-changing. She had told him that she was proud of him, that he had been a good friend to Timmy. That he had been brave. And he had been grateful then, for the punch. Grateful for Timmy's shite shoe. Grateful for all of it.

He closes his eyes and tries to picture where she is right now. Is she mad at him? He hurt her with that comment about the park. Not because she believed her job was something to be ashamed of, but because she thought he was ashamed of *her*. He knew his mother was immensely proud of her job. It made her complete. Even as a little boy after school, he understood somehow that her happiness when she worked was not something he could share. When he sat under trees watching her hunched over the flower beds, he did everything in his power not to bother her. He was happy to watch her movements like a meditation: digging, planting, pruning. He liked it when she forgot he was there and he would catch her lost in her thoughts, standing over a flower or bush, stroking the leaves slowly between two fingers and looking into the middle distance. It was her own peace. When he was about six or seven, he begged his ma for a pet. Instead she brought home three geraniums from work and she helped him pot them. See if you can look after these, she said. They're living things, like pets. They need air, water and light. He did it all in the shadow of her, her ponytail sticking up on the top of her head, while she administered gentle doses of encouragement. He remembers watering them with zeal, until their trays were overflowing. And her showing him how to take the plant out of the pot and shake off the wet soil, then plant it again in dry soil. She always said they were 'generous' plants. That as long as you removed the dead flowers, they would keep coming back, again and again. When he was small, he used to get the words generous and geranium mixed up.

TJ takes a deep breath. He can smell the faint lemon trace of fabric conditioner, mixing in with the wood. His stomach groans loudly and he sees himself suddenly. Jesus, what must he look like folded into this fucking wardrobe? He heaves himself up and out of the wooden frame and starts to pull his trainers back on. He likes to think that he knows his mother inside out, but telling her about the New York dream was always going to be risky. Why did he have to drop it straight after insulting her about her job? He sighs heavily as he walks out of her room.

CHAPTER 8

MARY, 1999

May was her favourite month. It was the letters of her name. It was new beginnings. It was warmth from the sun that soaked through her skin. She liked to sit with her face tilted up towards it, like a sunflower.

She was sitting on a park bench in the Botanic Gardens, by the glass house and the red brick turrets of the old Queen's University building, under the shade of a row of oak trees. In front of her was a large square green that was framed by neat footpaths and manicured flower beds. Fresh blooms peppered the landscape and new bees drifted between them. Her bench was far away from the cafe and the playground, but close enough to the green to watch and observe the visitors to the gardens.

A few feet down the hill, a toddler was running. Caught in the momentum of her moving legs, she careered sideways, like a drunk. She fell face first into the grass, and stayed static in that position, arms splayed out, nose buried into the green, until a woman jogged up behind her laughing and scooped her up, cooing sympathetic tones and smothering her in kisses.

Mary was in her school uniform. She had got the bus in the opposite direction after school, seduced by the sunshine and disenchanted with the idea of another quiet afternoon in the library. Her skirt was rolled up around her waist three times, exposing a few inches of pale thighs above her knees. Her thin ribbed knee-socks hung in rolls around her ankles. In the last year, the roundness in her face had fallen away, giving her facial features new angles and a slightly sunken appearance. She had drawn in her eyebrows with a pencil; they were over-pronounced, like thick caterpillars squaring up to each other on either side of her forehead. Her hair was piled up on top of her head in a messy bun with straggly bits falling down on either side. Friday was her eighteenth birthday.

Her school days were increasingly filled with stern warnings from her teachers about the passing and failing of her A-levels. She worried about sitting the exams every night: that her pen wouldn't work, that her mind would go into paralysis and all the neat boxes in her brain, filled with ordered information, would disappear. Her three chosen subjects were Biology, Geography and English. She studied hard and she was doing well enough in class, averaging on Cs and the odd B. Louise wasn't nearly as conscientious as she was. The house phone would ring frequently in the evenings, with

Louise eager to talk through her agenda of boys, teachers and family members. Mary listened patiently, all the while subtracting the time she had been on the phone from how long she had left to study before she would fall asleep.

Louise was in love. His name was Mickey O'Dowd and it all started at their bus stop on the Falls Road. He lived three streets away from Louise. Mary had been aghast at how shamelessly he had stared at Louise. And even more aghast at Louise's reciprocation. First, she started sitting beside him on the bus, shining her huge goofy smile all over him until he was rendered speechless. Then, one afternoon when Mary was in the library, head bent over her books, Louise French-kissed Mickey in the park. Now he was never far from the edges of their conversations. When he was with them, Louise spoke to him with a warm, jokey affection, like she saw Rita speak to Frank.

Mickey O'Dowd, would you ever brush your hair, she would say, running her fingers through his brown tufts, arranging it in funny styles and then nestling her head into his neck like he was a particularly comfy cushion. She was five foot ten now, and she moved with an endearing gawkiness that showed off her youth, like a baby giraffe, knock-kneed and soft-boned. Her blonde hair was straight and shoulder length and cut into a blunt fringe which gave her face an impish look.

Mary had been talking to herself a lot recently, telling herself that it was okay for Louise to have Mickey, that they would still be friends, that nothing would change. She still went over to Arndale twice a week, but on two of those visits over the last few weeks, Mickey had accompanied them. The last time they were there, Mary noticed that he didn't say thank you to Rita when she gave them dinner. She wanted to reach out and slap him sharp and hard on his blushing cheek.

Louise had initially told her about what it was like to have sex, but now she didn't discuss it any more, and Mary was acutely aware of this deepening chasm of communication between them. All those feelings Louise was pouring into him. All the things Mary didn't know. She tried not to think of Mickey O'Dowd now. Of his body intertwined around Louise, of his penis poking hopefully around her skinny thighs.

A groan sounded from the depths of her stomach as she watched two college students lick their ice cream cones on the grass below. She sighed and tuned her ears into the low hum of traffic in the distance. She was grateful for these long, light evenings, grateful to feel like part of the fabric of a beautiful day in the city. She reached down, scratched her ankle and pulled her socks up. It wouldn't be long before she was out of this uniform forever.

What about you, Mary?

She was suddenly cast in shadow by a figure standing right in front of her. It was Sean's friend Danny Donnelly, wearing an ill-fitting suit and and shiny, pointed brown shoes.

Hiya, Danny. Where are you off to?

I've just come back from a job interview.

His face was so square that his chin was close to having

corners. His shirt was pulled taut over his broad, stocky frame. His suit trousers were far too tight. She thought it must be hard to dress right if you were Danny Donnelly. Too baggy and you'd look small, but too small and you looked even more stocky. Mary realised he wasn't going to elaborate. She forced herself to speak.

What job are you going for?

One in the civil service. I don't know if I'll get it, like.

He raised his eyebrows and sighed out as he said it, gazing into the rose bushes behind her.

Okay. Well, good luck.

He gave her a nod and turned to walk away. She quietly exhaled.

Mary? He had stopped and turned around. His cheeks were pink in the afternoon sun.

Are you going to St Frances' on Friday? I'll be there . . .

A baby screeched nearby. Mary's head was ringing.

I think I might, yeah . . .

Cool . . . see you . . .

He raised his hand and turned away, a slight swagger in his step. She knew he knew she was watching him, because he pulled his shoulders back and stretched his head up to make himself taller.

Louise had already decided they would go to St Frances' to celebrate Mary's birthday. St Frances' was the local church hall. It was open for a 'disco' every second Friday of the month and everyone went. Mary sat for a few minutes in a daze, trying to process the conversation with Danny. He had always taken more of an interest in her than any of Sean's other friends had – and she always thought that he was just being polite. Did he just ask her out? As she walked up University Road that evening, she felt a low thrum of excitement, and wondered what it was like to feel things she had only imagined.

Friday came with a twenty-pound note and a smile from her father over the breakfast table.

Ye can go and buy yourself something nice.

She took it shyly, delighted he remembered. Sean grinned at her on his way out of the kitchen and promised a proper present when he got his pay packet. She spent the evening after school at Louise's. Rita called them down for dinner and, after their chips and fried eggs, she turned out the lights in the kitchen. Louise led her mother and brother in a loud and tuneless rendition of 'Happy Birthday' while Rita walked to the table, her smile illuminated by the candles of the sponge cake she had made for the occasion.

Make a wish, Mary!

Mary flushed with pleasure. She closed her eyes to make a wish, but before she could think of one, Frank bent forward and blew out the candles.

Ha ha! He giggled, his six-year-old face screwed up in mischief.

Frank! said Louise, pushing him back off the kitchen bench. He fell to the floor and screamed.

Rita shouted.

Louise! Get him back up here right now! Jesus Christ!

Mary was relieved not to have to declare a wish. She laughed at the chaos of it all, as the sugary sweetness of the icing on her slice of birthday cake melted in her mouth. After they cleared the table, they got ready in Louise's room. Louise bellowed at her, bent over the bed with the hairdryer on full blast.

I think you should wear my black minidress. Wear it with your Converse; it'll look really cool!

Mary stood at Louise's wardrobe, flicking through the strappy tops and backless dresses. The chips and cake felt heavy in her belly, and she thought briefly about running home to curl up in her bed and sleep. She pulled the mini dress off its hanger.

She and Louise had tried on so many clothes in front of each other, and had seen each other in their underwear so many times, but Mary never stopped feeling shy about it. She saw a flash of her ribs as she pulled the dress quickly over her head and smoothed it out over her stomach. She pulled the hem down, swivelling her hips as she did so. The sleeves were long, and the neck was round. The material was thin, stretchy cotton that clung to every part of her body. She felt obscenely exposed. She pulled her Converse on over her trainer socks and tied them loosely around the ankle.

She looked in the mirror now and stared at her reflection. She could see the soft shape of her breasts over her ribcage.

Her hair was washed and brushed and coaxed into a loose, wispy plait that hung down around her left shoulder. She had painted her face with help from Louise, and her friend had even put a pair of false eyelashes on her with some glue and a pair of tweezers. Mary thought she looked exaggerated, like a cartoon version of herself.

Louise came up behind her and said, Oh *bonita*! in a faux-Spanish accent. She put her fingers in her mouth and wolf-whistled loudly.

Louise! Mary turned round to gawp at her.

Mary, for once in your life, realise you are gorgeous.

A short while later, Mary sat in the back of the car with her hands tucked under her thighs, staring out the window and replaying those words again and again in her head.

Realise you are gorgeous.

Realise you are gorgeous.

The perfume she had borrowed from Louise was giving her a headache. Rita pulled the car to a stop on the Andersonstown Road.

Louise O'Mara, you better be home by midnight, or I will send a search party for you, do you hear? I'll have helicopters with floodlights looking in every corner of West Belfast.

Yesssssss, Rita, drawled Louise as she clambered out of the car. She was wearing a tiny black PVC miniskirt and a pair of platform sandals with ankle straps. She said she couldn't walk in them unless they were strapped on to her.

On top, she wore a pink cropped T-shirt that hung just at the waistline of her skirt. She looked like a wayward Spice Girl. Once again, Mary whispered silent prayers of thanks that Louise had chosen her as a friend.

Louise pulled Mary around the back of the church hall before the two old ladies at the door could spot them. They stood looking out over the playing fields as Louise rummaged in her bag and took out a plastic Coca-Cola bottle.

Drink, she said, unscrewing the lid and holding it up to Mary.

What is it? Mary said, sniffing the bottle.

Louise winked. Just a wee vodka Coke.

Mary had drunk with Louise before, of course. When she was fifteen, Louise had fed her a 'cocktail' that she had fashioned out of the leftovers of a family gathering, and Mary had ended her night vomiting behind Louise's wheelie bin. She had been cautious of overdoing it since then. But now she took a sip, and then another sip straight away. The Coke tasted bitter and sickly mixed up with the vodka. She winced as she handed the bottle back to Louise and said, We could have gone to the pub.

Nah, too expensive, Louise said.

Louise was looking from side to side, as if she was waiting for someone to join them. She took the bottle from Mary and gulped from it, shook her head and licked her lips.

The next time Mary had a turn, she gulped, too. She winced and nearly gagged, but almost the moment she swallowed, she felt looser, like someone had shaken her.

Just then, Mickey strode around the corner and Louise's face lit up. He put his arms around her, his palms grazing the top of her buttocks, and he kissed her for a long time on her lips.

Hiya gorgeous, he said, smiling. He turned to Mary, who was concentrating on her feet, and said, Hiya Mary, you look nice.

She blushed.

Doesn't she? said Louise, looking at her in admiration.

Mary said, Can we go in now?

They downed the last bit of vodka and Louise left the bottle on the ground by the wall. There were no bouncers at St Frances' Church Hall and the only ID you needed was your St Frances Parish ID card. The two old ladies stood at the door, inspecting people who looked like they could be holding drink. Louise flashed them an enormous smile as she held her card up and passed them in one stride. One of the ladies stared at the back of Louise, taking in the amount of naked leg on show as Mary followed in her slipstream.

It was one big square room, dimly lit apart from the cheap disco lights that flashed circles of faded colour over the walls and ceilings. Mary felt the music wash over her and into her, throbbing through her chest. It felt good. Louise cupped her mouth with her hands to speak into her ear.

Okay, you know the plan, right? If he comes over, you have to only dance with him if he asks you to. Let him come to you, okay?

Mary nodded solemnly. She realised she was standing with

one foot on top of the other and fixed her feet firmly to the ground. She didn't want to dirty her laces. The room was filling up. Mickey passed around a plastic cup full of whiskey he had decanted from a bottle in the toilets. The music seemed to get louder and louder. There was no point in talking, so they just smiled at each other a lot, and started to dance. Louise flung herself around the floor, limbs flailing recklessly, oblivious of rhythm. Mary nodded her head and pushed it forward and back in a nervous rocking motion. Her feet moved from side to side. As the alcohol dissolved into her bloodstream, she felt less and less inhibited, and when she felt a hand on her shoulder, she swung around easily.

Mary, I thought that was you!

His face was beetroot red, with a glossy sheen, his hair matted down over his forehead. Even in her loose state, she could see that he was very drunk. He swayed slowly, fixing his eyes on her boobs with a serious expression.

Jesus Christ, Mary, you look amazing.

Don't sound so surprised, Danny Donnelly! That was Louise who swooshed by them, a blur of blonde.

Mary laughed.

Thanks, Danny.

Happy birthday. I got you a card.

He handed her an envelope. She took it off him and put it in her handbag, then looked back up, blushing.

Thanks, Danny, that's very kind of you.

Will we get you a drink? Come on, it's your birthday!

He grabbed her hand and led her through the crowds to the trestle table in the corner. Once they were there, she leaned against the table to hold herself steady. She felt like she had just got off a boat on to dry land. She focused on the straight line of the table underneath her hands.

I'll have a Coke, please, she said nonchalantly to Danny.

They stood side by side, facing the dance floor, and gulped their drinks down. Danny turned to look her up and down, and she stayed staring outwards at the writhing bodies. There was nothing to say.

The DJ spoke into the mic, his voice smooth, practised.

Okaaaaay everybody, time for the slow set . . . this is where you grab somebody and squeeze them tiiiiight . . .

The room was even darker now and Danny turned to her, a grave expression on his face.

Wanna dance, Mary?

She took his arm like she had seen Louise do with Mickey. She realised she was exactly the same height as him and silently thanked Louise for telling her to wear her Converse. They walked through the bodies, and he pulled her round to face him. A voice rang around the room, nasal and earnest, singing of seeing people in dreams and of not wanting to miss a thing.

She felt Danny's arms encase her and press her tightly up to his chest. She could smell his sweat and aftershave. She forced herself to put her arms over his shoulders, and when she did, she could feel his hands running up and down her back until one of them rested on her bum. It sat there heavy on her buttock like a dead weight. Now his tongue was thick and squirming in her mouth. The words were still ringing out around the hall, singing about the moment, and wanting to stay in it forever. She forced herself to keep her mouth open.

She pulled away eventually, and rested her head on his shoulder. She saw Louise's face flash past her, sparkling and exuberant as she was dragged somewhere by Mickey. Louise gave her a comedic double thumbs-up. Mary willed herself to feel the importance of it all. She squeezed her eyes shut as Danny's hand roughly kneaded her right breast. It hurt. She felt something pressing on her groin area, and had the stomach-sinking realisation that his penis was erect. He whispered in her ear.

Let's get out of here.

He gripped her hand so tight that her fingers pressed together painfully. She could feel her heart drumming in her chest as he pulled her through the dark shapes of intertwined bodies and crashed them through the fire exit and down a set of steps to the playing field below. The air was cool on her face, and she tried to breathe it in deeply as he pulled her along. She heard giggles from the darkness in the distance.

Danny, where are we going?

Somewhere no one can see us.

They walked to the corner of the field, where it was coal black. She could just make out a small triangular red flag signposting the corner of the playing pitch. He turned to her and grabbed her head in his two hands and thrust his tongue into her mouth. His hands were frantically searching her body; they squeezed her boobs roughly, then kneaded her bum, then moved up between her legs. Then she was on the ground. Afterwards, she didn't remember how she had got there. But she did remember him roughly pulling up her dress around her waist and pulling her pants down to her knees.

She did remember the heavy weight of his penis in her hand, surprisingly thick and short.

She did remember a *fucksake* as he fumbled to find her vagina.

She did remember him pulling her legs apart and thrusting and thrusting until he was inside her and she did remember the feeling of pain then and his panting and that feeling like the most disgusting thing, his sour breath right in her mouth.

She did remember the long drawn-out groan that came out of him, and the feeling of something wet and dripping around her thighs.

She did remember him rolling off her to lie on his back on the ground.

She did remember the feeling of queasiness coming over her like a thick fog; her stomach lurching and her retching into the grass.

She did remember him asking her was she all right over and over again, and her telling him to fuck off.

She did remember his legs walking away from her, his hands

pulling up his flies as he walked, and his face lit up pale and gormless in the moonlight as he turned to look back at her.

Louise found her in the bathroom, bent over the sink, trying to wash her face as reams of drunken girls clambered around each other to get a glimpse of themselves in the mirror.

Well, you've got a lot to tell me about, she said, eyes wide, searching Mary's face for clues. Jesus, Mary, the state of your face. Let's get you home.

Mary felt like she was going to be sick again any second, so she sat in the back of the taxi with her eyes closed and the window open, head flopping from side to side. Louise held her hand tightly and promised her she'd ring her the next day.

Late into the night, Mary sat cross-legged on her bed, feeling hyper-awake. She couldn't brush the taste of the vomit out of her mouth. There was a dull throb of pain between her legs. She rubbed her sticky thighs and touched her fingers to her lips. She gulped water hungrily from a bottle. She unzipped her bag and pulled out the envelope Danny had given her earlier on that night. It was a card with a bunch of pastel flowers on the front. She opened it up.

To Mary.
Happy birthday.
From Danny.

She stared at it for a long time and fell asleep, her knees curled up to her chin.

CHAPTER 9

MARY, 1999

On the morning of her last A-level exam, Mary closed the door softly behind her and stepped out into the sunlight, eyes fixed firmly on the ground.

Well, Mary?

Mary jumped. Her next-door neighbour Dolores was standing at the bin in front of her house.

Hey, Dolores.

Dolores had lived next door for as long as Mary could remember. She worked as a seamstress in a factory downtown, sewing pillowcases on a machine.

What's up with you? Dolores said, her face cocked to one side, her hand on the lid of the wheelie bin.

Nothing . . .

Are ye getting any sleep? Dolores asked, staring intensely at Mary's face now.

Not much.

Mary shrugged. Lately, she was inhabited by a ceaseless fatigue. Her muscles felt tight all the time. She often skipped meals, using cans of Diet Coke every morning and evening to give her the chemical energy to get through revision. By the time darkness fell, her head felt enormously heavy on her neck. When she did collapse into bed, she slept fitfully, and in the mornings, even the simplest of tasks seemed to take a Herculean effort. Pulling herself out of bed, putting on clean clothes, tying her hair back – it was all too much for her.

Dolores was waiting for an explanation. Mary looked at her briefly.

A-levels.

Aaaaah. Dolores nodded knowingly. She wasn't much taller than the bin. Her work had given her the beginnings of a hunch, Mary noticed, as Dolores bent down to pick up a bag of rubbish.

A-levels means the formal. Have you got yourself a dress?

Mary sighed. The whole of her year were going to the formal that night at the pink hotel at Finaghy. Louise was consumed by it, but after her night at St Frances', Mary knew with absolute certainty that she would not attend.

Naw. No dress. Too much money.

I'll whip ye up a dress, said Dolores, swinging the rubbish bag into the bin. You can show me the style you want and you just have to buy the material.

Ach, that's lovely, Dolores, but honestly I just, I don't want to go.

Dolores was not a person who frightened easily. Her garden was on the end corner of their street and the soldiers used to jump over her wall as a short cut to the alleyway when Mary was small. Dolores used to shout at the soldiers when they trampled on her flowers. She was on first-name terms with the Colonel and would give out yards to him, pointing her finger up at his face like he was a child. There was something about her laser focused gaze that saw right through all the walls in your head.

She took a deep breath and summoned the strength to look back at Dolores. Her hand was on her hip now, and she propped her elbow up on top of the bin lid. Her dressing gown was mint-green and it gave her face a sickly tinge.

You know when your ma and da moved in here, yer ma, she hardly had anything. No books, no pictures, just a suitcase with clothes and shoes. She was so proud of you, used to dress you up like a wee doll, she did. You were a wee quiet thing, hardly cried at all. And here you are off to do your big exams. She would have been proud of ye, Mary.

Mary was numb. She couldn't find words to speak.

Will ye be going to college? Dolores persisted.

Louise had it all worked out for herself. She wanted to be a TV presenter, holding a mic and talking into the camera like she was having a chat. She wanted eyes on her, lights on her. Mary really didn't know. She thought of Rita changing nappies and spoon-feeding toddlers in her kitchen while they dripped food all down their faces. She thought of the mail sacks and forklifts of the Royal Mail sorting office, and her daddy, dead-eyed in the middle of them. She thought of her mother, hoping things for her. She felt an overwhelming urge to cry. She felt like she could cry enough tears for a whole lake. She wanted to sink in them.

I don't know.

She looked away from Dolores, on down the street, willing Dolores to let her go on. She had to be at the exam hall at 8.30 a.m.

I'd better . . .

On ye go, said Dolores. Good luck, Mary.

CHAPTER 10

MARY, 1999

It had been fifty-three days since her last period.

Sean had told her about new positions at Atlantic Homecare and she had secured herself a job on the shop floor. It was a useful distraction from the panic rising in her like a high tide. On a Sunday afternoon at the end of her first week at the new job, she sat next to Louise on her bed. The July sun was beating through the window and Mary could feel a pool of sweat gathering on the small of her back. She felt too tired to move. Above the bed, on a poster for the film *Cruel Intentions*, Reese Witherspoon glanced sideways in conspiracy, her heart-shaped face bathed in orange-yellow light. It was five-thirty and soon they would hear Rita yelling that dinner was ready from the bottom of the stairs. Louise sat forwards on the bed, arms folded on her legs, leaning towards her bedside table, where an over-the-counter pregnancy test lay flat. She was staring at it intensely, as if it were an egg about to hatch.

I can't be pregnant, Mary said, scratching her left breast under her jumper absent-mindedly.

Louise sighed deeply.

He came inside you. So you *could* be pregnant.

But there was sticky stuff on my legs.

It doesn't all stay inside you, though, does it, Mary. It all mostly falls out, apart from a few little tadpole things that swim up your tubes.

Louise had pestered Mary relentlessly for the whole story of her sex with Danny. Mary had finally found the words to answer her at the end of a visit to Arndale, when Louise had followed her out on to the street.

Mary. Danny didn't hurt you, did he?

Mary swallowed.

Why are you asking me this *again*, Louise? Did you tell Rita?

I . . . maybe. I just said you haven't been yourself and she said to make sure and check, just, like, that he didn't take advantage of you.

Mary sighed. I'm fine, she said in a quiet voice.

Louise grabbed Mary's hands and squeezed them. Mary could smell her sweat.

Tell me, Mary.

Mary felt tears tickle the back of her eyes.

Okay. It wasn't nice. It wasn't nice at all. It hurt.

Louise was bug-eyed.

Did you tell him to stop?

No. I puked. And I told him to fuck off. At the end. When he kept asking me was I all right.

And did he fuck off?

Mary nodded as her eyes filled with tears. She was as tall as the bottom of Louise's chin. She focused on Louise's collarbones sticking out under her round-necked top.

Louise hugged her then. And Mary allowed herself to melt into her chest for just a few seconds before pulling away and heading to the bus stop.

When Mary missed her period a few weeks later, Louise marched into MacKenzie's pharmacy, found the tests on a shelf and put one down on the counter, staring at the cashier with wild, combative eyes. They were new contraptions, just released into Belfast, and Louise walked out waving it in the air like she had just won a trophy. Mary couldn't even bring herself to laugh.

Now Louise was staring at the stick, talking quietly and without pause.

Come on stick, don't let us down. Give us a line. One simple blue fucking line. Danny Donnelly's penis is tiny, there's no way his sperm got up there high enough to actually do something . . . not a chance. Hang on, how long are we at now?

Mary had her head in her hands. There was a fluttery feeling in her stomach, moving up to her throat, like a tiny bird flapping its wings.

It's been two minutes, she said into her palms.

Okay, I'm looking at it now.

Louise pulled the lid off the stick and gawped. She handed it to Mary.

Mary.

Mary kept her head in one hand and reached out her other one to take the stick. She opened her right eye just enough to see the thick blue cross. She slid off the bed on to the carpet with her head still in her hands. There was a long silence between them.

Fuck fuck fuck. Mary was chanting the words into her palms.

Louise slid down beside her on to the carpet.

Fucking hell, Danny Donnelly got you fucking pregnant. The little fucking shit thinks he can drink a load of booze and then fuck you on a fucking football pitch and walk away and you have to deal with it all? Mary, we can go to England. We can find money . . .

Mary couldn't speak. When she did, ten minutes later, she directed the words at the wall in front of her.

I have to go, Louise.

Where?

Mary pulled herself up from the floor and walked out the bedroom door without looking back. Louise called her name as Mary ran downstairs, grabbed her bag from the bannister at the bottom and pulled the door shut behind her. As soon as the cold air hit her face, she let the tears come. She walked briskly up Arndale Street towards the Falls Road, wiping them with her sleeve.

As she made her way across Broadway and over the round-about to the bottom of Boucher Road, she remembered the bitter taste of his tongue, the weight of his whole body on hers after he came. She turned left up the long, slow hill of Tates Avenue. She walked faster, locked into the rhythm of her footfall, head down, hands shoved into her jeans pockets; she didn't bother to wipe the tears away now. She remembered his face turning back towards her as he walked away, his mouth hanging open. She turned right on to the Lisburn Road and walked alongside the heavy tea-time traffic, past the big police station, past the supermarket, past the quaint coffee shops and upmarket gift shops. In front of the New York Pizza Co. a delivery driver fastened his food packages on to the back of his moped and mounted the saddle, twisting the handle to start the low rumble of his engine. She turned down a residential street and kept walking, past wooden gates and big driveways with estate cars and Land Rovers. Past windows framing large, light-filled, opulent rooms with chandeliers and thick, handmade curtains. She remembered the letters of her name spelled out in his childish handwriting on the birthday card. She saw her father's face, twisted into rage. She walked past the manicured flower beds of the residential roads until the beep of a car in the distance jolted her out of her thoughts, and she turned around to walk back the way she came.

That's when she saw Belfast. She realised, her heart beating fast and loud, that she had never seen her city from afar like this, all vast and teeming with life. There was the faintest pinky hue to the clouds and she watched a plane fly through them, down into City Airport, over the yellow Harland and Wolff gantry by the shipyards on the lough. She could see the Europa Hotel. The tip of the ornate green dome of City Hall. There was the Royal Victoria Hospital, the football stadium. She could see the tops of the trees poking out from the Botanic Gardens. She sighed into the dusk, as the cars whooshed by behind her, and she felt totally emptied, light enough to float away into the breeze like a balloon.

It took her forty minutes to walk back down the Malone Road. By the time she walked through the gates of the Botanic Gardens, the light had turned inky blue in the dusk and the shadows of the trees looked like dark figures dancing on the grass. She went to her bench and sat down. The birds were burbling melodic exchanges above her in the branches. Groups of drunken students lay about on the green.

She pulled her feet up on to the bench and pulled her jumper over her knees and down to her ankles. Her tears had dried on her face and their salty residue cracked on her cheeks when she blinked her eyes open. She rested her chin on her knees and breathed deeply. She remembered the last time she was sitting here, watching the tiny toddler fall on the grass. Watching the child's mother pick her up and pour her love over her – so ordinarily, as simple as being alive. What a thing – to have a person! All to yourself. To love them and for them to love you. She sat until the trees were dark shapes in the distance. Until the park keeper gently reminded her he had to close the gates.

It was four more days before Mary had a day off to visit Louise. Louise waited for her at the front door, tapping her foot and flicking her hair impatiently. She wore a bikini top and denim cut-offs, and her pale legs looked extraordinarily long. She had yet to get herself a summer job. When her eyes rested on Mary, her expression darkened into worry. She walked out of the gate and up the street towards her. She grabbed Mary's shoulders, one in each hand, and talked just a few inches from her face.

Are you okay? Did you tell your dad?

Mary stepped back and took Louise's hands and held them firmly.

Louise, I need you to shut up about this. I'm going to figure out a plan, okay? I promise I am. But I need a clear head to think.

Louise was looking over Mary's head, into the distance.

Well, if you need a hand with figuring out how to say it to your da . . . maybe I could come with you.

Lou-lou. I've got to do this on my own. I just need time to think.

Okay. I'll shut up.

She led Mary by the hand through the house to sit on the deckchairs in the back garden. She kept her word, but Mary could see the question burning in her eyes all evening.

On the first Friday of August, Mary arrived home after work and cooked a lamb stew. She had been experiencing a new level of hunger; it felt alive inside of her, growling and insatiable. In the last few weeks, she had found herself cooking hearty meals and enjoying the sensation of heavy calm that came over her body after eating them. It felt like ballast, giving her balance and heft to prevent her from turning upside down.

The stew was simmering in the pot on the hob and she sat at the table reading her book. There was an open packet of black olives on the table beside her. The back door was propped open by the bin, and the evening sun shone right through the doorway. She hadn't bothered to change out of her work uniform.

Good timing, Daddy, she said, nodding at the pot on the hob as her father walked into the room.

I could smell it. Nice smell to wake up to, he said into the pot as he ladled himself out a full bowl and sat down at the table. His hair was wet from the shower. His whole forehead was lined with deep wrinkles that moved as he raised his eyebrows towards the open book on the table in front of her.

Can't get enough of the studying?

She blushed deeply. She was fixated on the chapter in her biology book that showed the different stages of the foetus. The page showed drawings of the earliest stage of pregnancy. It looked remarkably ugly to her; an alien-like clump of flesh and cartilage all curled up, already protecting itself from the dangers of life.

Just interested in it, that's all.

She closed the book, brought her bowl over to the sink and busied herself washing up.

How are ye getting on at the job?

Good. It's just tidying the shelves. It's really easy.

He nodded, his mouth full, and kept his eyes on her until he swallowed.

When do you get your results?

Any day now.

She shifted her weight on her feet. Willed herself to tell him. But she was still slowly washing dishes as he dropped his bowl into the sink and headed out the door.

The following evening, Mary walked up to Sean's room and knocked on his door. He had been making more appearances at the house lately, and she had surmised that his relationship with Julie was over. Sean never knew how to tread softly; his steps were big, weighty thumps on the carpet. The dance music coming from behind him and the smoke drifting out the door gave his bedroom the impression of a nightclub. His torso was bare. He had filled out over the last few years; his shoulders and chest were thick and tight with muscle. He had developed the same stooped posture as their father, pushing his head into his neck to try and curtail his height. His nose was slightly crooked over his mouth, which was small and thin-lipped.

What's up?

Sean, I'm going to the chippie. Will I get ye some?

Aye, see you soon.

He closed the door quickly, leaving a puff of smoke lingering above the bannisters.

When she came home, cheeks flushed, eyes sparkling, he was in the kitchen, dressed and leaning against the counter, and he was looking at her.

How's it going at the shop?

Good. It's dead easy, like.

Paul will move you to the tills soon, I bet.

They sat down and spread their newspaper-covered packages out over the table. They ate in silence for a few minutes. Sean had put a pirate radio station on, and it was playing choppy garage music. It sounded tinny on their radio.

What about your results? What are ye gonna do?

He bit the end off a battered sausage and spat it out on to the newspaper, blowing on the other half in his hand.

I don't think I did as well as last year, she spoke into her chips. But it'll all work out one way or another. Sean.

She looked at him intensely, her face filled with hope.

I'm pregnant.

He stopped chewing. He looked at her for a long time. He swallowed.

What the fuck, Mary.

He sat back in his chair, blinking rapidly, and slowly shook his head. Who the fuck . . . who . . . are you with someone? Do you have a boyfriend?

He was staring at her.

I want to keep the baby.

Sean was holding a chip in his left hand and he squashed it so that it broke, and the long end fell down on to the floor.

Who is he, Mary?

His voice was low and flat. The kitchen was filled with the vinegary smell of chips. Mary felt uncomfortably hot.

It wasn't. I didn't.

Just tell me!

Danny Donnelly.

There had been no contact. In two and a half months. No chance meetings outside the chip shop. No walk by in the park. No cards or letters. The birthday card was under her mattress. She couldn't bring herself to throw it out. She didn't tell Louise about it. She knew she would find it appallingly simple and hilarious. She was grateful for the card in a way. It helped cement her path. She knew she wanted to do this on her own, but she felt like maybe he could support her somehow, some day. If he could write her a birthday card, he could write her a cheque. Right now, he didn't want to know her and that was definite. What she didn't like was the feeling of not knowing him, or what he would want in the future. She didn't like the unpredictability of his needs.

Sean stood up quickly, knocking his chair backwards on to the kitchen floor. He stood for a few seconds, looking at the floor next to Mary's feet, breathing heavily.

Sean, she said quietly.

He walked out of the kitchen and upstairs. She heard him thump around, heard his music being turned off and heard his footsteps on the stairs before the house shook with the slam of the front door. She made herself breathe out slowly through her mouth. The table was a mess of chips and batter. She ran to the phone and dialled Louise's number.

3 – 2 – 9 – 2 – 0 – 6

Hello?

Hey Rita, is Louise there, please?

She's out with Mickey, darlin'. She'll be back around ten.

Mary sat for several minutes with the phone to her ear, listening to the dull line of dial tone. She didn't sleep that night. She didn't sleep because Sean didn't come home.

Sunday afternoon and the phone was clanging her slowly out of a deep, dreamless sleep. She was on the sofa, curled up, hugging a cushion, with a bowl of cereal on the carpet at her feet. It was four o'clock. She sat up just as her father walked in from the kitchen. He seemed surprised to see her.

I've got it, Daddy, she said as she picked up the phone.

Hello.

Hi, doll.

Hi, Louise.

Her head was pounding; the sleep had felt dangerously deep, like she had gone too far into her subconscious. It felt hard to wake up.

Jesus. I think I've been asleep for ages.

She pulled herself out of her blanket and walked over to the kitchen door. Her father was putting on his coat, a cigarette already dangling out of his mouth. He waved goodbye and she waved back before closing the door.

What's up, did you not sleep last night?

No, hardly at all, I was up half the night.

Sean's crestfallen face flashed up in her memory. She remembered the sound of the door slamming and the pictures trembling on their hooks in the hall.

Louise took a breath. Her words were sped up and whispered: Mary, Mickey heard that Sean found Danny Donnelly last night and beat the crap out of him. Like, bad. Like, he had to go to hospital, Mary.

What the fuck? Sean wouldn't do that.

Mary felt panicked. She was sitting up on the sofa now. Her hand was absent-mindedly cupping the small mound of her belly.

Mary, what happened? Did he find out?

Yeah, he did. I told him last night. That I was pregnant, and that I wanted to keep the baby.

Whoah. You want to keep the baby, Mary?! Jesus Christ.

There was a long silence on the phone. Mary's voice was flat.

I will manage, Louise.

Are you sure, darlin'?

Mary felt rage form inside her. She spat out the words.

Do you think I haven't been thinking about it every second of every day? Yes, Louise, I'm sure. I will manage. And Louise, I think it would be nice if you and Mickey don't go round telling people that my brother put someone in fucking hospital unless you saw it with your own eyes.

Jesus, Mary, I just thought you would want to know!

Well I don't. Because I don't believe it.

The line prickled with tension. Mary could hear Louise breathing down the phone.

So, what did Sean say when you told him?

None of your business, Louise.

Jesus, Mary, what's got into you?

Just fuck off, okay!

Mary hung up the phone. The house was deathly quiet again. She stared at the fireplace, feeling sick all of a sudden. She dragged herself up the stairs to the bathroom. She was sitting on the toilet with her head in her hands when she heard the front door open and click shut.

She came out to watch Sean walk up the stairs. He stopped halfway up when he saw her. She started to cry.

Sean, what did you do?

He sighed out heavily, one hand still holding the bannister.

What did you do to him?

Nothing that you need to be concerned with. He walked up to the top of the stairs and gently pushed past her on the landing. He stank of stale booze and cigarettes. She saw the dried mud on the back of his coat.

Sean, tell me what you did to him, for fuck's sake!

Her tears were dangling off the end of her nose.

He turned around and held her gaze for a few seconds and then sighed again, closing his eyes.

I need to sleep, he said, opening his bedroom door.

As his door lock clicked shut, she screamed. It was a jagged-edged sound, serrated like a bread knife, and it terrified her.

CHAPTER 11

MARY, PRESENT

She is driving up the Upper Newtownards Road. She sits upright and leans into the wheel, eyes wide and set on the road ahead. Every few minutes, without taking her eyes off the road, she absent-mindedly lifts her hand from the wheel and rubs the thick callouses on her palms with the thumb of her other hand. She hurried out of the cemetery at dawn and has been nervously revving her car around the roads of Belfast ever since. Her leggings are still damp from the wet grass. Even with the heating turned up to full, she can't shake the cold from her bones. Her head is beginning to throb.

At one point she drove up the Cave Hill, but there were too many people there, people with cameras and raincoats and picnics in bags. On her way back down she saw the ocean and the jagged line of the coast, and she knew exactly what she had to do. She will bring him to the sea. She knows the general direction, she just needs to put petrol in the tank. She sees the green horizontal line of a BP garage on the right-hand side of the road in the distance. Her stomach rumbles loudly as she indicates right and turns across the oncoming traffic to a bay in the garage. She pulls on the door to open it and then swiftly shuts it again. She's got to hide him. She looks around inside the car and then she takes off her hoodie and gently lays it on top of him on the front seat. She exits the car and shivers in her T-shirt.

She is clumsy and clammy-handed and fumbles with the petrol tank lid before inserting the hose. She steadies herself on the side of the car as the petrol pump whirrs into action. A man is filling his black BMW on the bay opposite and she catches eyes with him, then looks away immediately. He is wearing sunglasses, but she is sure he is still looking at her. It feels as if everyone in this garage is looking at her. She keeps her eyes to the ground as she hurries into the shop and straight to the fridge, where she grabs a can of Coke. As she pays for the petrol, she watches the girl behind the till and imagines what she is thinking about her. Her dirty nails and her messy hair. Her disgusting face. The state of her. She swallows and gestures to the shelf of medicine behind the counter.

Can I get some of those paracetamol, she says and the girl reluctantly pulls herself off her stool and adds them to the transaction.

That'll be fifty-four pounds fifty, she drawls, staring out the window.

Mary fumbles in her purse, pulls out her card and sticks it in the machine. She feels a stab of panic because she can't remember the numbers. The only number sequence she can conjure up in her mind is seven-four-seven-eight. The last four digits of his number. The number she hasn't been able to give a name to on her phone. What is her card number? She looks at the girl and giggles nervously,

I can't remember my number.

The girl faces her now, a look of scepticism on her face. She has to try something. She goes with her instinct.

Five-eight-four-five.

Pin error flashes up on the screen. She swallows and pulls the card out, then re-inserts it, stealing a glance at the girl behind the till who is raising her eyebrows at the people in the queue behind her. She closes her eyes. Come on, Mary, come on, Mary. She presses the buttons.

Four-eight-five-five.

Pin accepted.

Remove card.

She feels light-headed with relief, and she thinks she might fall over. The girl is staring at her. She has asked her something.

Sorry? she says, holding on to the counter.

Would you like your receipt?

No. No, thank you.

Mary takes her tablets and can of Coke out of the shop and back to the car. She sits with her hand on her hoodie and allows herself a deep breath. She blinks rapidly, then jumps as a car beeps behind her. They are queueing to get out and she is in their way. She quickly starts the car and it jolts forwards violently.

Shit shit shit shit, she is saying and as she turns the key in the ignition again she looks up and sees the girl in the shop staring at her from the window. She pulls the car out of the bay and on to the road, following the traffic. Big, slow drops of rain start to hit the windscreen. She turns on her wipers and sighs as the rubber from the left wiper drags across the glass, making a sad honking sound. Of course she never got them fixed. She clicks open the ring pull and takes a long gulp of Coca-Cola. She blinks and sniffs. She has to keep moving.

CHAPTER 12

TJ, PRESENT

The rain has been stopping and starting all morning. He is pacing the kitchen, feeling the need to do something useful. He will make them something to eat. She always has toasted banana bread in the cafe for a treat. He takes his phone out, googles banana bread and finds a recipe, then roots around in the drawer by the sink and finds her apron. It's bottle-green and grubby with old stains, like something you'd see a butcher wear.

He writes a note on his phone to buy his ma a new apron for her Christmas present. He puts it on over his head and ties it at the back and takes a photo of himself with it on, sticking out his tongue in a silly face. He looks at it and frowns. He looks so greasy! He thinks he must do that thing again soon where he puts his head over boiling water in the sink to steam his skin. His ma showed him how to do it last time. He remembers that he couldn't stop laughing, he felt like such an idiot, with his body bent over the sink and a towel over his head. He kept rearing himself up to protest, with the towel still on his head and his face all dripping. His ma was trying to tell him off, but she couldn't stop laughing, telling him it wouldn't work unless he stayed there. It did work in the end. His skin felt supple and gleaming and he was able to squeeze all his spots without them getting all red and sore. He'll do it again soon.

Everything is lined up on the worktop. Bananas, eggs, sugar, butter, flour. The only thing he can't find anywhere is baking powder. His ma has her own system in the kitchen; all the powders and herbs are in lots of different containers and tins. Only she knows what's what. So far, he has found three different containers with white powder in, but he doesn't want to risk it. He decides he'll call in to Dolores next door. He leaves the door on the latch, walks outside and turns immediately into the adjoining house to theirs. He notices how decrepit the house looks. The paint is peeling off the window frames. He knocks two times and waits. The dogs yap frantically until Dolores pulls open the door. It takes longer than usual.

Ach, Dolores.

Ah, would you look at this angel! In an apron and all! Well that's a first! Her laugh is wheezy and gleeful. TJ had forgotten about the apron. He looks down at himself and starts to blush, shifting his weight from leg to leg with a shy grin.

Are you in the bad books? Dolores looks up at him over the rims of her glasses. She half smiles.

Well . . . I'm trying to make banana bread for Ma. Have you seen her, Dolores? She's not been in this morning and she's not answering her phone.

Mm, didn't see her coming or going at all this morning.

She'll be back soon, I'm sure. So yeah, I don't have any baking powder. Well, I might, but I don't know which one is which and it's only half a teaspoonful, so can I borrow some?

Jesus Christ, we'd better get this one right. What did you do this time? Let me go and get ye some, come on in.

She turns back into the hall as she talks, on the assumption that he will follow her. The dogs stand halfway down the hall, eyes locked on him in suspicion. They are tiny Scottish Terriers, groomed adoringly by Dolores. There are photos of them all over the house, glass-eyed and panting. One of them has a tartan ribbon round its neck now, tied in a perfect bow.

Out of the way, you two, she says and her words catch in her throat. She starts to cough as she walks, a rasping bark that affects her enough she has to hold on to the bannister to steady herself.

He calls out after her, I can't, Dolores, I left the door on the latch! Are you okay?

She pulls herself up and shuffles on. Ach aye, I'm grand, son, it's just a wee cough.

He feels self-conscious all of a sudden, standing on her doorstep with his apron on. He quickly takes it off and folds it over his arm. Her use of the word 'son' reminds him of his conversation with Aiden before they left the pub on Thursday night. Aiden told him that his father was an ex pro-boxer and ran a boxing club up in Ardoyne. Aiden opted out of a boxing career for his job at Devaney's and a sideline selling hash, coke and ecstasy to the student population of the Holylands, who he both despised and admired in equal measure. He snarled into his pint as he spoke about his father.

He thinks he's fucking Clint Eastwood, but instead of Hilary Swank, he gets ratty wee boys from the estates and scares the shite out of them. I had enough of that as a kid. Fuck going back there.

At least you have a dad, TJ said. Mine fucked off before I was born and my ma pretends he doesn't exist.

Aiden looked up at him.

Where is he? Do you want to find him?

TJ swallowed his gulp and put his glass down.

America, apparently. She hasn't narrowed it down any further from there. I have a hunch he's in New York. Obviously I'm curious, like. But it's on him to find me. He's the one who fucked off.

And let's be honest, added Aiden, he could be a prick.

He can hear Dolores opening cupboards in the kitchen. He steps into the hall and peeks through an inch-wide gap in the door leading into the sitting room. It seems so much smaller than theirs, with all the trinkets and clutter. He can see the back of the easy chair, where Dolores's husband Freddie used to sit. He wonders if she sits in it now Freddie's gone. He remembers his ma helping Dolores when Freddie became too hard for her to care for; she'd be in there every evening, helping him up to bed, and every morning before work to help him downstairs again. They set up a fold-out bed downstairs for him, but he had to go into an old folks' home in the end. TJ went with his ma and Dolores to visit Freddie once, and was shocked at how depressing it was. All these shrunken people sitting in silence, with faraway looks in their eyes. His ma drove Dolores to the home every week until Freddie died.

TJ puts his hand up on Dolores's wall and examines the faded, greasy, brown-and-cream thick-striped wallpaper. There is a wooden plaque with a tiny container of holy water hanging on a nail just inside the front door. He gently pushes the wood sideways to reveal a perfect square of bright matt wallpaper underneath. He sighs as he thinks of all the presents he has received from Dolores in his life. Cards for every occasion, boxes of biscuits and chocolates, socks and scarves, and most recently, a thirty-pound voucher from M&S for leaving school.

It makes her happy to give, his ma told him when he opened the card and balked at the value of the voucher.

But I can't repay her.

You don't have to repay her, you just show her kindness in other ways; go and check on her, bring her things.

So, TJ checks on her at least once a week. Checking on her consists of calling at the door and seeing how quickly he can get out of the conversation. He has learned various techniques to help this endeavour – calling in just before dinner time, or calling in on his way somewhere, and most commonly, leaving the door on the latch.

She is making her way back up the hall. She leans quite heavily from side to side as she walks, using the heft of her body for momentum. She is squinting through her glasses at a little white container.

Take a look at that, will you, TJ?

TJ takes it from her and reads the label.

That's it, Dolores. Thanks a million! I'll drop it back when I'm done.

Ach, take it for as long as you need it, son. Hope it does the trick.

She waves as she closes the door behind him. He walks back down her drive, gripping the container tight.

CHAPTER 13

MARY, 1999

The weeks sludged by, and Louise called several times a day. Mary sat at the top of the stairs, watching the phone on the hall table. There was a freshly bloomed anger in her, shimmering and new, that eclipsed every other emotion. Louise filled her thoughts, but she never moved to answer the phone. It trilled through the house like a forlorn bird, maddening her brother and her father. But whenever they answered it and called for Mary, she shook her head at them and ran to her room. She pictured Louise's forehead furrowed under her fringe, imagined her nervously picking the skin around her fingernails with the phone tucked into the crook of her neck. She picked her own skin, pulling small strips of it around her thumbnails until she bled, and then she picked more. The sharp jolts of pain reminded her that she was there, in her body, alive.

On the first Monday of September, she spent an hour dawdling through the aisles of Primark looking at maternity clothes. She started to feel light-headed and took herself out-side to sit down on a bench near the bus stops on Donegall Square. The air was thick with fumes. She gulped down a can of Coke from her bag and watched a group of young teenage girls burst into spontaneous laughter at the bus stop. They reminded her of a shoal of fish she'd seen on a nature programme the night before.

Across the road, a figure pulled himself along on crutches, heading towards the bus stop. He stopped and looked up every few seconds to gauge the distance between him and the stop. His leg was in a cast and he had a bandage over his left ear and around his whole head. She stared now. He winced every time his cast touched the ground. There was something about the proportions of his neck to his shoulders that was familiar to her. The tightly packed density of his body. She held her breath as she recognised him, her stomach lurching as if in freefall, as if she had been pushed off the edge of something without warning. It was Danny Donnelly.

That's when he looked up at her. He was a few feet from the edge of the road. Their eyes locked and Mary watched his face twist into shock as he recognised her. She could see his chest heaving the air in and out of his lungs. She was paralysed on the bench; eyes wide and unblinking. Inside her head, she was screaming. They were both startled by the loud beep of a horn, which propelled Danny to hurry to the edge of the road, swing himself up on to the kerb and keep swinging himself along the road away from Mary, behind the bus stops, until he was out of sight. She still hadn't moved. Pigeons landed in a flurry of feathers around the benches. She had no control over her tears any more, and she sat, helpless to stop them as they streamed down her cheeks.

In the middle of the month, she went to her twelve-week scan alone. She took the bus all the way down the Falls Road and walked into the jumble of buildings that made up the Royal Victoria Hospital, feeling petrified. She watched the couples walk out of the dark room, looking tender-faced and softened. She thought of Danny Donnelly and how her dreams were filled with sequences of his face on a loop, walking away from her, sometimes in the moonlight, sometimes in the daylight. Always stumbling, hobbling, sometimes bleeding, face twisted into pain. Of how she was woken that morning, by her tears, soaking the pillowcase in a damp halo around her head. Then she heard her name.

Mary McConnell?

The nurse was kind to her, politely avoiding the conversation around her age and her lack of partner, and after she flinched from the cold of the ultrasound gel on her stomach, she relaxed back into the bed.

Here is your baby! the nurse exclaimed softly. Mary watched in awe as the grainy shape of her baby appeared on the screen.

There's the wee hands, there, see? Baby is jumping around

in there! laughed the nurse, deftly moving the wand around her belly.

It's a boy, isn't it? Mary whispered.

They'll tell you that for sure on your next scan. It's too early to tell now.

I don't know how, but I just know it, Mary said, eyes fixed on the moving shape on the screen in front of her.

A mother's intuition, said the nurse, typing into her keyboard. Mary wiped away her tears.

It was nearly lunchtime and she went straight home, preparing the words in her head for when her father woke up from his sleep. When she walked into the hall, she frowned as she saw the light of the television screen through the open living room door.

Daddy, you're up early. He was splayed out on the sofa, stained tracksuit bottoms under a black T-shirt, remote control in hand.

I couldn't sleep.

He glanced briefly at her before turning back to the television. The room was filled with the high-pitched nasal drone of the engines of Formula One cars. She watched her father's eyes move with the cars as they set off on their course around the track. He scratched at his beard. She forced herself to take a breath.

Daddy. I need to talk to you.

He looked back at her and narrowed his eyes. He lifted the remote and turned the TV silent.

She moved forward a few steps and cleared her throat.

I've just come from the hospital. I'm pregnant.

He stayed staring at her and blinked once, slowly. She felt frozen in her limbs, a block of ice. She remembered her lines and forced them out.

You're going to be a grandfather. The baby is coming in February.

Another blink from her father. He slowly moved his legs so his feet rested on the carpet and dragged himself to a sitting position.

I'm doing it alone. I don't need money.

His brow furrowed over his eyes. He stared at her feet.

Who's the father?

He's a friend of Sean's. Danny Donnelly, his name is. He won't be getting involved. I don't want him to.

Did he . . . ?

Her father sat up straight on the side of the sofa now and hesitated, looking confused, as if something had just dawned on him.

It's fine, Daddy. I just want to do it on my own.

And where will you do it?

His voice was low. She felt a bolt of fear in her chest.

Where will I . . . ?

Where do you intend on bringing up this baby?

She had felt the force of this look from her father a few times in the past. She had watched it wither her brother. It was contempt, pure and pointed and as visceral as if he had slapped her. Her voice shook.

I would like to bring my baby up here. In this house.

Something seemed to collapse inside him then and he leaned back into the chair and covered his eyes with his hands.

Jesus Christ, Mary. You had your whole life ahead of you. You could have gone to college.

Mary clenched her teeth together and willed the tears not to come. Her A-Level results had come in the post, at her request. They were just enough to go to university.

I could maybe do both. My life's not over, Daddy. This is what I want.

Is it now. Mary, you have no clue.

He shook his head slowly with his eyes closed, and then, suddenly, he let out a growl and stood over her, drawing up to his full height.

Just . . . get out of my sight, will ye!

And she fled, like a small creature, to pace the narrow width of her bedroom carpet until her heartbeat slowed down. Downstairs, her father pressed unmute on the remote control and she felt the drone of the Formula One cars vibrating through the walls.

You're going to have to speak to Paul. About your situation, Sean said to her as they sat side by side on the back of the bus, a few days after Mary told their father her news.

She was frightened of her own brother now. Of the storms

that raged inside his head. She spent hours lying awake in the dark, squeezing her pillow into a suffocating hug over her face, thinking of all the things that could happen to him now that he'd put someone in hospital. Thinking of the things he was capable of doing to other people.

He glanced in the direction of her stomach. She wore her grey elasticated trousers and the red sweatshirt of the Atlantic Homecare staff uniform.

I don't want them pissed off with you for getting a job and then just fucking off.

She was grateful for the simple satisfaction of her job. Grateful for a purpose now that school was finished. She didn't want to stop. She felt heavy with nerves when she knocked on the door of Paul's office and she held her breath and watched his eyebrows jump as he took in her news. Then she watched them join together, and then dip down towards his ginger beard, deep in thought.

She heard herself say, in a small voice, The baby's not due till February . . . I can work a full five months for you, and I can come back after the baby's born, too.

We'll make it work, he said, and she gripped on to the door frame on the way out. She felt light-headed all the time these days, as if she was always on the brink of falling over. But this was like a weight had been lifted off her. This was relief.

Louise stopped phoning three weeks into September. When Mary wasn't working, she couldn't bear this fresh silence in the house, so she took buses at random, moving in a trance-like state around the safe parts of the city, sitting on park benches if it wasn't too cold. She spent whole afternoons in the library, re-reading all her emails from Louise, speaking them out loud to herself like a mantra. She couldn't escape their last phone call.

Whoah. You want to keep the baby, Mary? Jesus Christ!

When people noticed her bump, she had all her answers polished and ready.

Six months now . . .

Ach yes, the daddy is delighted, so he is. He's dying for it to be a boy . . .

No! We deliberately didn't find out; we want it to be a surprise on the day . . .

She thought about 'the day' a lot, daydreaming of how it could have been with Louise and Rita. She played out entire scenes in her head, Louise gently making fun of her shape, marvelling at the movement of the baby in her stomach. Making a big deal of being overprotective. She imagined Rita taking her aside at Arndale, giving her advice about the labour, offering to come to the hospital on the day. A safe pair of hands.

And, of course, she saw Louise eventually. It was the last Thursday in September, and she had just sat down on the back of the bus setting off outside the Europa Hotel. She noticed a flash of white-blonde hair from the corner of her eye, and there she was, walking down Great Victoria Street with Mickey and his friend Freddie and another girl. The sun was glaring through the window and she shielded her eyes with her hands and squinted out the window to watch. Louise was wearing new black wedge sandals and a black choker around her neck. She was in full show-off mode, waving fingers and head bobbing, doing an impression of someone or something, Mary assumed. There was the fluid slip of her hand back into Mickey's as she basked in the laughter of his friends. Mickey's friend Freddie spat out his chewing gum as he walked, and stamped on it, his face still smiling from Louise's joke.

Her world was black and she couldn't see out of the shadows. She sat on the bus, rigid, for the whole circuit, until the driver came upstairs to shout at her to get off.

CHAPTER 14

MARY, 1999

According to the weather reports, Belfast was due a perfect blanket of snow for Christmas Day, but it still hadn't arrived by Christmas morning. Mary woke early and perched herself by the living room window to watch the lights of the houses on their street flick on one by one. The light was thin this morning, she could see the cold in it. The McIntyres across the road didn't pull their curtains and she had a perfect view right into their front room. There were the three children, still in their pyjamas, tearing open their presents under the fairy lights of their Christmas tree. She watched their silent screams of delight. There was their mum, Carol, on her knees on the floor, bent over her young daughter, helping her open a present. There was the dad, Dave, pulling his wife up on to the sofa beside him and kissing her on the cheek.

As winter had set in and the weeks fell away in a blur, she bought herself a bigger work jumper, and swallowed her yawns. Paul had cut her shifts to three days a week, and she shyly accepted a wheeled stool from him, rolling herself down the aisles, turning and straightening things through the hours. Her stomach was swollen and hard to the touch and she couldn't get comfortable in her bed at night. She felt tiredness pulling at her all through the days.

She was haunted by the memory of seeing Louise from the bus, bathed in laughter and blonde light. The rage she initially felt at Louise's reaction to her keeping the baby had quietened down to a crushing feeling of rejection. Louise had clearly moved on with her life and forgotten all about Mary and her sad choices. The last few months of separation had exposed the landslide of feelings inside Mary for her friend. She couldn't allow herself to be flattened by them. She had to stay upright. She had to keep herself well.

Mary sighed, squeezing her stomach tighter, thinking of how her own father hadn't looked her in the eye in four months. How her 'situation' was never spoken of under his roof. But her baby was letting her know of his presence all by himself. She could feel the small, hard lump of his foot just below her left rib, and she massaged it as she talked quietly.

Happy Christmas, Squidge. One day, Santa's gonna come to you and we'll have fairy lights and a tree and all of it. I promise.

Later, she prepared Christmas dinner, and served it out on the table. She called her father away from the canned laughter of the TV and shouted at Sean from the bottom of the stairs. She had lit a candle, and its single flame was a focal point for their stares as they chewed through the food. Their father ate quickly and messily and was the first to put his knife and fork on an empty plate. He wiped his face and hands with the holly printed paper napkins that Mary had bought.

Well, that was lovely, Mary. He nodded agreement at himself, looking down at his empty plate. He stood up and brought his hand out of his pocket, clutching a roll of notes, and peeled off two twenties, leaving one in front of each of his children's respective plates.

You can buy yourselves something nice.

Thank you, Daddy, Mary said, smiling. Sean grunted in agreement.

Her father nodded at her and then grabbed his coat and went out the back door into the icy air. As always there was the slightest change in the atmosphere, an exhalation of tension. She looked at Sean and he said, Is the Glen even open on Christmas Day?

She laughed.

He'll find somewhere.

Then, he spoke quickly like he had been waiting to say it: I've got something for you.

Two minutes later, he walked back into the kitchen, carrying something large in his arms. It was a white wooden rocking cradle, with a heart cut into the centre of the head-board. He set it on the linoleum by her feet.

I guess you'll be needing this.

She cried, of course. She was touched most by the fact that he had hidden it in his room. That this sweet object had sat in his dark, smoky cave for goodness knows how long. She cleared a space on the table and lifted it up and marvelled at how perfectly put together it was.

Sean. Thank you.

He nodded and sipped his beer. His eyes were soft. She went upstairs to her room and brought down a carefully wrapped present.

He opened it and looked at her. It was an A4-sized black leather covered photo album. Inside, she had stuck all the photos she had of Sean and her over the years. Sean flicked through the pages. One of Sean as a tiny baby, in a nappy, with creases in his chubby thighs and shining eyes. One of Sean and Mary holding hands in their school uniform when they were very small. One of Sean in his room, taken by surprise, his eyes pink from the flash and spots on his face. One taken by Aunt Bridget, of their father flanked by a small Mary and Sean, in the front yard of the house, with their father raising his hand up to his forehead in a salute to shelter his eyes from the sun. One she had taken of Sean standing proud in his Atlantic Homecare uniform first thing in the morning. He was holding a cup of tea with two hands so as to warm them with it. He was mid-laugh and looking down at the floor to the side. Mary spoke.

I thought you might want something to show Julie, you know, about your life. But then you split up with her, so it'll have to be the next girlfriend.

Sean laughed into the photo album, flicking back and forth through the pages.

I left some pages free at the end in case you wanted to put your picture of Mum in there.

He looked up at her then and said, Or the baby.

Or the baby, she whispered.

CHAPTER 15

MARY, 2000

She woke up at 6 a.m. with a strange, loose feeling inside her and she knew. She pulled on her clothes, sat at her make-up table and put on her concealer, checked her bag and checked her bag again. She knocked on Sean's door.

Sean, wake up.

He didn't respond and she had to run to the bathroom. As she was sitting on the toilet, she felt an enormous surge of pain low in her body. She cried out as her bowels emptied of their own accord. She pulled herself up and out and back to Sean's room and this time had to shout.

Sean, the baby's coming, get up, get up!

She carefully walked down the stairs and instinctively put the kettle on for Sean. By the time her next surge of pain came, he was sipping his tea in front of her in the kitchen, bleary-eyed and grey-faced. Their father came home then, pushing open the back door with a face dark as a thundercloud.

The baby is coming, Mary said, with an urgency that propelled her father's eyes to move rapidly from side to side.

Sean, get her out of here. Mary, I'll call Bridget to come and meet you there.

No.

She was clutching her stomach and staring at her father with wild eyes.

No Bridget, she said. Let's go, Sean.

Sean had bought a second-hand black Volkswagen Golf a few months before. He told her he could use it to drive her to the hospital. That was always the plan, but they had never discussed what would happen when they got there. On Mary's instruction, Sean pulled over outside the entrance and put his hazards on with the engine still running. She clung tightly to the handles of her hospital bag.

I hope I'm not too early, she said.

I'll keep my mobile on and when you need me to come back and get you, just call me, okay? You know the number, right?

Aye, I've it written down in my bag.

She looked at him and he was looking back at her, worry on his face. He moved his hand from the gearstick and pulled on the door handle across her body.

Go, go, go. You'll be grand. You're braver than you think.

She let herself out and watched Sean's car pull out on to the road again. She held back the urge to bawl as he beeped his horn. She hurried through the door and immediately the faint smell of disinfectant in the air made her feel sick. She took the lift up to the obstetric assessment unit to find the receptionist filling the printer on her desk with paper.

Are you okay, love? she said, glancing briefly at Mary and then focusing back on her printer.

I've had five contractions.

Only five? Are you sure you're dilated enough, love? Have you been timing them?

The receptionist paused as her eyes rested on Mary's face.

Have you got someone with you?

No, Mary said. I just want to be here because it feels like it's really happening.

Take a seat over there and I'll get your files and have someone come and see you whenever they're free, okay?

She sat on a fold-down chair in the waiting area. Beside her, there was a table covered in leaflets: The Centre For Pregnancy Nutrition, Family Planning, Hearing Tests. She watched dust motes float in the stream of sunlight coming in from the high window above her and wished she had remembered to put on her good bra and not the sweat-stained, flesh-coloured one that she was wearing now. There was a plant on the table. She saw that the leaves were covered in a thin layer of dust and she reached out to wipe off one of the leaves. It was plastic. She felt another contraction coming, and held on to the side of the seat of the chair as an enormous wave of pain built up and then crashed down inside her.

How could the pain just disappear so fast? She wiped away tears and locked eyes with a woman on the other side of the waiting area.

Are ye all right, love? she asked.

Mary shook her head and swallowed, trying to catch her breath. The woman was in her fifties, and was massaging the shoulders of another woman – her daughter? – who was also in labour. The daughter was sitting with her head bent right down between her knees. Her legs were spread wide so that her swollen stomach could drop through the gap between them. Their faces had a similar landscape to them; eyes close together, thick nose, pointed chin. There was a harmony to their bodies, a closeness. The woman looked towards the reception desk and then back at Mary.

They need to be coming for you.

Mary couldn't think what to say back to the woman. What would my mother say to this? To me? Here? she wondered. She would be cross, but she would be here with me, she decided. She would be holding my hand. The sound of a piercing scream came down the corridor. She tried not to cry at the thought of the next contraction and switched her thoughts to Louise's goofy smile. Of Sean's words in the car. You're braver than you think.

The girl across from her moaned deeply and Mary felt another wave mount inside her. She tried to take in the room around her, to focus on things that were solid and real. Pictures of painted hearts and baby's feet were screwed to the pale-yellow walls. She thought she would be sick then. She looked around for the toilets, but it was too late. She vomited all over the floor of the waiting room. Her head nodded as waves of nausea washed over her. She squeezed her eyes shut and tried to breathe through the pain. Resting her elbows on her thighs, she leaned forwards and opened her eyes. She could see the girl's mother looking at her, her face suspended in shock. She could hear voices asking her questions.

What's your name? Judy, clean that up, will you, I'm taking this one down to B.

Mary.

Mary what?

McConnell.

She was in a wheelchair, being pushed down the corridor.

How old are you, Mary?

Eighteen.

And this is your first?

Yes.

Do you know your blood type?

Type A positive.

She was being helped on to a bed. A face loomed over her, cragged with wrinkles.

Hello, Mary, I am your midwife today. My name is Linda.

Mary had seen that weary look before. It reminded her of the expression on Mr McNulty's face when she had to call in to get the football they kicked over his wall when they were small. Sean always sent her because Mr McNulty didn't shout at her as much. As Linda talked, she removed Mary's clothes and helped her into a green hospital gown, tying the strings around her neck and back.

Now Linda was reading a clipboard of notes and chatting to another midwife quietly.

Anything of note?

No, Linda. Straightforward pregnancy.

Where's the father?

There is no father recorded.

Linda frowned and looked up at Mary on the bed.

These girls. She exhaled the words with a shake of her head.

Okay! Let's check and see if you're ready to have this baby.

Mary was gently pushed back on to the bed by the maternity nurse as Linda poked around with her fingers. Okay, we're about seven centimetres dilated, Mary, which means you're well on the way, but you're going to have to do a wee bit more, okay?

She could hear a woman somewhere close braying like a farm animal. Beeps and moans punctured the air around her, and she heard herself start to make a noise as the next wave of pain crashed through her.

Here, breathe into this; it will help.

Linda shoved a large nozzle-like mouthpiece into Mary's mouth. She gripped her teeth over it and bit down hard, tensing every muscle in her body, bracing herself against the contraction. The pain made her buckle her back and twist over into the foetal position.

Whoah! Whoah! Steady, Mary.

Her fingers found the metal railings on the side of her bed and she clung on with both hands. Linda was gripping her arm tightly.

Breathe through this next one. Big deep breaths now.

Somewhere in the middle of the next contraction, she heard what sounded like a champagne cork popping and she felt a huge pressure release inside her and a big gush of water between her legs. She was self-conscious through the pain.

What, what is that?

That's your waters breaking, Mary, Linda said.

But she couldn't respond because the pain continued for longer than ever before, and when she emerged through the other side, she felt desperate. The pain had to stop. She was going to break open. She searched and searched for Linda's face and heaved herself up to rest on her elbows to find her. She was there, with her back to her, talking to someone.

I can't do this any more.

Linda turned around, her face set into a harder expression. She busied herself between Mary's legs again.

I can't do it any more. Please.

Another one came over her now and she was bellowing.

I CAAAAAN'T DO IT ANY MOOOOOORE!

While her body twisted sideways, curling into itself, she clamped her teeth on to the gas and air nozzle and gasped in the chemicals until they made her vomit again, into and all over the nozzle.

She saw Linda's face in front of hers, her gold cross glinting out from behind the collar of her scrubs.

You, young lady, are going to get this wee baby out of you. Do you hear me? You're nearly there now. Push!

The pain crashed through her again and she heard the sound of the scream coming from her as she saw the top of Linda's head, grey lank hair tucked behind her ears, bent down over her. She squeezed her eyes shut and she could see Sean's face contorted into rage as he kicked and punched Danny, and then Danny's face, inches from hers, as he thrusted inside her.

She fought for breath and felt a searing pain from between her legs.

Linda looked up and said, I can see the head. One more push, Mary!

Mary's face crumpled. Her whole body was leaking liquids, seeping into each other. And now it was coming again. She could hear muffled shouting, as if it was coming from far away.

Push! Mary! Push!

She could see the shape of Linda, blurred through her tears into one big moving, dripping mass by her feet. She saw the photo of her mother, watching her over her shoulder with sloped eyebrows and her half-smile. And she could feel the pulsing lump of blood and soft bones of her baby, moving through her, inch by inch, closer towards air.

Then, through the blur of noise, Mary heard a tiny bleat. There was a flurry of activity by her feet. Her whole body was trembling, low and steady, like the engine of an old car. Her eyes stuck to Linda and what was in her hands. There was a flash of dark, wet hair and tiny folded shoulders. She watched her roughly wipe the wriggling blue shape with a towel and lift his legs like she was stuffing a chicken. She watched her deposit him on some large metal scales and write down numbers on a clipboard. She saw the tiny feet kicking up and down, rising up over the edge of the metal bowl. Her head lay sideways on the pillow, eyes glued to the metal scales. She watched as Linda lifted the baby and wrapped him in a blanket and brought him to her.

It's a boy, she whispered as she tucked a pillow under Mary's neck and placed him in her arms. She was crying so much that her tears rolled on to his bluish tinged cheeks. There he was. He lay completely still and stared at her, mouth slowly opening and closing, taking her all in with the tiny wet depths of his eyes.

CHAPTER 16

TJ, PRESENT

In the mornings when he walks into the kitchen, she stands in front of him and her expression softens as he fills her gaze. She inspects him like one of her plants, smoothing down his hair and scraping off dirt from his clothes with one of her nails. Her first question to him is, What can I do for you, love?

He is so used to this little ritual now that if she is busy or in another room, he stops by the table and waits to sit down, until she is ready to see him.

The banana bread sits in two sad lumps on a plate on the table. It collapsed when he tried to lever it out of the baking tin with a spatula. He tried to eat some, but the queasy feeling in his stomach meant he stopped after one bite. The kitchen smells nice at least. It's 3.30 p.m. He is feeling panicky now, and he is questioning himself. Is he allowed to be worried? Because he doesn't know when she actually left the house, he doesn't know how long she's been gone for. But even if it was this morning, it's still just not like her. She would have left him a note. He sits back on the bench and rubs his forehead with his forearm.

He can hear Dolores's dogs yapping next door. He starts to scroll through his phone, wondering what numbers he has saved that are anything to do with his mother. There's Aunt Bridget under A. He hardly sees her and he knows his ma doesn't really speak to her. Something to do with a falling-out between grandad and her years ago. There's Dolores's home number under the Ds. She has no idea. He keeps scrolling, hoping for inspiration. His mother doesn't have any close girl-friends that he knows of. She works on her own, so there's no social life around work. He keeps scrolling through the letters until he stops at a name in the M section. McKee. He holds his thumb on the screen and lets his mind mull over this option.

Mr McKee gave her a job when she was in her early twen-ties, with no qualifications and very few questions. She was always grateful to him for that, and in this gratitude managed to forgive him many, in TJ's opinion, unforgivable things. He is a slug of a man. A miserable bastard.

TJ sighs out and tries to remember the last time he saw Mr McKee. It was back in April. He was on his Easter holidays and his ma was due to give him a driving lesson after work. He went to Ballybawn in the late afternoon and asked her for her car keys so he could sit and wait for her. He knew guys who went to Ballybawn to smoke weed, and he didn't want to be in a position to have to explain his ma and her mushroom hat to them. He had coursework to do anyway, so he pushed the seat back in the car and got his books out on his lap. Mr McKee pulled up in front of him in his Belfast City Council car and TJ slid down in his seat and watched.

The door opened and nothing happened for a full minute. When McKee manoeuvred himself out of his seat, the whole car lifted a couple of inches from the ground. He leaned back into the car and found his cane and shifted himself to the left so there was room to close the door behind him. TJ crouched himself down his seat further for fear of being seen. He watched as McKee leaned against the car for a couple of minutes, concentrating on getting his breath back.

His ma wasn't far from where they were, and he saw her wave quickly at McKee before getting back to work turning the soil. He knew she would not want McKee to feel self-conscious about the time it took him to get to her. He shook his head slowly, in silence, as he watched McKee lumber himself through the gates and up to the flower bed. He was consistently astounded at McKee's diametrical proportions.

He watched their exchange through the glass, McKee using his cane to point at things over his ma's shoulder, his ma, pale and serious, nodding in acquiescence.

Afterwards, they sat in traffic on the way to the industrial estate. She was quieter than normal.

What did McKee want?

Ach, he was in a right mood today, she said. He gave out to me about the state of the rose bed.

He gave out to you? he said, turning to face her. He's fucking lucky to have you.

She raised her eyebrows and grimaced.

I was trying to introduce some new colours, God forbid.

The traffic lights turned green in front of her.

This memory of his ma, quiet and pale, leaning into the steering wheel after getting shouted at by McKee, makes the heat rise in him now. She takes such pride in her parks. At home, she draws out diagrams that he doesn't understand, different planting formations for different seasons. She knows the regular visitors by name: tired mothers pushing prams, lonely old people perched on benches with plastic bags full of breadcrumbs, and even some of the kids who come there to be free of the rules of school and home. It is these kids she struggles with the most, as to her they have no respect for the gardens at all. Often, she will come home looking visibly upset, after another run-in with a drunk teenager who didn't want to take the time to understand why it was important to give the plants space from their cigarette butts and empty tins. She puts up with so much shite, and this wobbly prick had shouted at her for it.

TJ stares at the name on his screen. His ma insisted on putting McKee's number in his contacts when she got him his first mobile. Just in case TJ needed her in an emergency and she wasn't near her phone. She is useless at answering it anyway. TJ sighs. He doesn't have to be friends with McKee.

He just needs to know one thing. He presses the small phone icon and listens as it rings. It is 3.44 p.m.

Four rings and then there's the click of an answer and the grunt.

Hello.

Is that Mr McKee?

Aye.

Mr McKee, it's TJ McConnell here. Mary's son? I was . . . I was wondering, did you know if my mum is working today?

McKee is heavy breathing down the phone in big rasps like a pervert.

She doesn't work weekends. Hasn't for a while now.

There is a long silence. TJ feels like there is something thick and suffocating wedged in his throat. He shifts his focus to breathing. He breathes through his nose. McKee is still there.

Have you lost her?

I . . . I . . . She's not at home today. I went to Ballybawn to find her but she's not there. I just wanted to double-check. Thanks, Mr McKee.

There is the sound of a phlegmy cough.

You should try Sid. I'll send you the number.

Then, nothing but the cold flatline of a hang-up.

Sid. The old guy from Bedwood? Surely not. Do they still see each other? She never mentioned him.

He needs to think.

CHAPTER 17

MARY, 2000

Her father was waiting for her. She saw his stooping silhouette through the glass of the back door as they walked into the kitchen. He turned around on hearing the baby's cries and opened the door to greet them.

There was a smell of rotting food coming from the direction of the bin. In a saucepan on the hob, a thin layer of white mould grew on some vegetable soup, like morning frost. Mary stood in the middle of the room, her arm wrapped around her son, who was locked into the crook of her hip. She wore a tracksuit, with white congealed stains around the sweatshirt collar, and a pair of fluffy slippers and socks. Her bag was slung over her shoulders, holding a week's worth of baby things inside. Nappies, wipes, nappy bags, nipple cream, his bottle, his formula, his soothers, his blankie. It was endless, the list of things her baby demanded.

She named him Anthony. She liked how strong it sounded, how it commanded several different parts of your tongue to say it. It was a commitment. His middle name was her father's, Joseph. Somehow, in the chaos of the first few months, she didn't know how or when, he had become Tony, and then TJ.

Y'all set? her father said, as his eyes took them both in.

I don't want to go.

TJ had been crying on and off all morning. She knew he carried her tension with him, soaked up into his little folds of flesh. He looked wearily at her father and started to cry again, his tiny fists pushing against her shoulders. Her father frowned at his grandson and huffed out the words.

Sure it's for your own good. The nurse said.

I'm grand, she said crossly. But she knew she wasn't grand. She had read enough magazines and seen enough mothers, cooing into their prams, to know that it was all wrong.

She exhaled and watched as her father stubbed out his cigarette, closed the back door behind him and walked to the front door, beckoning her to follow. He awkwardly manoeuvred the pram out the door and stood back as Mary laid TJ inside.

It was a perfect spring morning, bright with birdsong and blossom. They walked to the roundabout side by side, her father nodding at passers-by, Mary staring straight ahead. A man, skinny to the point of malnutrition, scuttled across the road ahead of them, scratching his arm absent-mindedly. She heard her father sigh at the sight of him.

Everyone's on the drugs now.

She swallowed and concentrated on ignoring the prolonged stares of the residents of Purves estate. She hated feeling this exposed. Why was she letting this happen? Was it TJ they wanted to see? She looked down at him asleep in the pram, his arms raised above his head in surrender. She remembered walking out of the hospital a few months earlier, holding this tiny fragile thing in her hands, and feeling like every moving thing was a mortal threat to him, from the cars, with their engines roaring like lions, to people, peering into his face, breathing their air all over him. She had not ventured out of the house since then to show him off. Her father and brother didn't interfere.

It was the health visitor who intervened. Lynn was an older woman, somewhere in her fifties, who was bigger than the clothes she wore and seemed to melt out and over them. She smelt of cigarettes and her hair was dyed a fluorescent auburn that made Mary's eyes smart. She visited three times in total. The first Mary couldn't even remember; the second involved Mary taking a lot of persuasion to let Lynn into the house at all. Once inside, she could see her behaviour reflected on Lynn's face, and she couldn't do anything to stop it. She drifted from tears to maniacal giggling, then back to sobbing. The third time, Lynn gave no warning. Mary was asleep, sitting upright on the sofa. TJ was asleep on his back, splayed out across her knees. Her left breast was exposed between a muslin cloth and her shirt. Lynn knocked four times at the door and eventually peered through the window and knocked on the glass until Mary woke up.

There was no small talk.

When's the last time you washed?

I give him a bath every second day, so I do, in the bath upstairs.

No, yerself.

I . . . I . . . I don't know. He doesn't let me be away from him, ye see, he tells me that I have to be there all the time.

Are you getting enough sleep?

Her sleeps were like short deaths. They felt void. When she woke through the night, she had to fight through her confusion to find herself. To know herself.

He never stops feeding. He's awake all through the night. He just loves to talk. He's a wee chatterbox, so he is, aren't ye, TJ.

And is he in a cot in your room?

He . . . at the moment he sleeps in the bed with me cos he's always wanting milk.

So TJ talks to you, does he?

Aye, he talks to me all the time!

How do you think you're doing, Mary?

I don't know . . .

She knew there was something not right about the fact that day and night felt like the same place, and that when she looked in the mirror she saw a strange broken girl, someone she didn't know. In the darkest recesses of her thoughts, she knew that sometimes, this broken girl wished bad upon her baby. The voices came and went, vivid as dreams; they spoke of the bad things that could happen to him if she didn't look after him. They spoke of the bad things that would happen to her if she didn't feed him when he wanted. The worst was his crying at night; it pierced her like a blade. She would do anything to stop it.

You're not right, love, Lynn said, shaking her head at Mary, as if she was talking about the cup of tea in her hand.

She remembered the feeling of panic that overtook her when Lynn had asked to speak to her father. How strange to be reminded that her father was deemed a responsible adult when she had been doing the job of one since she was eight years old.

The conversation was stilted afterwards.

She said you're not coping well, he said, scratching his beard, as she sat on the sofa staring into the middle distance.

She remembered wanting to scream at his face, why can't you help me to cope. She remembered the tears streaming freely, as if she was beyond embarrassment, and him reaching down to pat her shoulder with a look of complete helplessness on him. She remembered TJ, sitting on her lap, with his solemn stare, into her eyes and right out the back of her head, as if she wasn't there.

And she had dragged herself through the week as if she was in slow motion, dreading the moment when she had to put herself in the hands of strangers. Now here she was in her slippers, in broad daylight, climbing into a taxi, clutching TJ on her lap as her father cursed under his breath and kicked at the side of the pram, trying to find the catch to collapse it.

Her father sniffed big loud sniffs all the way up the main road, sneaking little glances towards her. The sniffs burrowed into her head and became huge. Each one felt like an aggression. She tried to focus on the air going in and out of her mouth. When they arrived at the building, she was taken aback. It looked more like a house than a medical institution.

It'll be good to get some help, her father offered, with a sideways glance, as they waited at reception. She signed her name without asking any questions.

Make sure and call and let us know how you're going, he said.

She clenched her teeth and firmed her mouth into the shape of a smile, and he was gone, the doors swinging behind him.

CHAPTER 18

MARY, 2001

She wore her green apron over her sweater and concentrated on tying thick, ribbon-like twine around the towering bunches of bamboo in front of her as if she was putting the finishing touches on wrapping a present. The canes were exposed at the bottom, waxy and yellowish, and as they grew taller, they became dense with leaves. These were black bamboo, one of three types that they sold in the garden centre of Atlantic Homecare. She could hear the rattle of a trolley in the distance and glanced over to the sliding doors to check for a customer. It wasn't spring yet, but Mary was aware of every second of extra light in the evenings, every half degree of warmer sun. She stood back to survey her work.

Behind her, on the wall opposite the entrance, were the rows and rows of planters, stacked up on top of each other. At the end of their row were the garden ornaments. Dominating the metal shelves of the animal section was a troop of twelve plastic elephants, their trunks curled over their heads in perfect harmony. Beside them were the Buddhas, cupping their faces in their hands with beatific smiles. To their left were the monkeys, their hands over their eyes, ears and mouths, seeing no evil, hearing no evil, speaking no evil. They looked heavy to hold, but were surprisingly light when lifted.

The garden centre was split into two sections. The 'green' section of the space, which housed most of the live plants and flowers, was under a huge canopy that held strip lights with pigeons huddled on top, resting from the cold. The instant-gratification flowers were stacked near the doorway: primroses and pansies and daffodils, hyacinth bulbs, White Pearls in pots. Then there were whole corridors of herbs and shrubs and saplings.

Outside of the canopy were the huge metal shelf structures that held everything else you could ever need to build and maintain a garden. In one corner, the wheelbarrows stood in rows, shiny new and stacked with their wheels in the air and their handles on the ground like legs. There were freshly made bird houses, huddled together in the corner like gossips. There were wooden pallets weighed down with large rectangular sacks, tightly packed on top of each other like a game of Jenga. Sacks of compost and soil, gravel for driveways, sand for cement, all different colours and textures of pebbles called things like Sorrento Blush, Icy Blue and White Alpine, names that reminded Mary of Sean's deodorants.

Hello? she said brightly to a confused-looking young woman clutching her trolley in front of a wooden slat of compost sacks.

Hi, the woman said apologetically. I've got these new flowers and I want to give them the best chance, but . . . she trailed off, looking overwhelmed.

Where are you planning on planting them? Mary said.

In our front garden, but I haven't planted anything there before. It's just grass.

Ah, okay, so you'll be digging yourself a new flower bed.

Aye, I guess so.

Okay, so we want some top soil over here.

Mary pointed and walked over to a stack of soil sacks in the corner.

How big do you want your bed to be?

The girl showed Mary with her arms, stretching them out.

So we'll get you two bags of this, Mary said, bending down at her knees and lifting each sack on to the woman's trolley.

And then you need Growmore, over here.

She beckoned to the woman to follow her over to another stack.

You can put this in with the soil and it'll help a lot, she said, lifting it on top of the soil sacks.

Great, thanks so much! said the woman, smiling straight at Mary.

Mary reciprocated the smile and breathed out a sigh of relief. From the second she arrived in to work in the mornings, she felt a prickly fear under her skin of finding herself face-to-face with Danny Donnelly or one of his family, and having nowhere to run. Louise had shown her his ma once. She was waddling out of St Michael's Mass and they were walking on the other side of the road.

You know where he gets his shortness from, Louise said.

She knew he had a father, too, and a brother and two sisters. There was a web of Donnellys all over the city who could lay claim to her child any day. She imagined scenarios where she would be called on the tannoy by Sharon on reception and walk up to the customer services desk to find Danny, square-jawed and sullen, demanding to talk to her. She dreamed of a day when her heart didn't jump every time someone new walked into the garden centre. Fuck him. Fuck him. She walked towards the two large green doors that led to the staff-only area. She would spend an hour before lunch at the potting bench with her gloves on, making up hanging baskets. And at 5 p.m., she would jump on the bus back in the direction of home and pick up TJ from the childminder's.

It had taken eight months for her to summon up the courage to leave her son and return to Atlantic Homecare. The air still smelt of musty wood, and the staff welcomed her gently, as if she was the same scared pregnant girl facing off in the paint aisles, but she felt wholly new, like she should have to start all over again; and in a way, she did.

You couldn't have come back at a better time, Paul had said on her first day back as they walked through the shop. We're understaffed outside.

She had visited the garden centre occasionally when she worked there before TJ was born, but she had never spent any time there. She knew it was as far as possible from the hustle and bustle of the cashiers and car park and nearly always empty of staff.

She had followed Paul past the insect repellent and hanging baskets, and through the sliding doors, and had felt the soft breeze on her face as she took it all in. It wasn't until she was standing on her own in a corridor of shrubs later that morning, a plane crawling through the blue overhead, that she allowed herself to remember her precious fact about her mother's love of the garden. When she learned that as a young girl, she had started collecting leaves and flowers, eager to feel the things her mother did. She thought on that first day back at Atlantic Homecare that maybe this new assignment was a sign from her mother. Three months into the job, she knew that working there made her feel still, like water on a day with no wind.

She stood at her bench in the corner of the staff area. The forklifts were parked behind her and the huge bins were overflowing, ready to be collected at the end of the day. She started to turn the small pots upside down and tap the bases gently to coax the flowers out. Her thoughts drifted to her brother, who had left Atlantic Homecare and gone to work for one of his friends' brothers, who had a delivery company. His days were spent driving large vans delivering precious antique cargo all over Northern Ireland. She missed seeing glimpses of him charging around the shop floor.

A pierced bag of compost lay on its side, spilling out on to the bench in front of her. She grabbed a trowel and started to fill a basket. A year had passed since her visit to the Mother and Baby Unit. There was an unopened box of pills tucked into the back of her bedside drawer. She tried to forget about them because they reminded her of when she was a stranger to herself, and she had a hold of herself now. She had a hold of TJ, too. She knew about the different tones of his cries: the defiant protests, the tired whinges, the frustrated hungry wails. She understood them like a language and she felt enormous strength in being able to quiet them. He was all hers to love. As she pressed the flowers into the compost, she remembered TJ's cries when she'd handed him over that morning.

At weekends when she worked, she left TJ in the arthritic hands of Dolores next door. She was no expert, but she had a capacity for love that was more than enough for Mary. Even so, she worried about him plonked in front of the TV in the stuffy living room for hours, the dogs sniffing at his feet. On weekdays, he went to a childminder on the other side of the roundabout. She catastrophized about the chaos of the place, imagining TJ's nappy bulging and unchanged, his cheeks red from screaming. When she left him there, she was always brought back, with a painful jolt, to Arndale Road. To Rita, leaning on the counter, staring fondly down at the chubby toddlers at her feet.

Louise had gone now, off on the boat to Liverpool. Sean told her and she didn't ask how he knew. It was easier somehow, living in a Belfast without Louise. Like when your eyes adjust to the dark. She didn't have to look in the mirror any more. She could forget herself.

She pushed the remaining compost around the roots of the flowers so that there were no air pockets, and filled the basket with half a watering can of water. It dripped down around her feet as she reached for the next one.

CHAPTER 19

MARY, 2002

Mary was roused slowly from the depths of her sleep by the movements of TJ beside her in bed, stretching and yawning and clenching and unclenching his chubby fingers. She smiled at him and when he saw her, he said Mamma, in a soft voice.

Hello, baby boo.

She stood up and pulled on her dressing gown, then turned back to the bed, where TJ was standing up, arms raised in the air, waiting to be lifted. She carried him downstairs, still warm and floppy from sleep, and put him in his baby chair. The midsummer sun was already pouring through the kitchen window. She inspected her row of plants on the windowsill. There was a small sapling of a fig tree that she had been allowed to bring home from the garden centre as it was broken down the middle. She fixed it with garden twine, and she wasn't sure whether she was imagining it, but it seemed more rooted today, as if it had staked its claim in its brown plastic pot. She filled the kettle and poured an inch of water into the soil of the pot before putting the kettle into its holder and flicking it on.

TJ banged his plastic spoon on the side of his chair.

Okay, okay, Mary said softly, I'm getting it for ye now.

She poured some oats into a saucepan, poured milk on top and started to stir.

TJ was eating his bowl of porridge and Mary was peering into a saucepan on the hob, lid in hand, as Sean walked into the kitchen, yawning.

He hasn't eaten any dinner again, she said, frowning.

Sean rubbed his eyes and spoke with a croak.

He got kicked out of the Glen last weekend, I heard.

For what?

Mary turned to him, looking horrified.

Fuck knows. Mary, he's a mess.

Why has it got so bad, Sean? Should we do something?

Sean shrugged and held his hands up in a gesture of helplessness. He leaned down to TJ and blew on his cheek. TJ giggled and said, Moooore.

After breakfast – TJ giggling hysterically at Sean making faces while he ate his porridge – Sean went back to bed and Mary got TJ dressed for a trip to the playground. The air was already warm and hazy at 9.30 a.m. and Mary could smell the faintest tinge of burnt rubber in the air as she stepped out the front door. The drums had been booming in and around the Suffolk estate over the last week or so, and the tension had climaxed yesterday with the Orange Marches.

Mary was relieved that the drums would subside now and Belfast could get on with the rest of summer.

The McIntyres across the road had their front door open, and the little girl, Susan, was crouched on the step, solemnly talking to her doll. She looked up as Mary opened the door and, after a brief moment of recognition, returned to her conversation. Mary's shoulders were naked under a halter-neck sundress. She had put a tiny peaked cap on TJ and he clapped and sang to himself as Mary lifted the buggy down the step.

Then TJ was pointing from the buggy.

Gandad! Gandad!

There was the body of a man lying face down on the paving stones of their front yard. His arm was raised halfway towards his mouth, and under his hand was a half-crushed can of Royal Dutch. His head was turned to the side and his mouth was wide open, suspended in anticipation of his next gulp. There was a thick, acrid smell of urine coming from his trousers.

Mary was quite certain that her father was dead. She knelt down beside him and felt his pulse on his right wrist, closing her eyes in concentration to feel the reverberations through his skin. When she knew he was still alive, she jumped up, opened the back door again and shouted.

Sean. Come here. *Now.*

She knelt down in front of TJ in his buggy and tickled him to make him laugh, avoiding looking at the shape of her father on the ground. Little Susan McIntyre was staring over at them now, her doll hanging upside down out of her hands. When Sean came to the door, she gestured at the buggy.

Mind him.

She went straight to the cleaning cupboard.

Jesus Christ, Sean said as he saw the shape of his father on the ground. He took the buggy and moved it out of Mary's way as she walked past them with a mop bucket filled with cold water. He watched as she slowly poured it over the matted hair of her father.

Give it here.

Mary gesticulated for Sean to hand her the pram and, as their father coughed and spluttered his way back to consciousness, she turned and walked out on to the road and away from the house at a brisk pace.

The playground was in the furthest corner of Ballybawn Park and was warming in Saturday morning sun when Sean arrived half an hour later. She was pushing TJ on the swing, and when she turned around he was standing behind her, watching her, holding his bag. His hair was wet and combed back from his face, and his eyes were luminous blue.

Mary . . . I just packed a bag. Like, with stuff for a while. I can't be under the same roof as him any more . . .

Mammy, push me, TJ yelled, and she turned back to him to push him without saying a word.

Sean stepped forwards and stood beside her, dodging a small girl as she ran across the playground.

Mary. I think you guys should go, too.

She continued to push, staring into the back of TJ as he held on tightly to the ropes. The motion seemed to hypnotise him into silence. It was usually a peaceful time for both of them.

Mary!

She turned to face him then. She kept her expression flat, neutral.

The state of him, Mary! He's a fucking nightmare! Shit. Sorry, he said, side-eying TJ, who was still in his trance.

Mary nodded at him.

I know. I get it, Sean. I get it.

I'll be staying at Daisy's.

When she didn't respond, he added, Bye, bye, big man.

She stopped the swing and held TJ suspended in the air so that Sean could reach down and kiss him. He turned and looked at her straight in the eye.

Call me if you need anything, okay?

She watched him walk off, bag slung over his shoulder, until she couldn't see him any more.

That night, their father came home, heavily drunk, and lowered himself slowly into the chair by the kitchen table. Mary was making up a pasta bake for the next day. Her father sat, propping himself up on the table, his smoke stench curling into the air around them. Without a word, Mary put a cup of tea down on the table in front of him. It hit the wood with a dull, familiar thump. She saw his shoulders move out of the corner of her eye, and realised the movements were the jumping shoulder-heaves of a sob.

I'm not a monster, he said, with a low moan. He folded his arms tightly into his chest and hid his head, rocking forwards and backwards, knocking into the table. There was a puddle of tea around the base of the mug. She walked up behind him and spoke down into the back of his grey-streaked hair.

No. You're not a monster. You've a serious problem though, Daddy. Sean's gone. We'll have to go, too, if you keep going like this.

He nodded his head into his arms, still rocking back and forth. Slowly he rocked himself still, sat back into his chair and sighed.

Did you skip work? She asked into his hair.

I'm a fucking mess, he croaked. She focused on the wall in front of her as she rested her hands on his shoulders and took a deep breath.

Well fix yourself up, then.

When Sean realised that Mary was staying at home, he ordered her to move TJ into his room. Mary had spent a full ten days stripping off the wallpaper, sanding down the woodwork and painting the walls a brilliant light blue, the colour of a cerulean sky. The ceiling was stained with the brown-yellow residue of years of Sean's cigarettes. She painted it late into the evenings after work, perched awkwardly on a step ladder, her back aching from the arching of it. TJ's old cot lay in the corner, filled with teddies. She thought of that Christmas a couple of years ago, of Sean's eyes, full of light as he walked into the kitchen carrying it in his arms. I'm painting over his entire existence in this house, she thought as she brushed, he can be anyone he wants now. She wondered about Daisy; about what it was like for Sean to share a bed with someone he loved night after night. He had never told Mary how they met. He just started speaking about her one day as if she had been around forever. His face illuminated, she thought, like there was an electric bulb behind his eyes that turned on at the mention of her name.

On a balmy August evening, Sean picked up Mary from work to take her to buy TJ a new bed. As he walked through the shop in front of her, dangling his keys from his fingers, Mary took him in. He had been living with Daisy for over a month now and he looked taller and more . . . finished, like a man from a magazine, with his denim shirt tucked into his jeans and new white Adidas trainers. He seemed to fizz with excitement as he examined all the kids' furniture, suggesting things that TJ would love. Afterwards, he drove her home and carried the bed to the front step. He shifted his weight from one foot to the other as he dug his hands into his pocket and took out a black leather wallet. His fingers briskly unfurled three twenty-pound notes.

For the bed, he said, offering them to her.

She hesitated, opening her mouth to say something.

Take it. Also, Daisy wants you and TJ to come over next weekend. Are you around?

The rev of his car engine roared through the estate as she waved him off.

Daisy lived in a ground-floor flat on Carmel Street in the Holylands. Mary had learned from Sean that she was twenty-seven years old, three years older than him, and worked as a hairdresser in a salon in the middle of the city. Mary knew the salon; it was a place full of heat and noise and sharp angles. A place that compelled her to speed up her pace as she walked past it.

Mary brought a small bunch of lilies, still in their buds, and some home-baked soda bread that she knew Sean loved. She pushed TJ in his buggy through the Botanic Gardens, stopping at the playground, and then they made their way down Carmel Street, watching the numbers on the doors until they reached the final house on the street, overlooking Stranmillis Embankment and the River Lagan. Mary stopped for a second to enjoy the view, imagining how it would feel to live right next to the water. Daisy opened the door in a cloud of sweet floral perfume and enveloped Mary in a tight hug. Sean stood behind her, smiling down on them. Daisy held her by her shoulders.

Mary, you look so like Sean. What is it? Is it the eyes?

They're a different colour, said Mary, smiling

Maybe the mouth, is it? she said, looking from Sean to his sister and back again. Sean shrugged.

Daisy bent down to TJ, who backed away from the hug and mutely accepted a high five.

TJ, look at you! What are you into? Batman still?

The flat was small and scrubbed sparkly clean, with magazines lying on the coffee table, and candles on the mantelpiece over the fire. TJ's eyes widened at the plate of chocolate biscuits on the coffee table and it wasn't long before he was happily watching cartoons with a biscuit in hand while Daisy got out her kit and made a big fuss of cutting his hair.

Mary and Sean sat side by side on the sofa and watched her. She had close-cropped hair that was the bleached an ashy blonde colour, and a thick silver nose ring with a ball in it. Mary could see how easily Daisy would fit in a hair salon, moving through clouds of hairspray, mouthing along to the words of the pop songs that blared through the shop as she sculpted shapes into shiny hair. There was an absolute lack of self-consciousness to her, with her soft curves and her breasts pushed up out of her purple blouse. She had a large bottom that was neatly wrapped in a pair of black leggings and seemed to have its own set of movements separate to the rest of her body.

Mary, what about your hair?

Daisy was looking at her over the top of TJ's head.

Mary looked surprised.

What about it?

Daisy laughed and Sean smiled at her.

When's the last time you got it cut?

Mary looked from Daisy to Sean, then back to Daisy. Sean seemed embarrassed for her. Daisy's eyes moved between them.

About a year and a half ago.

Daisy looked at her for a long time, scissors suspended an inch from the down of TJ's head.

Okay, girl, you're getting on here after TJ.

Mary felt the heat rise into her face. She did as she was told. Daisy chopped a four-finger measure of hair clean off.

Afterwards, as she walked to the bus stop, she felt lighter, as if her hair had been made of lead.

CHAPTER 20

TJ, PRESENT

So she isn't at work. He is still clutching his phone and he is breathing in through his nose. IN and OUT, he tells himself. Keep going. He lays his hand on his heart and feels the reverberations against his palm.

Okay. I will text this Sid.

Sid. My name is TJ. I got your number from Mr McKee. I am Mary McConnell's son. Sorry to bother you. Please can you give me a call when it suits?

He presses send and walks into the living room to the desk and sits down. He boots up the computer and types in, How do I report a missing person in Belfast?

The results take him to the Police Service of Northern Ireland website.

If you cannot get in touch with someone and are concerned for their welfare, it is important that you contact us as soon as you can to report the person missing.

In order for us to start looking for the person, we will need to know some important information, including:

- The person's details and a physical description of them.
- Where the person is missing from.
- Any clothing the person may be wearing.
- Whether their absence appears to be planned (clothing or valuables missing).
- Any vehicles the person may have access to.
- Any distinguishing features the person may have.
- Any telephone number or social media accounts they may have.
- Any addresses the person may go to, or friends they may have.

CALL 101.

Was her absence planned? Of course it wasn't planned, because if it was, he would know about it. It's only 5 p.m. He needs to calm down. It's only been a morning and an afternoon. And maybe a night, if she left last night. He will call them tonight. Will he? CALL 101. He's never had to call the police for anything in his life. But he has had a few run-ins with them recently. He sits back on the chair and stares at the screen until the letters became blurry in his vision. He remembers the Friday night of his last day at school.

He was on his back, arms outstretched, fists clenched, the lights shining so intensely down on him, all cut up and kaleidoscopic, a fuzz of blue and yellow . . . he had lain silently for what had seemed like a long time, toes and fingers unfurling and clenching like a starfish, and he felt like he was floating up towards the light, totally weightless. The lights were getting heavier and there were sounds, too, then . . . were they voices?

Then a hand was on his shoulder, shaking him.

Oi! Are you okay there, wee lad?

I think he had one too many pills, a female voice said.

Hello? More shaking of his shoulder.

He had forced his eyes open, squinted into the light and heaved himself up on to his elbows. It took a few seconds for the shapes to make sense. A car was parked a few metres in front of him, the headlights shining straight at him, and above, silent electric-blue LEDs flashed left, then right, then left, then right. They were quite beautiful to his enlarged pupils.

I . . . I . . . I was just having a wee lie down, he said.

There were two faces peering down at him. A round, earnest face belonging to a man bent over with his hands on his knees. The other face belonged to a woman a bit further back, who was trying not to smile. They both wore the dark green hard hats of the PSNI. The woman's radio started to buzz and a voice came through. She turned around to talk into the radio as the man started to talk to him.

You better move on, son, you're not allowed on the grounds of the uni at this time . . . Go on, move along or we'll have to search you.

He had stumbled into the darkness, away from the cop car, through the big red-brick arch of Queen's University. He looked back across the road at the students' union. The doors were closed. Last thing he remembered was getting another pill off Jamesy, flying, hugging Aiden. He remembered him and Aiden, locked in an embrace, tripping over each other and falling on to the dance floor, and laughing so hard they had to be pulled up. The police car was driving out of the university towards the Malone Road now.

He had walked through the quad and sat down in a dark archway, getting his breath back. How long had the police been sitting in that car watching him? Laughing at him? Had he been kicked out? He leaned back against the stone wall and smoked a fag. The quad was a perfect rectangle of grass surrounded by the old red-brick arches and towers of the university. He remembered loving the feeling of being in this little stone cocoon. He wished now, with the benefit of hindsight, that he had had the good sense to go home then, high and happy and satisfied after a great night out. But he went to Aiden's, of course. There were girls there, and more drugs.

His head had still been fizzing when he had knocked at the small terraced house on Cairo Street. Aiden greeted him with his lone middle finger stuck up in the air and a barrage of words.

TJ followed his friend down the hall towards the kitchen. Olly was in the corner of the living room with his face stuck in a bong. He raised his hand slowly to greet TJ without moving his face. Two girls he didn't recognise were on the sofa, their heads close, talking quietly to each other. It was the same small kitchen in every small house on every street in the Holylands. Empty pizza boxes were folded into the bin and there was a bumper family pack of six 2-litre bottles of 7 Up wedged under the table. Aiden opened a jar and took out several different small plastic baggies. He arranged them in a row on the kitchen counter.

Take your pick, he offered. As TJ held each bag up to his eyes for a closer look, Aiden poured powder on to a plate from another baggie and arranged it into neat, straight lines with a razor blade.

He reached down and snorted a big line, then handed the straw to TJ.

That's strong enough stuff, man, so take your time with it. What the fuck happened to ye anyway? Them two girls came back with us, they're sound, we'll get ye laid yet, big man.

Aiden playfully punched TJ on the shoulder and aimed an exaggerated wink at him. That's why he loved Aiden's house. It was easy. You went there, you got obliterated. There were always good drugs. Always new people to talk shite to. And always Aiden lording above everyone, stirring up the conversations, not letting anyone be a dick.

It took an hour to be out of it again, laughing at Aiden's impression of one of the girls, telling them his story of being caught gurning by the police, arguing over what music to listen to. One of the girls was trying to talk to him and when he looked down to his lap, he realised he was massaging her hand in his.

So, do you go to Queen's?

Hahaaa, he's only just left school! Aiden had said, exploding into laughter. The girl opened her mouth, shocked.

Are you serious?!

She turned to examine him with massive round eyes.

Fuck, you *do* look young. What are you, eighteen?

Aye, said TJ, smiling.

Don't you worry, TJ, she loves a toy boy, her friend said.

Get in, TJ! Aiden shouted, and punched the air. Aiden was particularly wasted now, sniffing absent-mindedly every twenty seconds while creating a little mound of perfectly rolled joints on the side of his armchair.

So, what are you going to do with your life?

The girl was still looking at him. He remembers his silent relief that his age didn't seem to put her off.

I wanna go to New York.

It was the first time he had said it out loud. It sounded cool.

And then it was 8 a.m. Olly was snoring in the corner. The girls were looking at their phones. Aiden was in the corner in a puff of smoke. The blind had a hole in it, about the size of a ten-pence piece, and the morning light was piercing through like a laser right on to his face. Even though it was Saturday and he didn't have work, he knew he had to get out of there soon, because if he didn't, he would never be able to face rainy Belfast. And most of all, he knew he had to go because of Ma. So, he left quickly. He pulled on his puffa jacket and drew the hood over his face as he walked down the road. He checked his phone. The girl had given him her Instagram. He copied and pasted her name into the app and found her. He clicked follow. She was Emily. Twenty. Final year at Queen's. She had a Derry accent and mad big green eyes. He didn't think she was, like, *beautiful*, but she was pretty, and she had lovely long hair and she seemed sound.

A ten-minute walk and a bus ride later, he walked through the front gate of the house. There was movement on the other side of the road. He kept his face down to avoid eye contact as he pulled out his keys and pushed open the door, trying to stay as quiet as possible. He heard the radio from the kitchen and the sound of his ma humming. He bent over to take his trainers off at the bottom of the stairs and knocked over her umbrella, which was propped up against the hall table. Then she was there, in her dressing gown, all rumpled and cross.

TJ, I presumed you were in bed. Jesus, would you look at the state of ye.

She was right under him, peering closely up at his face.

Jesus, Ma, will ye leave it.

She stepped back to survey him.

TJ, as long as you live under my roof, I am not okay with you staying out all night. I know what this means.

Ma, what are you talking about? You don't have a clue!

Well, give me one good reason why you are getting in at eight a.m., TJ. One reason that makes sense to me.

Her jaw stuck out. The frown line between her eyes was a crevice. He thought you could stick a coin in it.

I went out, Ma. With Aiden. There was a party after, Ma, it was nothing bad.

But it *was* drugs, was it, TJ? Were you taking drugs?

She pointed her finger in his face. He rolled his eyes.

Do *not* roll your eyes at me, young man.

He pushed past her and ran up the stairs.

TJ! Come back here right now.

There was panic in her voice. He slammed his door, knelt down on the floor by his bed and punched his mattress over and over again, as hard as he could. Eighteen punches. One for every year of his life. He lay awake, eyes closed, colours flashing on the inside of his lids for what seemed like hours. He ignored the soft knocks on his door later that morning. They never talked about it after that day.

He squeezes his eyes shut now and opens them to focus on the screen in front of him. What would *she* do now? What if *she* hadn't heard from *him* since yesterday? And the last time she saw him was last night? And he wasn't answering his phone? She would be raging. It occurs to him now that he could be angry, too. He pulls his chair towards the desk and hovers his hand over the mouse. What was she thinking? How dare she put him through all this worry? The phone's electronic trill pierces the silence and makes him jump. He swipes to the right and presses the speaker button.

Hello? he says.

Hello? A voice, frail but friendly.

Hello, is that Sid? TJ replies.

Sure is.

I'm so sorry to bother you, but I wanted to ask you about my mother. She's . . . I . . . I can't find her.

Oh dear! Well, since when?

The lightness in Sid's voice is gone.

Since, well, sometime last night or this morning. I rang Mr McKee to see if she was in work today and he said she wasn't, and I should ring you.

How strange that she has, that you can't find her. I haven't spoken to her in a while, I'm afraid, TJ. But I will start thinking now, trying to remember if there are any clues in our conversations.

TJ feels his face sag. His mouth hangs open.

When *was* the last time you spoke to her?

I think it was around the start of the year. To be honest, it has been less and less, and I was sad about that, as we used to talk a lot. She used to invite me out to her parks, and I would sit with her on her lunch breaks. But she hasn't invited me in a long time, so recently it's been me trying to catch her on the phone.

TJ is silent.

Listen, Sid continues. She is a dear friend and I would love to help in any way I can. Come and see me and I will tell you everything I know. It's Buss Buildings, off Woodstock Road. Number eighty.

Okay, I'll maybe do that if we still can't find her later.

Absolutely. Just let me know when you're on your way. Don't worry if it's late. Bye, TJ. Try not to worry. She is a very capable woman.

The phone clicks dead. TJ stares at the phone in his hand for a long time.

CHAPTER 21

MARY, 2003

She started her job at Bedwood Cemetery in early December. Two months earlier, she had met Mr McKee for the first time when she served him at the garden centre. He was impressed with her, so much so that he came back the following week with an application form. She went for her first job interview and talked her way into a job with the Belfast City Council. It was a better paid job than Atlantic Homecare. It was a job where they sent you on courses to learn.

Bedwood was known for being one of the nicer cemeteries in Belfast; it won awards for its manicured landscapes and beautiful trees. It didn't harbour any history of sectarian violence. No grenades were thrown there. Mary was wholly aware of Bedwood because it was where her mother's grave was. She had visited once as a young girl, with Sean and her father and Aunt Bridget. She remembered Bridget's gloved hand squeezing hers too tight, and the silhouette of her father looking down over the plot. She remembered her father shouting at Sean for throwing stones at the ducks in the lake. After Bridget fell out with their father, she never took them back there. Now Mary would be near her mother all the time. She knew what to say when her father's face clouded over at the realisation of where she would be every day.

I'll be able to make sure her plot is nice and neat, Daddy. And she meant it.

On a freezing grey Monday, she got off the train from Dunmurry in her box-fresh council green overalls, turned up on the leg, and walked through the gates. Remembering McKee's directions, she took the east path around the outer edge of the cemetery, walking hurriedly until she arrived at a cluster of buildings tucked away behind some pine trees. Two large open gates revealed a yard full of vehicles. She stepped through them, feeling sick with nerves. McKee was there to 'see her in'. He was a mountain of a man with no discernible jawline in the pillow of flesh that spilled over his collar. His glasses looked comically small on the enormous expanse of his face.

This is Mary, she is the new member of the team, he wheezed to two weathered men, who nodded shyly in her direction. She forced a smile. There was a prolonged silence.

Where's Sid? Mr McKee asked them, and before they could answer, she heard a voice from behind them.

Aha, it's our new recruit!

Ah, here he is, said Mr McKee with a hint of a smile. The man stood in front of them, grinning widely.

Mr McKee, ye keeping well? he asked brightly.

Aye. Mr McKee turned to Mary.

Sid will show you the ropes.

Mary stared at Sid. His nose was large and protruding under two giant, wiry white eyebrows. He wore a Belfast City Council beanie hat pulled over his head and a lanyard weighed down with keys around his neck.

Come on then, let's go find those ropes, shall we? he said, with a dainty flicking gesture of his hand.

His accent was pointed and exotic. Mary couldn't place it, but he definitely wasn't from Belfast, she thought as she followed him around the facilities. He talked at her as they walked.

Don't mind those grumpy fuckers, darling. They'd complain if they won the fucking lottery.

His gait was hindered by extreme bow legs. She followed him into a door beside the manager's office.

This is the drying room. You have a locker here to put your stuff in and you hang your wet clothes and boots up over there.

She nodded, looking at all the coats strung up on hangers across the room. A large patch of paint had peeled off above them, revealing the raw brick underneath. Two garden benches, painted green, served as seating, and the opposite walls were covered in lockers. She took in the soggy boots under the benches. They all looked enormous.

Sid said, as if reading her thoughts, We had a woman work for us for years, but she retired last year.

He led her into a small, shabby room with several tables and chairs, two microwaves stacked on top of each other on a fridge, and in the corner, a sink and a kettle.

This is where we eat. We're not allowed in the crematorium cafe because of the dirt on us. But if there's no funerals on, you can use the toilets there to save you coming all the way back here. You get an hour off a day and you can take it how you like. Sections or one block.

She nodded and smiled politely, following him out and across the yard. They walked through an assortment of diggers, mowers, tractors and trailers.

Mowers over there!

He gesticulated as he walked.

And this is the gravedigger, he said, pointing at a fluorescent orange Hitachi excavator, its blade folded in on itself and covered with wet mud.

That's not our concern, though. The other lads have to be called in to help with the grave-digging when it's a busy time, but us horticulturalists get to stay out of that. We just make sure the plots look good after the burials. There's lots of turfing to be done there, and then the spraying with the weedkiller. Do you know about spraying?

Mary looked at him, panic rising. She thought of the rows of weedkillers on the shelves inside the sliding doors of Atlantic Homecare. Is that what he meant? She was afraid of saying the wrong thing. Sid had stopped and was looking at her.

Are you able to talk? he asked, deadpan, eyes twinkling.

She smiled nervously.

Yes!

Excellent. We do get all sorts of people coming and going from ground maintenance. Some people I wish really couldn't talk. But it does help to not be mute. At the start, anyway. Don't worry if you don't know things, I can teach you or we'll put you on a course.

As he talked, he looked down at his lanyard and sifted through the keys. He pulled one out while walking towards a garage behind them, and opened the padlock hanging off the shed doors.

Stand back! he shouted, pulling back both doors theatrically. She peered into the darkness and her eyes adjusted. She made out the shape of a white pick-up truck, the doors embossed with the Belfast City Council logo.

Hop in! he said, and she jumped in, feeling a twinge of excitement as he turned on the ignition. He drove out and into the cemetery, cranking up the heating in the van as he talked.

We must drive slowly at all times here, Mary. Everything has to be done as quietly as possible and with respect for the mourners. The ground maintenance guys will dig the graves, chop down trees and plant the bigger ones. They're busy this time of year. They're also in charge of fencing and a lot of the grass-cutting and spraying, but we muck in on that stuff, too. In spring, it's all hands on deck.

The neat rows of gravestones fell away behind them as the van circled around the outside of the cemetery.

We'll have to get you some gloves, said Sid, stealing a glance at her hands, pushed under her thighs.

That would be great, she agreed, as Sid slowed down in front of a copse of white tree trunks to her left.

Memorial trees, he said. Come and look.

He jumped out of the car and Mary followed him. A small brown plaque was stuck into the ground on a stake at the base of each tree. There were bunches of flowers, pebbles, laminated photos, even a small toy windmill at the bottom of one tree further into the copse. Some had circular fences that were ornate marble things, some were handmade, using rolls of small flower-bed edging like the ones she sold at the garden centre.

We have these all over the cemetery, said Sid. Much nicer than a stone, don't you think? We plant a lot of these. They come from the nursery at about five years old. You've to really soak the roots for a good twenty-four hours before you plant them. You get all different memorial trees, but I like these silver birches the best. They clean themselves. Look!

A piece of bark was flaking off the trunk. He pulled it gently, rolling it around the full circumference of the trunk, revealing a flawless smooth white ring underneath.

Good as new!

Mary laughed.

What are those? she asked, pointing to the small horizontal grooves dotted around the surface of the trunk.

Those are the gills, said Sid. That's where the air comes in.

Mary moved her head in closer and ran her finger over the grooves, lost in herself momentarily. Sid had moved over to a lopsided tree on the side of the copse.

That's the problem with these trees, he said, reaching out to it.

When you help something grow with a stake, then there's no message being sent down to the roots to grow and expand. The roots think everything is fine and dandy up there. Jesus, this is a doddle, the roots are saying. Then you take the stake away and the tree is out there unsupported, with these flimsy roots, and it's knocked over at the first gust of strong wind.

He pointed over to the other side of the road where, in front of a beech hedge, there was a small row of tiny saplings, no more than a foot tall. They were protected at the bottom by a circular plastic covering, to keep the rabbits away from gnawing at the bark.

See these whips? These ones are going to have to learn the hard way. The roots will get the message that the whips are fragile and need foundation. They will throw out roots quickly, and it might be a little harder at the start, but that tree is set then. It can fend for itself.

They drove around the whole cemetery that morning, past the children's Garden of Remembrance, past the crematorium and the cafe, and the stone memorial book statue outside, covered in tiny plaques, spelling out the words and numbers of lives lost. Sid pointed out all the formal beds and hedges that were to be under Mary's remit. They drove right out to the edge, where there was an empty field of uninhabited plots, and he stopped again at a small lake, where the grass grew wild and willow trees drooped into the water from the bank.

This is a conservation area here, he said, walking to the edge of the lake and peering down into the water.

You get bream in here sometimes.

And ducks! said Mary as two speckled brown ducks drifted by them. She remembered her father's gruff shout at Sean at this lake all those years ago.

Aye, ducks and coots, said Sid, following her gaze.

Coots?

She looked at him.

Aye – you never heard the phrase 'bald as a coot'? Sid said, smiling. He pointed to a small black bird, like a moorhen, bobbing its head in and out of the water on the far side of the lake.

Look! See the wee white patches above their beaks?

Mary saw and smiled.

We get the odd cormorant and a heron sometimes, too.

Wonderful, Mary whispered, looking out to the water.

Right, now you've got your bearings, Mary, are you ready to work? Sid said, baring his jagged-toothed grin at her.

She smiled and nodded, and they walked back to the van together.

CHAPTER 22

MARY, 2004

It was a bitterly cold morning and she jumped up and down a few times to warm herself up before lowering herself on to the grass. She pulled off her heavy-duty gardening gloves and unwrapped a tinfoil package, revealing two soggy tomato sandwiches. She could just see the lake glistening through the trees, and if she strained her ears, she could hear the distant clink of ceramics from the coffee shop next to the crematorium. She took a gulp of warm, sugary tea from her flask and looked around her as she screwed the lid back on.

Tonight was Halloween. She had to leave early to bring TJ out. She still had to prune and tidy the beds in the centre of the main entrance road. It was like being at home. Everywhere she looked, she could see work that needed to be done. TJ's capacity for making a mess never failed to irritate or amuse her, depending on how tired she was that day. She could turn her back for thirty seconds and he would have scribbled all over a wall, stuck stickers all over a chair, swung his weight on a cupboard door until it was hanging off its hinges. She took a bite of her sandwich and leaned her head back against the wall.

During her first January, the rain came sideways and she worked with a dogged determination, with a scarf pulled over her face and a Thermos flask full of tea to thaw her freezing fingers. She saw the other gardeners' small nods of approval as they walked past and surreptitiously surveyed her work. In springtime, she did all the summer bedding with Sid, planting salvia, alyssum, lobelia, double-headed begonias, peony roses and dahlias. Then the grass-cutting started up in earnest, with both her and Sid and the ground maintenance team taking on sections of the cemetery to cover. When summer arrived, the heat felt oppressive at Bedwood, and her workload was intense as she tried to keep up with the rapid growth of her flower beds and hedges, the yellowing of the grass, the relentless weeds.

The ground maintenance team spent days driving down the rows between the graves, spraying out the weedkiller. Then they would get their packs on their backs, their spray guns and do the area around each gravestone manually. It was a vast, never-ending job. She didn't envy them. They knew very little about her, apart from that she had a son who she had to hurry to pick up after her shift every day. But she had been there for nearly a year, and although she didn't lift pints with them at the end of the day, she felt an overwhelming sense of relief to be an accepted part of the team. She was the quiet one, she was Sid's friend.

They worked together as much as possible. It took a long time to go anywhere on site because there was always something for Sid to show her, something for her to learn. She got used to the graves quickly, and found that she enjoyed deducing stories from the small amount of words, their font, the look of the stone, the years etched into it. Sid told her of the regulars, and introduced her to old Mr Linehan who came every day, always on his own, to tend to his wife's grave. Every day for ten years. It was always the men that came on their own, Sid said; women usually liked to come with family, and it was more often daughters who came with their mothers. They would put in requests through the office for service to their graves. Mary and Sid would go and find the section and the number and make sure the grave was turfed okay, sow some grass seed if they needed to. She learned about Sid too; that he was brought up in Oxfordshire in England by his mother and a selection of nannies, and sent to a fee-paying Protestant boarding school in Bangor due to his mother's friendship with the head teacher there. He told her stories of getting hit by one of the teachers with a cane, whipped across his bare bottom. And he told her that the problem with an all-boys boarding school is that it's full of boys. He said this with a wink and a smirk.

Little did she know, Mary, that she was giving me all the ammunition I needed to be a raging queer.

Mary imagined an old cathedral school, where the pupils called the teachers Master, and everything was in black and white. She pictured Sid's mischievous face pulled straight, head bowed and full of fear and confusion at the feelings of arousal he was trying to quash every day.

Poor little you, she said.

And then there was his mother. He told Mary about how she teased him relentlessly about his effeminate tendencies, giggling at him in front of her friends. Of how, when he lashed out in frustration, she would switch off from him completely for days on end. Of how his mother never came to collect him for the holidays until the teachers sent for her. Mary had to take this out of her head and look at it again and again. In her mind, her mother was a construct of memory and desire, made up of snippets from her brother and father's memories of her: a laughing mother singing to her kids in the car; a beautiful young mother who hugged her children incessantly; a tough, independent young woman who could hold her own. Sometimes she was the Virgin Mary in the pictures she saw on Dolores's walls, kind face etched into marble, head bowed, cheeks perfect pink. Sometimes she was knowing and kind, as reliable as the rain, like Rita O'Mara. Every gesture of affection that she never received was stored in the vault of thoughts of her mother. She was everything good. Sid's stories of his mother introduced the notion that a mother could be flawed. They made her wonder what her mother's imperfections could have been. Was she selfish? Was she spiteful? Mary then turned the mirror in on herself, on the feelings of guilt that covered her at night like a heavy blanket, the sense that she wasn't good enough for TJ. A belief she was never able to articulate in the cold light of day. But after that conversation with Sid, she felt a quiet reassurance that she had done all right for her son. She wasn't Sid's mother. She would never be Sid's mother.

She stood up, dusting the crumbs off the overalls, and walked to the nearest row of gravestones. Her mother's stone was under the spread of an ash tree. She liked to come here during her lunch breaks sometimes, just to be beside her. Once a week, first thing in the morning, before the gates opened and the hearses crawled through the gravestones like giant insects, she spent time tidying around her mother's grave, and placed fresh flowers down at the base of it, next to the framed photo of TJ in a plastic sandwich bag. She knew the order of the words on the stone off by heart.

McConnell
In Loving Memory of
MARY
Beloved Wife and Mother
Died 11 February 1984

It was like the kids' graffiti you saw at bus stops. Mary McConnell was here. Right here in this city. She filled up space with her body and her laugh and the songs she liked to sing. She existed with all her flaws. With her blood and bones and hair. Mary often wondered if her mother had suffered with frizzy hair like she did. She brushed the stone with her fingers before walking back down the path.

Later that night, she sat in the kitchen with her son, after they had completed their tour of the estate. The estate was overflowing with groups of little shapes moving through the dusk, dressed in costume and clutching bags. The door knocks were slowing down as the darkness closed in, and Mary and TJ had already completed their bit. TJ was four years old and superhero obsessed. He was still dressed in his Batman costume, merrily counting his money and eating his way through his wares in the kitchen, when there was a loud knock on the front door. Outside the window, the sky was filled with the splintered light of fireworks. TJ jumped off his chair and grabbed his mother by the hand.

Mammy! Come on!

He dragged her to the door, and she stood behind him as he reached up and opened it himself, a large bowl of sweets and lollipops tucked into his left arm. Sean was on the doorstep, face hovering inches from the door, swaying on his feet, with a pull-along suitcase behind him. She saw the faraway look in his eyes and her stomach lurched. She closed the door behind him as he stepped inside.

Uncle Sean! TJ yelled excitedly. Mary leaned down to him and spoke sternly.

TJ, go and put a film on, okay? Do not answer the door. Do you hear me?

Sean, what's going on?

She was right up in his face. His breath was sour with alcohol. He lost his balance and held out his arm to the bannister to steady himself. He swallowed and tried to speak, but nothing came out.

It took all her strength to get him upstairs to her bed. He crashed down on to it, knocking her lamp off the side table, and he was asleep in less than a minute.

The next morning, Sean sat on the sofa watching television with TJ squished up beside him as close as he could be. The radio sing-songed in the kitchen, a high falsetto singing of sexy independent bodies, of goodies. Mary, dressed in her uniform for the cemetery, was buttering bread for TJ's packed lunch, her face set into a deep frown. She had folded herself into bed with TJ and slept fitfully, waking up every few hours to check on her brother. In the dead of night, she tried to piece together what was going on.

She realised that it had been a full year since she had been to Carmel Street. The last visit left a ball of worry in Mary's chest. On answering the door, Daisy's face had immediately rearranged itself from anger to smiles. They stood in the kitchen, in a haze of Marlboro smoke, while Daisy made tea. Next door, someone put on heavy metal music and it raged through the thin wall as Daisy lit up another cigarette.

Wow, that music is loud, Mary said, but Daisy hardly seemed to notice it. She was wiping the crumbs off the sideboard on to the floor with her hand.

Aye, that's Paul. Sean is in his house a lot these days.

Sean had walked in then, his face in a frown, his hand massaging his forehead. He took a beer from the fridge and beckoned Mary and TJ into the living room. She had told them about the job at Bedwood, relishing in her good news, and Sean was genuinely happy for her, until Daisy, leaning against the door frame, absent-mindedly flicked her cigarette and the ash fell down on to TJ's head. Mary had instinctively jumped up and wiped it off with her hand. Sean had glared at Daisy and said, Jesus, Daisy, what the fuck, are you gone mad!

Daisy shook her head at them.

Fuck! I'm so sorry, Mary. Sorry, TJ!

TJ had a look of utter confusion on his face. Sean was still looking at Daisy, shaking his head in disgust.

It's fine, honestly, Mary smiled, but she was interrupted.

Oh, fuck off, Mr Martyr here, acting like you've never done anything wrong in your life. It was a mistake, for fuck's sake.

Daisy turned back into the kitchen and Sean jumped up from the sofa and followed her in.

Don't you speak to me like that in front of my family, do you hear?

He closed the door behind them and Mary heard Daisy mutter something low from behind the door, and then Sean's louder retort.

You're a fucking cunt sometimes, Daisy.

They walked out of the house with the kitchen door still shut and she could hear the heavy metal music raging all the way to the top of Carmel Street. Sean had apologised, and Mary had said, Don't even think about it! But there were no more invites after that and she didn't see Daisy again. She'd had the odd afternoon with Sean, meeting up in playgrounds and parks. He was almost always wincing through a hangover and when she asked about Daisy, she never got more than a 'grand'.

Daisy must have kicked him out. Was he home for good? She put the sandwiches in TJ's lunchbox and closed it up as her father walked into the kitchen, hair still wet from the shower.

Morning. Where's TJ? he asked, and Mary turned around.

Daddy, he's in there, he's with . . .

Her father was already walking into the living room and stopped abruptly in the doorway when he locked eyes with his son. Mary knew that Sean's pull-along bag was open by his feet, with his clothes strewn all over the carpet. She heard him say, I'm only here for a couple of weeks, okay?

Mary swallowed by the kitchen counter. Her father looked back through the door to Mary for affirmation. She smiled a big, easy smile at him.

You'll provide for yourself so, he replied, as he turned back into the kitchen again. He pulled the kitchen chair out from the table and sat down, deep in thought.

Mary buttered some toast and put it on a plate in front of him. Her father looked at her in silence, his face full of questions.

He must have split up with Daisy? she whispered.

Gandad!

TJ came running into the room and wrapped his arms around his grandfather's leg. Mary's father picked him up with one arm and settled him on his knee.

I know you, ye wee scamp. You're only after my toast.

TJ giggled and took a piece of toast off his grandfather's plate, then snuggled into his chest as his grandfather ruffled his hair. TJ's presence had softened and sweetened Mary's father over the years, like fruit in the sun. Watching TJ on her father's knee, Mary felt a twinge of excitement at the return of her brother. Having Sean around would be nice. For them all. She walked over and glanced in the door of the living room. Sean was texting on his phone and looked up at her with a sheepish smile.

On New Year's Day, she woke up early, pulled her coat on and stepped into the icy air with her phone in her hand. The estate was deathly quiet.

Inside, her father, son and brother were all still deep in sleep. Sean was using the sofa for a bed. When he wasn't working, he was horizontal all day, and they had become used to his presence in the middle of them all, moving around him like he was the dining table. She thought back to Christmas Day, to Sean either dozing or blank-faced and silent, staring at the TV. There was a heaviness to his moods now, and when he smiled, it was as if he had to dredge it up from a deep and distant place. It never reached his eyes. While her father was working less over the holiday period, he grew more impatient. His exasperated sighs were like pinpricks for Mary, drawing up old memories of door slams and blood on the linoleum. She had caught him on the stairs on Christmas night, his face like thunder.

Daddy, he's heartbroken He just needs time.

But she was frightened. She didn't know heartbreak could physically flatline someone in the way that it had her brother. It was like he had lost the essence of who he was.

She had listened to the muffled pop and splutter of the midnight fireworks from the warmth of her bed the night before and made a decision. She had to do something. She shivered as she waited for the phone to ring.

I didn't want to bother you. I need someone who he will listen to, she whispered to Daisy.

She paced up and down Purves Road, face set in a frown as Daisy talked her through their break-up. How Sean had always had a jealous streak, and how it became worse with his drinking – to the point where she couldn't even go to work without him accusing her of flirting with other people. How she felt smothered by his love and weary of his rages, and how she dealt with it by drinking herself.

We stopped together, she said. We lasted a few weeks, but we went out for dinner and I met an old school friend and spoke to him for a few minutes, and it just set Sean off. He started drinking again and so did I, and by the time we were home, we were fighting, like properly fighting, and I locked myself in the bathroom and called my neighbour to get him out of the house. It wasn't pretty, Mary. He doesn't realise how aggressive he can be.

There was a long silence as Mary stared at the ground. Daisy sighed.

And then he's so . . . soft at the same time. He rang me every day for a month. I really loved him, Mary. But we weren't good for each other. I'm sorry, I can't help you.

Mary walked back into the house, shivering. She pushed open the door to the living room. TJ was curled up around Sean's feet on the sofa, watching cartoons. Sean was softly snoring, mouth gaping open.

Hi Mammy, her son said, without looking away from the TV.

CHAPTER 23

TJ, PRESENT

TJ is trying to eat chips at the table. He left them for too long in the oven and they are browned and hardened. He picks one up and dips it into the dollop of tomato ketchup on the side of his plate and crunches it between his teeth. He is watching the clock above the fridge. Time is moving torturously slowly. It's 6.57 p.m. In three minutes, he will not have seen her for twenty-four hours. In three minutes, he is supposed to call the police. He can't get his head away from one part of the guidelines on the missing persons page on the police website:

Whether their absence appears to be planned (clothing or valuables missing).

Could she have planned this? No. No way. Did something he said trigger this? Slagging off her job. Saying he wanted to go to New York. Maybe. But really? He didn't say anything definitive. It was all just floated casually in the conversation. He thinks back to them in the kitchen. She had cancelled that phone call she got. Who was calling her? At 7 p.m. on a Friday night?

He has looked through her clothes again. Her coat is still on the hook in the hall. Her work boots are not here, but sometimes she leaves them in the boot of her car. He can't see anything else missing. He has tried and failed to log in to her Hotmail account, using varying incarnations of the spelling of his name as passwords.

Earlier, he found her old address book in the desk drawer in the living room. It was a narrow thing, hardbacked, with flowers on the cover. One of those old ones that have sections for doctors and dentists and next of kin, from before smart phones existed. He had to prop it open with two hands to read the names. There were no fresh-looking entries at all. The only one he didn't recognise was Louise O'Mara. The number was written in pencil and was faded into the page. He called the number but it rang out. Fuck knows what he would have said if she had answered, anyway.

Will he go and visit this Sid guy later? Talking to him had felt slightly unsettling, and he couldn't figure it out at first. He had always assumed that he knew everything there was to know about his mother. She didn't talk about herself. Or maybe he just didn't ask. The idea that she had a life beyond him was new for him. But she never *did* anything . . .

Or did she? He tries to think of the times they have spent together recently and he can't. This summer, his working hours meant he had stayed out later at night and got out of bed later in the morning. At the weekends, he mostly hid in his room, nursing his hangovers. In the last few weeks, he has been starting the day with a joint, and floating around the house in a clumsy haze until it is time to go to work. Sometimes, he leaves for work before she gets home, because he can't stand being under her constant cloud of disapproval.

And she is always either coming or going. It's always either the sound of her car engine turning out the front or the sound of her quiet sigh as she arrives home at night. It's always her, on her own. He remembers a few weeks ago, her walking into the kitchen after work at Ballybawn, looking pale and exhausted, saying brightly, You're the first person I have spoken to all day!

He remembers feeling frustration at having to be the one sole conversation she was going to have that day. What if he didn't want to talk?

He sighs, squeezes his eyes shut and opens them. The clock says 7 p.m. She is officially a missing person. Missing.

Is he really going to do this?

Fuck it, he whispers, shaking his head and reaching for his phone.

He dials 101.

Hello. I'd like to report someone missing, please.

Okay, what's your address?

Forty-two, Purves Road, Belfast.

In which case, are you able to come into the station, to file an official missing persons report? We need you here to sign a few things.

Aye, I'll be there in half an hour.

What's your name, please?

TJ McConnell.

CHAPTER 24

MARY, PRESENT

Mary follows the roads. The car is moving down the A2 from Belfast, snaking its way down the slow curves of the east coast towards Bangor. Her head is throbbing again and a cloud of nausea drifts slowly through her, causing her to open her window and swallow down big gulps of air. The evening sun is low. She reaches into the pocket between the seats with her left hand and feels about for a pair of sunglasses without taking her eyes off the road.

The autumn colours are beginning to blend through the trees on the edges of her vision, leaf edges framed with yellows and browns. She is attracted to the idea of the trees starting again every year, growing and then shedding themselves of everything when nature is at its most brutal. Like taking off all your clothes and standing outside in the snow.

Images flash up in her head, of dried flowers, pressed under Sellotape on to coloured paper. She was five years old when Granny Olive died and Aunt Bridget left them to go back to the farmhouse in Maghera. Suddenly there were no boundaries. Sean was giddy with the freedom, running around the estate like an escaped animal. She tried to follow him at first, but was hindered by an uncomfortable fluttering feeling in her chest that grew stronger the further she ventured from the house. She found ways to occupy herself at home. She collected flowers and leaves from the green and rushed home to press them between her school books. She learned that leaves didn't press and keep like flowers did. She was fascinated by how the life died out of them, leaving these tiny fragile skeletons behind. She spent whole days at home on her own, with her dried flowers and her colouring pencils, listening out for footsteps at the door.

She hears a long beep of a car horn, getting louder, and then turns to see a car overtaking with an old man gesticulating at her, his face screwed up in rage and fright. She sees his mouth open and he looks like he is screaming. *Fuck!* He is so close to her! Her car has veered right over the cat's eyes in the middle of the road. She swerves violently back to her side of the road. The car is ahead now and still beeping. She slows down to let it drive away. Her heart is hammering. She realises she is moaning, a high-pitched, wavering note, and she swallows and sits back into her seat, concentrating on breathing deeply through her nose.

She sees a sign that reads Helen's Bay. She indicates left and winds the car about half a mile down a road until she reaches a small village. There is Helen's Bay train station. She slows the car right down and peers out her window, looking for any signs to the beach. She is rocking slightly, forwards and backwards in her seat, and, after realising she is driving in a circle, lets out a *fuck sake* and slams her foot down on to the accelerator. She heads back up to the dual carriageway. She will have to find another beach. The road falls down into a valley. The houses are sleek and angled, set back from the road. She drives past electric gates and big cars catching the light with their polished shine. She steers slowly through the town of Bangor. The streets are lively: the pastel pick-and-mix townhouses line the road on her right, and as she drives down the hill into the marina, there are the neat grids of yachts moored to their jetties, like leaves on a branch. Everything is polished and perfect. The people are smiling, wholesome, hopeful. She has a compulsion to drive fast, back to the empty roads.

She drives out of Bangor and follows the coastal road signs until suddenly the road is flat and level with the surface of the ocean. The water is the colour of heavy steel, metallic under a dense blanket of clouds that stretches all the way to the horizon. She drives slowly and glances out to the sea intermittently as she bends the car around the coast. Directly overhead, the clouds break to reveal a triangle of brilliant blue. Flashes of white light pierce the windows every few seconds, as the car is exposed to the sun's reflection off the sea.

It is dusk now, and she is driving through a small town called Donaghadee, past the yacht club, past the bakery, turning into a common recreation area where there are spaces for motor homes and angular outdoor gym equipment sits in manicured grass. Too much potential for being seen, she thinks, and turns the car back around on to the road out of the town. A minute later, she sees an empty, unkempt car park on the right-hand side of the road. She turns quickly without indicating and spins the car into a stop. She takes a second to adjust herself, to try and quell the dizziness.

The car park is deserted but for a pair of seagulls hopping around a bin in the corner. Beyond a small hillock of long grass and ferns in front of her, on the other side of the road, is the sea. She pushes two more paracetamol out of the foil packet and washes them down with the dregs of her Coca-Cola. She holds her forehead in her hands, trembling under the weight of its ache. The pain scares her in its intensity. She remembers the panic and fear of TJ's birth, the desperation for knowledge, for someone to tell her that it would end soon. She could end it all soon. She remembers after TJ was born, going to the Mother and Baby unit and refusing to take their pills. They took TJ to a different room to sleep at night. They told her that she could catch up on sleep, but she lay awake all night, worrying about her son. In the morning, a nurse carried TJ into her room. He was chattering and bright eyed, oblivious to her absence.

Seeing her son happy in the arms of this nurse made her heart crash open. She imagined the ways she could quietly end her existence with the least amount of fuss for anyone. She took the pills after that.

She shivers suddenly, reaching to turn on the ignition of the car, to twist the clunky heating button up to full. It makes a loud rattling noise and immediately the car is filled with warm, stale air. Her stomach turns and she gags; quickly she turns the heating back off and winds down her window again. She breathes deeply through her nose and lets her head flop down towards her chest, listening to the gentle collapse of wave after wave on the beach in the distance. A car speeds past. From the outside, with her head bowed and her eyes shut, she looks like a woman praying.

CHAPTER 25

MARY, 2005

She stood at the classroom door, panting for breath, her eyes wildly scanning the classroom for TJ. Mr Allan had informed her on the phone that TJ had vomited all over the floor in the middle of phonics class, with no warning. She saw him in the corner, dragging himself off his chair and swinging his Batman bag over his shoulders. His face was pale as the moon.

Darlin'!

She enveloped him in a big hug. He took it, but didn't stop walking away from the classroom. He allowed her to take his hand.

They sat on the back seat of a taxi as it trundled down the Stewartstown Road, her arms wrapped around him, her chin resting on the crown of his head. She could smell the vomit on his trousers. She didn't try and glean information about his school day as she usually would. Usually, towards the end of her shifts, Mary's mind conjured up pictures of TJ. His round face and enormous eyes, crinkling up when he laughed. His right foot turning in slightly when he walked. His sleeping face, and fingers, clinging on to his dino teddy as if it was his last lifeline from an otherwise certain death. By the time she got to the school gates, she was hungry for him. He was five years old now, and recently he had been highly strung and hyperactive after school, not wanting to tell her anything about his day. He talked about running to the playground as soon as he could after lunch time, about leaving his packed lunches because his friends did, too. Mary had been meaning to speak to his teacher, Mr Allan, about someone watching over him while he ate. She knew it was all down to lack of food.

She opened his lunch box now – everything was there as she had packed it: an apple, a Tupperware box of grapes, crackers and cream cheese. She felt a stab of guilt for enjoying this opportunity for extra time with him when he was feeling so ill, and pulled him closer to her. She thought she would let him watch a movie when they got home. Maybe they could watch it together under a blanket. She remembered the living room this morning before they left. The carpet was strewn with toys of all different shapes and sizes, and TJ was in the middle of them, in his uniform, blowing raspberry noises with his mouth, building something out of his Lego. In front of him on the sofa was the naked body of her brother, who was sitting underneath a duvet, clutching a mug of coffee with two hands, his face crumpled from sleep, staring at the wall.

In the last few weeks, Mary had found it harder and harder to wake Sean in the mornings. Sometimes she thought he was awake and she would come back to say goodbye, only to find him in the exact same place she had left him, upright on the sofa, but asleep. She pictured him now, his bare feet stumbling through the scattered Lego, his unshaven face peering into the light of the fridge. Finding a clean mug and spooning three tablespoons of instant coffee into his cup. She had to brace herself for the sight of him. The taxi pulled to a stop at the roundabout, yielding to the cars coming from the right. Mary sighed out as she slung her canvas bag over her shoulder with her left hand, still clutching TJ with her right. His mouth was turned down into a grimace.

Baby, time to get out. Just here, please, she said, and fumbled in her purse for a five-pound note to give to the driver. Mary and TJ yawned in perfect sync as they walked hand in hand towards the house.

The living room was dark, the curtains were pulled, and she could see the shape of her brother under the duvet on the sofa. Mary winced as the pungent smell of stale sweat hit her nose. She went straight to the medicine box, took out the Calpol and guided TJ up the stairs to his room.

I'm hungry, Mammy, he said, his eyes big.

You shouldn't eat anything, darlin', not with an upset stomach, she said, tucking his duvet around him.

Ooh.

Let me take your temperature and we'll see.

She wrote down the time and his temperature in her notebook:

3.30 p.m. 38.

Then she spooned Calpol into his mouth. She would check his temperature again in an hour.

When she went downstairs, nothing had changed. The kitchen was untouched. Had Sean moved, since they left? Or had he simply lain back down as soon as she had closed the door? She felt a swell of anger as she went to the sofa and moved the duvet off his face. She could see a light film of sweat on his forehead. His eyes slowly opened, and he blinked. He pulled his lips together and tried to lick them moist. She spoke quietly.

Sean.

He blinked again, so slowly, like it was an effort. And shook his head ever so slightly, before he allowed his eyelids to close again.

She felt his forehead. He was hot.

It occurred to her that maybe TJ and Sean had the same thing.

Sean, are you ill?

His eyes stayed closed.

Jesus, she whispered as she ran back upstairs. How could I be so stupid? They've got a virus.

TJ was asleep in the bed. She kissed him on the forehead,

then grabbed the thermometer from beside his bed and ran back downstairs. She pulled the duvet back, took Sean's arm and wedged the thermometer into his armpit. She held the thermometer steady with her right hand and held his forearm with her left hand. She looked his arm up and down as she waited for the beep. Her eyes stopped at a mark, tucked into the side of his elbow. It was a deep purple circle of a bruise with a tiny red pinprick in the middle, right in line with a thick blue vein underneath it. The thermometer beeped. She didn't move.

CHAPTER 26

MARY, 2005

She had been spending a lot of time creeping around the house at night. Hoping to find a clue. Checking he was still alive. At 4 a.m. on the first morning of May, she climbed out of bed and pulled on her dressing gown and tiptoed downstairs. She could still hear her father's long, low snores as she pushed open the door of the living room. There was the outline of her brother in his makeshift bed. She thought about the hours she had spent studying the sleeping face of her son and tried to imagine him taking up as much space as her brother did now, his legs hanging over the end of the bed, his arms splayed out as if to show off the length of them.

Sean's clothes lay in a heap at the base of the sofa. She saw the handle of his sports bag sticking out from behind the sofa, and gently pulled it out and unzipped it. She searched through every compartment and pocket. Clothes, underwear, phone charger, batteries, sunglasses. There were his car keys, tucked into the side pocket. She held them in her hand for a few seconds before padding out of the living room and out the front door.

She kept her eyes focused on his car as she walked, not letting herself look up and down the street for fear of seeing someone or something that would scare her. She turned the key in the lock and opened the car door. She looked across to the front door of the house to make sure it was pulled shut and then wriggled herself into the seat, closed the door and exhaled.

The car smelt of stale cigarette smoke. The carpet on the floor of the passenger side was strewn with empty plastic bottles and crisp packets, half empty packets of rolling tobacco and rolling papers. An air freshener hung down from the rear-view mirror; it was the shape of the island of Ireland, scented with a cheap lemony smell, like detergent. She ran her hands along the driver door compartment and picked up some scrunched-up pieces of tinfoil, staring down at them in her palm. She pushed the key into the ignition. Where does he go when he leaves the house? In what corners of the city does he find his drugs? She sighed heavily. A shiver of cold ran through her and she pulled the key out of the ignition. She quickly exited the car, locked it, and ran back to the house.

She stood in the stillness of the hall, allowing her breath to settle before going back to him. His hair was matted down over his forehead and there was a light smattering of stubble coming through around his mouth and chin. She reached down to hold her hand flat in front of his mouth. She felt the faint brush of air on her palm for a few seconds and then it stopped. There was an unnaturally long pause, and she felt the panic rise in her chest as she sat down on the sofa to feel his pulse. She blinked into the dim light of the room, feeling the soft bumps of his blood through the vein on his wrist until finally, after a frightening length of time, he inhaled deeply. It was like his heart was fighting to pulse as it should. She thought about how faces unfold when they sleep, how all the muscle tension is released, leaving them expressionless, a blank canvas of skin and cartilage. There's no difference between his sleeping face and his waking face, she thought, as she gently ran her fingers up and down the inside of his arm. She counted four small mounds of swollen, reddened flesh sitting on the lines of his vein. When she looked back to his face, his eyes were open and filled with tears. She inhaled quickly.

Sean.

Her brother shook his head slowly.

Sean. You're going to kill yourself.

Her voice broke as she said the words.

He stared down at his arm, still being held in position by her hand at his wrist. A lone tear sat suspended on his cheekbone.

Sean. TJ can't be around this.

He looked at her then. His voice was cracked.

I would never hurt TJ.

Yes, but he's not safe around heroin. Is it in this house?

He shook his head, pulled his arm out of her grip and turned his face away from her. She sat for a minute, looking at his shoulders curled into his chest, resisting the urge to shake him and scream in his face. He had her fooled. He had them all fooled. How did she not realise sooner? She spent the rest of the night sitting upright on the side of her bed, picking the skin around her fingers. She stayed there until the white line of light crept in between her curtains all the way up to her bed.

Happy Birthday, Mary McConnell, Sid said, walking out of the Cemetery Operatives' Office with a bottle and two plastic glasses.

Is that booze? she exclaimed, shielding her eyes from the sun. It was break time and they went to sit on one of their favourite benches in the Garden of Remembrance. It was a perfect spring day, and the cemetery was dotted with lone mourners slowly circumnavigating the pathways through the grids of gravestones. Midweek meant fewer visitors. It was always a more peaceful time for cemetery staff.

Mary watched Sid open the bottle expertly and tilt the glasses so the bubbles didn't spill when he poured. She tentatively took a glass and peered in, watching the fizz.

Cheers, he said, holding up his plastic glass to hers as if it was the finest crystal.

Cheers, Mary said, without breaking into a smile, and held the glass up to her lips, feeling the bitter wine slide over her tongue.

Look at them. They're just showing off, Sid said, pointing to a circle of poppies in full bloom in the bed in front of them. Mary nodded in agreement. He turned to her.

I want you to tell me what you are going to achieve this year.

Ha! she said.

Go on.

Mary rolled her eyes in mock exasperation.

Think. What do you want from your twenty-fourth year?

Em, I want to take TJ to the cinema at the weekend.

Mm hmm, said Sid, looking unimpressed.

I want to start bringing TJ to swimming lessons.

Mary, I understand that your son is the light of your life and the centre of your everything, et cetera, but I asked about *you*, said Sid, looking at her with a bemused expression.

I'm going to start saving for a car, she said with finality.

Sid nodded in approval and looked back out to the flowers in front of them.

Personally, I think you and I should rob a bank like those guys did in Donegall Square. We could escape on a helicopter and buy an island in the Caribbean. How much did they get again?

I think it was twenty-six million, she said.

That'll do, he muttered, turning to face her again. Is there a war going on in that head of yours today?

She looked at him, then looked away and slumped back on to the bench.

Something like that.

Sid sipped his drink and let the silence settle.

Sid, have you ever known anyone who was on heroin?

He raised his eyebrows. The sun slipped behind a cloud and the light left his face as he said, Sure have. It didn't end well.

Do you know how to get them off it?

You need to get them on a programme. It's a bitch to kick. I would get help if you can, darlin'.

The next day, a year older, she found herself walking past the entrance to Purves estate and following the curve of the road around to the left at the roundabout. Timmy's mum was to keep TJ after school for dinner until she could pick him up.

She turned left off the main road and walked through the car park. Her right hand hovered by her mouth as she bit at the skin around her thumbnail. She couldn't get her thoughts in a straight line. There was no one else to turn to. She needed help. But it was impossible to ignore the anxious feeling in her chest that swelled with every step closer to the Glen.

The building was flat and faded and housed an off-license at the far end. She could see the outline of a man behind a counter fortified with metal grills. The windows of the bar were protected by the same grills and the black paint was flaking off the wooden frames. Between two security cameras, a round harp sign stuck out at ninety degrees from the wall, beckoning passing pedestrians in from the footpath.

It took a few seconds for her eyes to adjust to the darkness of the bar. There was a cigarette machine glowing on the wall opposite and a decrepit pool table parked in the far corner of the room. The bar was central, long and open on three sides. Behind it were stacks of shelves lined with glasses and bottles, and above it was a crooked wooden shelf littered with stoneware jugs, dirt-brown coloured and thick with dust.

The barman was already looking at her, eyebrow raised, tea towel in hand, rubbing a glass. He was weaselly, with a thin film of silver hair carefully combed over a shining bald head, and his eyes stayed on her as she walked towards the bar. There were the outlines of two men sitting a couple of metres apart, facing the kaleidoscope of glass and mirror behind the bar. One was wide as a barrel and slumped down to lean on his elbow, half hanging off his stool. The other one bore the unmistakable hunched shoulders of her father. She smiled at the barman and nodded in greeting.

What can I get ye? he said, chin tilted towards her. Her father turned then, to see her. He could have been an extension of the bar itself; cracked and dented, soaked in stout. He looked her up and down, like he was having trouble believing that she was really there. She swallowed down a sudden and overwhelming urge to shriek. She wanted to rupture the dingy silence with her voice. To jump on the pool table and smash the cues on the hard wooden edge until they snapped. She wanted to pull the stool from under the other drinker's fat behind and smash it over his fat head. She wanted to slap her father clean across the face. She wanted to slap him for every day and night she spent alone as a child, when he was here. For everything he missed. She wanted to slap him until her hands bled. She could feel her hand trembling and she held it out to the bar and steadied herself. She turned to the weasel.

I'll have a Diet Coke, please. Her voice wavered.

Her father hadn't said a word yet. He was still staring at her.

Is this your stool? she asked, trying to break the silence.

If you mean is that where he always sits, then you're right. He might as well pay rent here, said the weasel as he set down the Diet Coke on the bar. There was a second's silence until her father lifted his pint and swallowed the last third in one gulp.

I do pay rent here, he said, and threw a five-pound note from his coat pocket on to the bar.

They watched in silence as the barman prepared a fresh pint of Guinness. When it was set, her father led her to a corner table.

He was too big for the chair, creaking it against the ground as he pulled it forward towards the table. Above them the ceiling was tacked with green GAA football tops. Mary felt like her mouth was sewn shut. Now she could feel a tickling sensation from behind her eyes and she willed herself not to cry.

What's up? he asked, pint raised to just under his chin. She nodded and took a gulp of her Diet Coke. The syrupy sweetness felt good. She swallowed and spoke.

It's Sean. He's on drugs.

Her father put his pint down deliberately softly. She observed a faint tremor in his hands before he slicked back his hair. He spoke quietly.

What kind of drugs?

Heroin. I noticed last month. I think it's been going on for a while now . . . I don't know how to stop him.

Her father stared blankly at her stomach area, and she followed the tiny lines of the spider veins crawling over his nose. She saw his chest inhale and exhale, but apart from that he was statue still.

She gulped more of her drink down and the ice clinked around the bottom of the glass. The dishwasher beeped from its position behind the bar. He was shaking his head now.

I know, she said. He did it right under our noses. All this time. Her father took another drink and looked her in the eye.

I'll deal with this.

She hesitated, thinking of years gone by, of the muffled clumps and thumps that came from beneath her bedroom floor.

Daddy. You wouldn't.

He looked at her sharply and she felt a flutter of fear in her chest.

You're not to worry, Mary.

When she came home from work the next day, the duvet cover was in the washing machine and the duvet was neatly folded on the sofa. All Sean's stuff was gone. When she phoned him, he didn't answer, but later on that evening, Mary received a text.

Moved out. Waiting on a flat. Speak soon.

CHAPTER 27

TJ, PRESENT

TJ had passed the fortified red brick walls of the police station countless times, but never, thankfully, had reason to go beyond them. He walked towards it now, hands pushed into his pockets, feeling scared. His ma had stories of this place. Of the soldiers that used to come from behind these walls and crouch in people's front gardens with rifles. Of how they were never allowed to walk on the same side of the road as a patrol, in case the paramilitaries took a potshot at them and missed and hit the children instead. She had only recently told him the most shocking story of all of them.

When she was a very small girl, around six or seven, she and Uncle Sean had witnessed a foot patrol get bombed. Just at the top of Purves Road, where the old folks' home was now, there used to be a field with a shortcut through it to get to the Stewartstown Road. The IRA laid a tripwire across the Stewartstown Road and sat in a car at the top of

Purves, with a direct view on to the road, waiting for the soldiers to come.

These young fellas, no older than you, darlin', she said.

They got one. She heard the blast, felt the shock of it, the windows shaking, then she heard the violent revving of the car engine and she saw the red flash of the IRA car making a getaway down their street. She ran out of the house and saw Sean at the top of the street with some other kids all staring over the wall. A soldier was dragging another injured soldier off the road. He was crying. She had never seen a soldier cry before. She told him that she looked down to the injured soldier, seeing his head lolling and bouncing off his chest under his helmet. Then she realised there was only half of him. His legs had been blown clean off in the blast. TJ looked at his ma differently after that story.

He sits in the main reception, waiting for the woman to call him up, and trying to figure out why this visit feels like a betrayal of some sort. It feels wrong, but he knows it's the right thing to do. He is wearing his best white shirt with red buttons, still smooth and uncreased from when she ironed it last weekend. Above him, a large sign urges him to stop crime by calling this number anonymously.

A man walks into the waiting area and up to the desk, followed by a tired and remarkably young-looking police-woman. Does he know her? She looks vaguely familiar. The man sways slowly, almost gracefully, until he reaches out to the counter with two hands, to steady himself.

Drunk and disorderly, says the policewoman, who is holding the man's arm and leaning over the desk.

The man slurs. I want my lawyer! I want my lawyer, for fuck's sake!

Protestant, TJ thinks. He looks like one.

The woman behind the desk speaks. You can call your solicitor when we have all your information and you are registered into the system, sir. I just need your full name.

She speaks like a robot, as if the words are programmed to come out of her mouth. She must have to deal with all sorts of shite in here, TJ thinks to himself.

Fucking pigs.

TJ sees the irony in that remark, as the man is swinishly pink-cheeked and snub-nosed. Now his boiled face is right up next to hers, spittle hovering on his lips.

Listen to me, ye stuck up bitch . . . I want my lawyer . . .

The woman behind the desk is rolling her eyes now and seems to be pressing a button under the counter. TJ is impressed by her nonchalance and makes a mental note to remember how an eye roll at the opportune time can be an extremely effective weapon. Almost immediately, two policemen crash through a door on the other side of the waiting area, making TJ jump. They nod at the young police-woman and grab hold of each of the man's arms.

He needs to sober up. C-three is free, the woman behind the desk says to them, calm as anything.

The men pull the drunk man away, his feet dragging over the lacquered grey concrete floor, still yelling. The young policewoman follows. TJ watches her bottom as she walks away; her tight PSNI trousers and her belt with the handcuffs dangling down give him flashes of pornographic scenes in his head, and he moves his head away quickly to face the desk in front of him.

The space is completely silent but for the faint sound of Saturday evening traffic outside. Above the reception desk on the wall is a star-shaped sign with Police Service of Northern Ireland written across the centre of it in sculpted silver letters. He remembers about a month ago, Aiden and he were walking home from Devaney's after a lock-in. It must have been three or even four in the morning. Aiden was veering off the pavement, laughing hysterically, when a police car pulled up on the road ahead. They were questioned by two police, asking them where they'd been. TJ managed to remember to lie, saying they were round a friend's house on Malone Avenue. When the policewoman asked Aiden what he did for a living, he turned around and started to twerk, shouting wildly, I work mah booty!

TJ shuffles in his chair and coughs a little but the woman stays staring down at her paperwork, writing conscientiously so that TJ feels bad interrupting her. He stands up.

Ehh . . . Hi . . . I'm here to report a missing person.

She looks up then, just seeing him. She stares at him, accusatory, her eyebrows raised in a question.

I think I spoke to you on the phone? About my mum?

Right, okay.

She gets up and walks over to a set of drawers behind her. She is barrel-shaped, with wide hips and narrow shoulders and a prim fringed bob that reminds TJ of the Lego figures he played with as a kid. They must be in the attic now, he thinks, boxed up and carefully labelled by Ma. She keeps everything that has any sort of sentimental value.

The woman hands TJ a two-page form and a biro.

Fill in everything you can, don't spare any details, then we'll talk through it.

CHAPTER 28

MARY, 2010

It was the last day of April and Mary was on her feet in the kitchen, wiping the counter in hurried circles. Her son sat at the table, shovelling cornflakes into his mouth. He was ten years old now, gap-toothed and long-limbed, and mostly ran or leapt around the house. It was only when he was eating that he was still. Mary jumped at the clink of TJ's spoon tapping off his cereal bowl, and rubbed her forehead between her fingers as she turned to him and spoke.

TJ, I'm worried about Grandad.

TJ looked up.

Why?

Because he was sick in the night and he still isn't out of bed. I'm going to see him.

Hokay, he said, staring at her, spoon in hand. He probably just drank too much.

The three of them had settled back into a quiet rhythm after Sean left. Her father never left the post office and never defected from the Glen, but he had mellowed over the years. All his sharp edges were rounded out. She cut his hair these days, with the radio softly filling the room around them, so that it was neat around his ears. She had even persuaded him to come and see her mother's grave.

See how smart it is now, she suggested, and after that one time, he started to go at the weekends by himself. The thought of him pulling himself on to the train, with his huge yellowed hands and his lumpy nose, puffing his way into his seat, made her heart ache.

It was TJ who had alerted her to a problem the Sunday before. Her father had ambled into the living room as they were watching football, waiting for the lunch to cook. They both turned to him and TJ said, Grandad, your skin is yellow.

There *was* a sickly yellow tinge to his skin. His eyes were puffed out and squinting more than normal, focused on TJ. He was holding on to the back of the chair. Over the past year, his tremor had settled in for good, and he liked to grip on to things to keep it at bay. He looked perplexed and shook his head quickly, as if to wish TJ's words out of existence, before collapsing into his armchair. Mary noticed that his belly seemed preposterously round, as if a beach ball had been pushed up his jumper.

Daddy, are you okay? You do look yellow . . .

Just tired, he grunted through his beard. I could sleep for a week.

She walked up the stairs now, straining to hear his snores.

She remembered the heaves and croaks and spits that woke her up the night before. How she heard a dull thud, and felt the floor underneath the bed shake for a split second. How she lay, paralysed in fear, holding her breath, until she heard a scraping sound, the slow open of the bathroom door, and the dragging sound of his feet on the carpet making their way across the landing to his room.

She was at his door now. She knocked softly and waited. Last night, she had waited five minutes and crept into the bathroom. The water in the bowl was a dark red pool. Where was the blood coming from? There was no answer at his door, so she gently pushed it open. The air smelt of sweat and stale stout. His Royal Mail coat hung on the open wardrobe door. There were newspapers everywhere, piled up on all the flat surfaces and on the carpet by his bed. She closed the door behind her and took a breath. He lay diagonally on the bed, with his head in the far corner and his feet dangling out the side. His toenails were yellow shells, whorled and hardened. His grey hair was straggled over the pillow. His head lolled to the side.

Daddy!

He didn't move. She sat down on the side of the bed.

Daddy, wake up!

He did not stir. She walked around to the other side of the bed, where his head was, and leaned into his face, hovering her hand flat over his mouth. She felt a surge of relief at the exhalation of warm air. She put her hands on his shoulders and spoke right up to his face.

Daddy, can you hear me?

His eyes opened slowly then. They were bloodshot pink and wet with tears. He was staring straight through her.

Daddy! It's time to get up!

His eyes slowly focused on her and he stared at her, intensely. She could smell the cigarette stench of his breath. Slowly, his face contorted into rage.

Ye didn't do it. Ye *didn't do* it!

I didn't do what?

She backed away from the bed.

Daddy, what are you talking about?

She never said you could do it!

He was shouting now, up slightly on his elbows. She saw spittle land on his beard.

Daddy, I don't understand. Daddy, it's me, Mary.

Just then, he pushed himself bolt upright on the bed. His eyes were bulging out of their sockets. He pointed at her.

You'll be a fool to do it. A fuckin' *fool*.

She heard a noise at the door and looked up to see TJ staring at his grandfather, a look of abject fear on his face. She moved towards him, but stumbled on some newspapers. She managed to catch herself from falling by holding on to his wardrobe.

Her father was leaning forwards now, and trembling, staring at the wall opposite. He was somewhere far away.

Go downstairs now and get me my phone, she said to TJ, as she closed the door behind her. She rang the ambulance then, one hand gripping the phone and one hand firmly clenched on her father's door handle. As she recited the address, she could hear the chatter of school kids on their way to the bus stop outside. It was a Tuesday morning. She was to plant sunflowers in the north garden that day. She stayed outside the door for fifteen long minutes, listening to her father shouting, then whispering, then shouting again. When TJ crept up the stairs to ask should he go to school, she held him tightly in a hug, repeating, He's not well, darlin'. He's not himself.

His slippered feet hung over the end of the stretcher as they carried him out. His mouth hung open in a gawp, eyes squeezed shut in pain. There was a group of school kids across the road, silenced and staring. Dolores hobbled out her front door.

Jesus, can I do anything?

Can you make sure TJ gets to school? Mary said, tight-lipped and pale as she climbed into the ambulance behind her father.

They took him to the Royal Victoria and a bespectacled doctor told her that his liver was riddled with cancer. Poisoned from the endless glut of alcohol. The cancer had spread so far around his body he was 'beyond treatment'. He was admitted to the St Augustus Hospice for palliative care, and for fourteen days he lay in a drugged-up stupor in a room with walls the colour of piss. Night after night, Mary sat by his side, TJ fidgety and wide-eyed behind her, his school books open on his knees. She ignored the dull ache of her back and her growling stomach, unable to eat the sandwiches she made for them both. She held her father's hand for hours. His tremble had stopped.

She politely thanked the nurses who changed his bedpan and turned him over, and after a week of him being there, politely listened when they advised her to go back to work. That he was in good hands, and they would ring her if anything at all happened.

So she did, and in the evenings she visited with TJ, and she rang Sean and urged him to go and visit, and when he didn't, she collected him one day and drove him herself. She busied herself telling him all the details of their father's illness, of the hospice and how great they were, of his room and his nurses, plumping his pillow, straightening his sheets, while Sean leaned back into his chair and looked at everything in the room but his father.

He died on a glorious May morning when the spring sun made everything glow. She was at Bedwood, in the van with Sid. Sid had the window open and his elbow resting on it, and they were comfortable in their silence as they moved through the cemetery. When her phone rang, she felt Sid's eyes on her.

Hello?

Hello, Mary, it's Ann here, the nurse from St Augustus's.

Hello, she said.

Mary, your father died this morning at seven-thirty a.m. He died peacefully, in his sleep and without pain.

She stared out the front window as Sid slowed down the van to a stop and quietly exited the van. The sun shone in through the front windscreen, warming her thighs.

There were absolutely no signs of deterioration, Mary, or we would have called you at once. He just went.

He died on his own. In that room that reeked of disinfectant. With Jesus on the cross hanging above the head of the bed. Her stomach turned.

I wanted to be there. I wanted to be with him.

I'm so sorry, Mary.

She hung up the phone then, and leaned her head down between her knees, down to her work boots on the filthy floor of the van. She squeezed her fingernails into her palms, pressing as hard as she could. She was in a state of suspended stillness, after the pin is pulled and before the explosion. She heard the sing-song of a lone blackbird from a tree nearby. She sat back up at the sound of the van door opening.

Was it your father? he asked, as he climbed back in.

She nodded at her feet.

Do you need to leave?

She nodded again and didn't allow herself to look at Sid as he turned on the ignition. He drove her back to the office, where she gathered her things and walked to her car as if in slow motion.

And a few days after, when all the forms were signed and her father's belongings gathered, she went back to his bedroom again. She sat on the carpet, surrounded by the piles of newspapers, yellowed and stiffened from the light coming in the window. She sat until darkness fell over Purves estate. And when it was dark, she lay in his bed and tried to find the shape of him in the mattress, tried to fit into it. She took the photo of her mother from the bedside table and held it to her chest. She found a shoebox in the bottom of his wardrobe and took it downstairs to the kitchen table. There were old letters from Paul, her father's older brother, written from Adelaide, Australia, telling her father about the shipyard where he worked, written in childish, shaky writing. There were black and white photos of her father's family at the farm, her grandfather's face shadowed by his flat cap, cigarette hanging out of his mouth in every shot, and her father a knock-kneed boy with dirt on his face, holding hands with his sister.

She found a plastic folder holding her mother's death certificate, stating her cause of death as a brain aneurysm and her age at death as thirty years old. She sat on the carpet, clutching the document, staring at the typed letters, and let the realisation that she was an orphan wash over her. She was rootless. She was flailing in the wind. Behind the death certificate, she found a photo that she stared at for a long time. It was a girl, sitting on a step, in front of the back door of a house. She had one hand on a mop that was resting in a bucket by her feet. She had a long-sleeved dress on, and old runners. Her hair was tied up in a tangled bun on top of her head. She looked as if she was in her mid-teens. Her face was set in a grimace, her forehead wrinkling over her nose. Mary recognised this girl as her mother. Not from the other photos she had seen of her, but because of the way she looked at the camera as if she'd been confronted with something. She recognised herself.

CHAPTER 29

TJ, PRESENT

He shifts his weight in his plastic chair and frowns over the clipboard on his knee, tongue stuck between his lips in concentration.

Full name of missing person: *Mary Margaret McConnell*.

He writes carefully.

Age of missing person.

He was born in 2000 and she was eighteen when he was born . . . and now it's 2018. So, eighteen and eighteen makes thirty-six. But her birthday was when? May twentieth. He tries to remember what happened on her last birthday as he writes down *37*.

What did they do? It was a weeknight, and he had made her breakfast that morning. It was scrambled eggs on toast, and they were terrible, all coagulated and rubbery. He remembers his mum laughing it off, eating every last bite, assuring him that it was the thought that counted. He remembers her flicking through her *House & Home* magazines. Did he buy her a bigger present? He can't remember doing that. He hopes he did. She'll remember, of course.

Last seen:

42, Purves Road.

Belfast BT17

Friday, 7 p.m., 14 September 2018.

He pictures the last time he saw her, her facing away from him, pinching the bridge of her nose. He swallows and moves on through the list.

Description of missing person.

She is small, but what height he doesn't know . . . he guesses at five foot four. Growing up, she measured him up against the door of the downstairs hall cupboard. When you open it now, you can see the etchings and the neat dates written beside them. He remembers how delighted he was when he overtook her in height. And when he outgrew the door, they stopped measuring him altogether. He writes:

Slim build, browny-red hair, green eyes. Hair is long but nearly always tied up. Not sure what clothes – maybe big work boots.

He finishes, stands up and pushes the form over the counter towards the woman. She picks it up and scans it, then picks up a biro and leans over to carry on writing. Without looking at him, she says, Okay, so you last saw her in your house. Was there an event that could have led to her being angry or emotional in any way?

TJ swallows.

We had an argument.

Was it violent? she says, without hesitation.

No! God, no. I, I went to my room, she left dinner out for me and I didn't check, but I'm sure she was in her room later on that night. When I woke this morning, she was gone. Her car is gone. She hasn't gone to work.

The woman scribbles on the paper.

Is there anywhere else you think she could have gone?

I just don't know. It's really not like her to not answer my calls or texts.

I see. So, let's say she's definitely been gone since this morning. What time did you wake up?

Me? TJ said.

The woman looks up slowly. Her lipstick is faded out of the centre of her lips and just outlines them now. She looks like she needs an early night, he thinks.

Yes, you.

Hmm, about eleven?

She scribbles more notes on the piece of paper.

And is there anything on her that would definitely make her identifiable as her?

TJ flashes back to films and TV shows he has watched, of people in morgues lifting up blankets and wincing at the bulging shapes underneath.

He looks at her in silence. The woman speaks.

It's handy for us to have really easy things to know that it's your mother. There's a lot of red-haired women in Belfast.

Any jewellery? She says that forgivingly, seeing the look of panic on TJ's face.

She wears a ring. A gold band on her finger.

So, she's married?

No. It's my grandfather's old wedding ring. It's the only ring she wears. She's a gardener, so she doesn't wear a lot of jewellery.

He yearns for the big, quiet presence of his grandad now. The smoky smell of him. The slow smile. His grandad was never assertive; TJ can't imagine how he would deal with something like this. He was happy to be looked after by Ma and she always did so. Fed him and brought him papers and Guinness, let him watch his favourite TV programmes over her own. After he died, the dynamic changed so much in the house. TJ knew his ma wouldn't move into her father's old bedroom, so he volunteered, suggesting that she could have his room and finally have more space. They spent hours scraping off the old wallpaper together, with the windows open. She got the carpet cleaned and she bought him a new striped rug for the floor. He thought that once his room was sorted, she would start sorting out her new space. That she would transform it. But she slept in his room just as it was for a good two years before she took a paintbrush to it. He was embarrassed at her in there, with the walls covered in Blu Tack marks and faded rectangles where his posters had been.

And does she have a partner, or any other family that are also looking?

TJ looks at her again, a slight pause before he replies.

No.

Does she have any mental health conditions that we should know about? Any vital medication?

No. She's pretty healthy.

Okay, do you know the registration of her car, TJ?

TJ screws his face up in concentration.

Can I borrow this? he says, pointing at the biro.

He tries out different combinations of numbers and letters.

I'm not a hundred per cent sure, but it's something like this. The first two are definitely right. It's like, shiny light green, old. Peugeot.

Not to worry, we can find it. Does it have any distinguishing marks on it?

Eh, the windscreen wiper rubs off the window and makes a racket. There is a dent in the back bumper as well, not sure which side.

Have you rung around her friends? Neighbours? Checked her address books for new names?

Eh, I've done some ringing, and checked an address book, but nothing new or out of the ordinary.

Did your mother have any links with paramilitaries? Or does anyone in your family?

He racks his brains.

No. Definitely not my mother, and not anyone else, as far as I know.

He watches as she carefully writes down the details and then reads over the paper again. TJ has the impression he is being tested by a teacher and he wonders what his grade would be. His A-level results were boringly below average. He remembers his mother's face struggling to hide her disappointment when he showed her the piece of paper. Her cheery lilt of, Not bad, son!

She was straight on the computer, her hopeful expression illuminated by the light of the screen as she looked up local college courses, and what grades they accepted. This was before he told her about his idea of living in New York, of course. He didn't have the nerve then. To shatter her hopes. They were so pure. He knew she would hate the idea of him going to New York with no work and no plan. And he knew she would suspect that it was because of his father. And he would say it was nothing to do with him. But it would make it easier *if* they were to ever meet. Like, just to be in the same country as him.

The phone rings then behind the desk, and the woman exhales a soft sigh as she reaches out for it without turning her head away from the form.

Police, she says on answering.

His gaze moves up to the wall behind her as the call continues. He remembers watching his mother from the doorway, running her finger down the screen, following the list of accepted grades for Belfast Met College, speaking the words under her breath. He wanted to get out then, to walk out of the house and keep walking, out of Belfast itself, up the motorway all the way to Larne, straight to the kiosk to buy a ticket to anywhere on the next ferry leaving this stupid fucking island. He remembers hating her and hating his stupid A-levels. His stupid school and his stupid teachers. He wanted an adventure. He wanted, as Aiden would say, *life* lessons.

Ma, I need to get out. It's results night. Everyone goes out.

She turned to him.

Sure, darlin'. Just . . .

I'll be careful. Don't wait up for me, please. I'll probably stay at Aiden's.

She was still hunched over the computer when he slammed the door ten minutes later. He got so drunk that night that he vomited all over himself and had to borrow one of Aiden's malodorous T-shirts to return home in the following morning.

He flinches at the sound of the receiver being slammed back on to the phone.

Okay. So, I'm going to add all these details to the system tonight and send out a preliminary missing persons description so that patrols can keep a lookout.

What if she's still not turned up tomorrow?

Then we will actively send search parties out and increase the search. It's likely you'll be called on again. Can I check this is your correct number?

She recites his number back to him.

TJ nods.

When you wake up in the morning, if she hasn't arrived home, then call the station with this reference number. Put it in your phone, maybe, so you don't forget it.

TJ types out the number in a note on his phone. He flicks on to his recent call history: Ma (18 calls).

He wonders how many more there will be before he finds her.

Okay. Okay.

He is nodding profusely and forces himself to keep still. He hasn't moved from the counter. The words 'search party' have crashed through him like breeze blocks. He is finding it hard to talk.

How old are you? she says, looking at him properly now for what seems like the first time.

Eighteen.

Are you sure there's nowhere you can go tonight?

He thinks of Aiden's house, the stench of weed and over-flowing ashtrays, reruns of the American *Office*. He thinks of the suffocating heat of Dolores's house. He shakes his head.

I just want to be be there when she gets home.

The woman is smiling now, or maybe she just isn't frowning any more, and her face looks younger all of a sudden.

Try not to worry, I'm sure she'll show up.

He nods at her and turns, hands in pockets, to walk out of the building. The door bangs shut behind him as he steps out of the caged porch and on to the main road. The sun's light is fading and the edges of the clouds are tinged with the lightest pink. A group of women walk past, huddled together, all clutching bags full of clinking bottles. He'd forgotten it was Saturday night. He starts to cry then. He tucks his head down into his shoulders and wipes away the tears with the back of his sleeve.

He looks at his watch: 8.30 p.m. He pulls his phone out and sends a text to Sid.

Sid, I'm on my way.

He lets out a large sigh as he puts his phone back in his pocket. He stands up tall, and starts to walk back up the road towards the roundabout.

CHAPTER 30

MARY, PRESENT

She has learned that this part of the road is a place for passing through. Every now and then a car whizzes past, but no one stops. There is no reason to. She doesn't know how long she has been here, but she knows she has watched the daylight collide with the darkness of the night. She has watched the thin, papery moon rise up through the clouds to hang over the sea. The paracetamol is useless. Her head aches right under the front of her skull, as if there is something raw and exposed in there, something bruised. She has to keep moving.

She turns to the passenger seat to pick him up, then sniffs and shakes her head quickly, as if to wake herself up and out of a fog. She opens the door and steps out. The wind whips her hair on to her cheeks and she pulls it away with her free hand. A lone seagull faces her; it is dappled and grey, its black beak closed firmly shut, head cocked in anticipation of her next move. She walks slowly, holding him close to her, out to the road and across it, without looking for cars. She walks into the wind, along the narrow pavement, until she sees a small opening of a path through the brush.

It is not a pretty beach. The sand is bedraggled with the residue of the sea, long black straggles of seaweed and driftwood, shells and plastic waste, all colour faded off by water and light. She feels suddenly dizzy with relief that she has remembered her purpose. She has found the place. She hears a crunching sound and looks down to see she has crushed a shell, worn thin from the weight of the waves. There is a used condom slung on the sand by her foot. She stares at it for a long time and looks around her again. This is a place for sex and excess, she realises. Accessible but hidden, this is a place where people come to lose themselves. Some deliberately, some forced, but always with the ocean close by, whispering and shushing in commentary. She knows what it feels like to lose yourself in the dark. Her head flashes to a triangular flag hanging off a pole, the bitter taste of vodka in her mouth, the heavy weight of him, pushing the breath out of her lungs. She keeps seeing the last digits of the phone number.

7-4-7-8

Three missed calls in a row. Taunting her. She feels the fear moving up into her chest and swallows it down, emitting a small moan into the air. Focus on the water, she tells herself. It is choppy this evening, but not rough. White foam crests whipped up by the wind appear and disappear in front of her. The tide is starting to creep out, leaving a thick strip of wet, shining black pebbles in front of her. She walks right up to the edge of the water. The seagull is flying in languid circles above her. She watches it for a while. There are stars twinkling through the gap in the clouds. She is reminded of the summer after her father died. His death felt like somebody had broken into the house and stolen all the furniture. There was all this new space that they didn't know how to fill. Even the air felt different. TJ took her father's room, and she was glad of the challenge to transform it. She took TJ's old room and welcomed a new perspective on the house. But she was such a light sleeper, and the cars on the road woke her in the night and the morning. When he was a small boy, she had stuck glow-in-the-dark stickers of stars and planets all over his ceiling. All summer, she had lain awake staring at their dull glow. She was numb. TJ followed her round the house a lot. She enrolled him into football camp at Andersonstown Leisure Centre and afterwards, he came on the train and spent the last few hours of the afternoons at Bedwood. He grumbled about it, but she suspected he was content there, sitting under the ash tree with his Nintendo and his chocolate biscuits and his ma nearby. That was before he started secondary school. When he was still a boy. A boy with no father. Did he wish for one? Her face screws up into a grimace. She gave him everything she could. Was it enough? She lied to him. A lie that has swollen over the years into something preposterous, something impossible to bear. Would he ever forgive her? She was a girl with no mother. And a father that was only ever half alive. A girl that dreamed of climbing into her father's bed at night with a knitting needle like the ones Aunt Bridget used, and perforating the thick skin of his belly. She imagined it bursting like a water balloon; with brown, bitter liquid splattering across the walls. In the morning, he would wake up sparkly eyed and smiling, and come and scoop her out of bed and ask her what she wanted for breakfast.

She can see the lights of the recreation area across the bay, but it is just her on the beach, and this is it. The darkness is closing in around her. She sits down on the pebbles, and the water laps at her toes.

CHAPTER 31

MARY, 2013

Saturday afternoon meant bad traffic. Every driver she could see was cross-looking, and she wondered why. The grey skies maybe, or just the inconvenience of it all. The realisation that their Saturday wasn't going to be special after all. She swallowed down a flutter of anxiety and checked her watch. She was right on time to pick up TJ. She reached out and ran her hand across the dashboard of her car, collecting a light film of dust across her fingertips. The year before her father died, she had invested in ten driving lessons, and passed her test first time. She bought the car with the help of Sean from an auction out in Ballymena. It was a metallic mint-green Peugeot 305. Third gear was almost impossible to engage and the heating system was loud and clunky. There was a substantial crack in the front windscreen where a stone had hit it. It was the single greatest thing she had ever purchased.

She saw her son from a distance. He was walking towards the carpark. His hoodie was tied around his waist and the red of his Manchester United football shirt looked garish against his skin. She pulled in off the Andersonstown Road.

I've been calling you for ages, but you never answered, he said, as he dropped himself into the passenger seat. His hair was tufty with the matt finish of a lack of shampoo.

God, sorry love, it must be on silent.

She smiled at him hopefully.

How are you?

All right, he sighed, staring out the front window. Actually, I'm freezing.

Score any goals?

Nah. I had one set up for me and I missed it.

Well, don't be hard on yourself, son, you can't score every goal.

Rooney does, he said, putting on his hoodie.

I'll put the hot air on. Here, I've kept these for ye.

She took half a pack of chocolate digestives from her bag and handed them over to him.

Thanks.

Are you ready for Uncle Sean, then?

He rolled his eyes.

Ready as I'll ever be.

On the first Saturday of every month, they went to visit Sean. Seeing her brother in the context of other people at their father's funeral had been a shock. He was so thin it was as if his bones were rattling inside his suit. She felt she needed to do something to hold what was left of her family together. That had been three years ago. TJ was thirteen now, in secondary school, and he didn't return her hugs any more. She was aware that she didn't have much time left until TJ refused to come on the Sean visits at all. A car behind her beeped.

Jesus Christ. What is it with people today?

They were in traffic, crawling along the Falls Road. She could see the clusters of colourful graffiti on the Peace Wall up ahead. They drove past Falls Road Library. She always loved the grandiosity of the building, its complete detachment from the domino rows of houses stretching out behind it. It sat right beside an end-of-terrace red-bricked house with an enormous mural of Bobby Sands painted on it. His hair was long and glossy; the artist had painted his face with a feminine softness that gave him the look of a middle-aged woman. Mary knew the words off by heart.

Everyone, Republican or otherwise, has their own particular role to play . . . our revenge will be the laughter of our children.

She liked that idea of revenge. That happiness could win over a weapon. She glanced over at TJ and saw him staring at the library, face set in a frown.

A few minutes later, they arrived. Sean had been rotting in Bedoin Close for years now. It was a neglected dead end of one-storey, red-brick terraced properties built in the shadow of the Peace Wall, and number nine was right at the end of the line. Mary could see the bottle-green corrugated iron cladding from her car, the metal fencing stretched so high it was as if it could pierce the dense blanket of clouds above. She turned off the ignition and they sat in silence for a short while before Mary opened her door.

The black wheelie bin was tucked around the side of the house, a soggy pizza box hanging out over the top, looking for escape. There was a grubby net curtain hanging over the bottom of the front window and a tasselled pull-down blind hanging over the top part.

I wonder how long it will take for him to open the door this time? TJ said, eyes rolling as they walked up to the door. Mary could just see through the gap in the blinds, and took in three empty glasses on top of the corner of the faux marble fireplace. TJ pressed the bell and stood back. He folded his arms and set his face into a sulking expression. His limbs were stretching, Mary thought as she watched him. His milky skin and thin frame exaggerated his facial features to a cartoon-like degree. She had a sudden urge for time to freeze. She could hug him close to her and they could remain on this doorstep, frozen in embrace, for eternity.

How'ryouse!

Sean's complexion was the same dull grey as the sky. He greeted them with a straight face and raised eyebrows, and stood aside as they shuffled in the door. He reached out and tousled TJ's hair as he walked past. TJ turned around to face him.

What'll we watch today?

I have the new Iron Man film downloaded for you.

TJ's eyes widened and he nodded, casting a sideways glance at his mother.

Go on then, but you might have to finish it next time.

Sean followed TJ into the tiny living room, and Mary walked into the kitchen. The sink was half-full of water and she could see that Sean had just started to soak some pans in it before she arrived. She opened the bin and was hit with the pungent smell of stale smoke. He had emptied his ashtrays too, she thought, so there was some small sense of shame in there somewhere. She put on her Marigold gloves and lined up various cleaning products on the kitchen table.

Do you two want a cup of tea? she shouted in.

No thanks! they replied in unison.

She surveyed the remainder of the kitchen. There was thick grime over every surface, even the vertical ones, with dark splatter marks on the cupboard doors and skirting boards. Cigarette ash had mixed with spillages on the floor and been walked into the grooves of the linoleum.

She started on her hands and knees, scrubbing with an old toothbrush. She used it again in the bathroom, which was so small she had to leave the door open and lean into the shower with her feet stuck into the hall. She scrubbed and shined the tiles in the shower, washed down the folding door, cleaned and disinfected the toilet and neatly lined up his mouthwash and toothpaste on the side of the sink. She could smell the lingering smell of his aftershave from his bedroom. She didn't open the door.

She got out the hoover from the tiny cramped cupboard by the fridge and moved through the kitchen and the hall, ending in the living room. The carpet was threadbare and crab pink and scattered with the drab confetti of loose tobacco. TJ and Sean lifted their feet as she hoovered around the sofa, stopping every now and again to pick up pieces of ripped Rizla papers that were wedged into the weave. TJ looked at his mum in frustration.

Mum, I can't hear.

Sean found the remote control and turned up the volume loud so they could hear it over the hoovering. When Mary had folded the hoover carefully back into its tiny holding place, she came back into the room and collected the empty cups, plates and glasses and brought them to soak in the sink. Then she went back in with a cleaning spray and wiped down the surfaces. She collected six lighters from different places in the room and held them in front of Sean's face with a questioning look in her eye. He took them out of her hand without moving his line of sight from a porcelain-skinned Gwyneth Paltrow on the screen in front of him.

The last thing she tackled was the dishes, and she hummed as she stood at the sink, looking out the back window. There was no outside space here, just a low wall that backed on to an alleyway where the local kids tore up and down on their bikes. There was graffiti on the wall outside.

Marko is a cunt was written in thick black marker with the 'cunt' underlined for extra emphasis. She smiled at that. She wondered if the act had provided catharsis for the person who wrote it. She thought maybe she should try it some-time. She could walk around Belfast at night with a Sharpie, spelling out all her frustrations on cement . . .

So, sis . . .

She turned around. Sean stood in the doorway.

You're very good to be doing this.

Well Sean, you're clearly not doing it yourself.

The sharpness of her retort surprised her, and the silence fell fast and heavy between them. She turned around from the sink and wiped her wet gloves on a tea towel. He was wearing his same old grey tracksuit. It had a centimetre squared cigarette burn in the chest, just above the black tick of the logo. She didn't look for the spots any more. She knew they would be there, peppered all over the thread of his veins like chicken pox.

Are you eating? she said.

He caught her eye briefly and then flitted his gaze to the window.

Aye, but only about one meal a day.

Mary sighed and started to fiddle with her gloves.

Mary. I lost my job.

He was looking at the floor now.

Did they find out?

No. Business isn't good and Richie said he doesn't need me any more.

Well you better sign on quick.

She turned back around to the dishes. She reached for a bowl that had cereal dried on to the inside. No amount of scrubbing seemed to be able to get it off. As she worked, her scrubbing brush slipped off the inside of the bowl and knocked against her thumb. She hissed, an inhalation of breath. It hurt. Irrationally so.

Sean went to the cupboard behind her, pulled out a six pack of crisps and walked back into the living room, leaving the cupboard door open behind him. She heard TJ's grunt of acknowledgement, and the rustling of the bags being opened. Mary thought of the hoovering she had just done.

She suddenly knew she had to get out. She left the dirty plate in the sink and quickly wiped the counters. She found the mop from beside the fridge and mopped the floor. The kitchen looked habitable again, she thought as she surveyed her work. She gathered up the cleaning products and left them by the door. She stuck her head in the living room and said, TJ, we leave in five minutes.

She picked up the three plastic bags she had brought with her and started to unload them. It was mostly groceries: long-life milk, eggs, bread for the freezer that he could toast. Some frozen pizzas and a homemade lasagne for the freezer too. She unpacked four ciders and lined them up in the fridge door, and put a double pack of some of his favourite Jammie Dodger biscuits in the cupboard.

The final bag had a cactus in it. It was a *Crassula ovata* – about a foot high, in the pot, with five bursts of green waxy leaves that she had polished to a glossy finish. She held it up to the window and looked at the light glistening off the leaves, and then carefully set it down in the middle of the kitchen table. Her handbag was on the table and she pulled out her purse and flicked through the notes. She was sure she had had a fiver in the zipped-up coin pocket. She took out a crisp twenty-pound note and left it beside the cactus.

Her coat and bag were on when she went to the living room.

Ooh, TJ said as he saw her, raising his tone in frustration.

We'll have to come back again, and you can watch the end of it.

Sean pressed pause and stood up. She hated the look in his eyes when they left.

Well then. I'll see yiz next time.

He looked down at TJ.

You be good for your mammy, okay?

Yes, Uncle Sean.

TJ flounced out of the room and opened the door. Sean stood in the doorway, lighting up a cigarette as they drove away. He had developed the hunch of an old man, she thought as she watched him get smaller and smaller behind them in the mirror.

CHAPTER 32

MARY, 2014

Sid's last working day fell on a Thursday, three days before Christmas. The holidays were looming and the mood amongst the team of gardeners was buoyant. Mary brought a cake to work, carefully placed in a biscuit box, which had sat beside her on the passenger seat all the way to Bedwood. She had stayed up late the night before, apron on, tight-lipped in concentration, determined to make it perfect. Apple cake was his favourite – due to his years in Germany when he was in his twenties – and Mary remembered how he had grumbled about how difficult it was to find in Belfast. She enjoyed seeing his gap-toothed, shy smile at the revelation of it at tea-break that morning. She also brought in custard, and the gardeners passed the carton of it around, pouring it into their paper bowls. They were all layered up, braced against the icy December air, and they stood awkwardly in a circle as they ate, murmuring praise for the cake, mouths full.

How many years have you been here, Sid? said Alan, their newest recruit, smiling into his bowl.

Dear God, said Sid. I joined Bedwood in 1990. So, twenty-four years now.

Twenty-four years of McKee, said Frank, shaking his head into his bowl of cake.

Well at least I'll be gone when Mr McKee is dead and buried. You'll need to call in extra help to dig that grave, said Sid.

A ripple of laughter moved around the circle.

What will you do? said Frank.

I don't know. But I better find something to fill up my days quick or I'll go spare.

McKee had appointed Mary the new head of the ground maintenance team, taking over from Sid. She was to get a pay rise, and have the word 'Senior' precede her job title, which was fitting, as she felt older than ever. Since the announcement, she had felt the parallel forces of resentment from her colleagues and anxiety from inside her head. She had been agitated all morning, as if there was a balloon in her chest getting bigger, and she tried her hardest to focus on the familiar routines of their labour to forget about it. There was a tacit agreement that she and Sid would work side by side for the whole day. He wanted to do all of the menial tasks; the emptying of the grass in the compost, pouring petrol into the lawnmower, the stacking of the pots on the shelves of the garage. She watched him from nearby, taking his time with the work, allowing his limbs to take on the shapes and movements of his tasks from muscle memory. She drove them around the site, giving Sid all the time he needed to jump out and deliver his instructions for her to keep everything in place.

At the north field, he climbed slowly out of the van and frowned over a row of fledgling silver birch memorial trees.

I don't think these are looking too good, he said, taking out his Stanley knife and cutting a small piece of bark from the trunk.

Mm. These roots haven't been soaked. They've dried out too quick, he continued, examining the small piece of wood. He looked at Mary then, his cheeks pink from the wind.

Mary. Bare roots. They're really handy cos they're light and they're easy to plant, but you can't forget about the water, Mary. Never forget the importance of soaking your bare roots. Soak them for twenty-four hours, right up to the point of planting. Time it in advance. Straight from the water into the soil.

Mary nodded. She had heard this before from Sid, but she relished it then.

At the end of the day, they stood, side by side, looking out over the lake. It was dark, and she had to allow her eyes to tune in to the black to spot the heron balancing on one spindly leg on the far side of the water, directly opposite Sid. They looked like they were squaring off at each other.

She sneaked a sideways look at her friend. His hair was

a white wiry brush. His bushy eyebrows cantilevered over his nose. He looked like an old man, and it still surprised her. She knew he had waited longer than he should have to retire. She had noticed him slowing down over the last few years, of course; she saw him wince as he bent over to pick things up off the ground, and getting up and down off his knees to plant took longer and longer. She took on some of his more strenuous jobs and he didn't protest. Sometimes he'd reach out his hand to her when there was no one else around and say, Help an old man up.

They stared out on to the inky sheet of water in front of them. She thought of the feeling of heavy calm that came over her when she saw Sid drive towards her in the van, his face screwed up against the light and his elbow out the window.

Sid. What will I do without you? she said softly into the darkness. He turned to her swiftly and looked at her. He took her right hand in his and wrapped his crooked fingers around it, pulling it to his chest.

You've got what it takes, Mary. Just give it time.

She wanted to cling on to him. They stayed facing the lake.

CHAPTER 33

MARY, 2015

She sat at the window of McGonegal's Seafood Restaurant, in the Cathedral Quarter. She tried to relax into her position, to enjoy the buzz of the open square outside, and the feel of a warm June evening in Belfast. But he still hadn't answered her reminder text and she couldn't help fidgeting. She twisted the slender stem of her wine glass back and forth between her fingers. He was only five minutes late. She forced herself to take small sips of her wine, so she could stretch out the time for as long as possible. It was her idea, of course. After another depressing visit to his house the week before, he had looked so utterly hollow and depressed that she said it to him on the front step.

Let me take you out for your birthday! I'll take you for posh fish and chips in town.

And he had raised his eyebrows and said, Aye. I suppose so.

She looked out the window. Opposite her, there was a

bar with the whole front window opened up and out so that the people sitting along the high bench were tipping their glasses into the naked dusk. There was a giddiness to them all. She focused in on a couple who were leaning on the bar and staring into each other's eyes. She noticed that the girl's leg was coiled around the guy's.

Sean had never had any girlfriends after Daisy, as far as she could tell. Since Richie let him go, he had been claiming benefits. There were always things on the horizon, of course, appointments and people who knew people who might have work. He always had a thing to tell her. She had thought that after their father's death, Sean might change. That it might be freeing in some way for him. But he only talked less; looked her in the eye less. She thought she would ask him tonight, did he miss their father? Maybe they could talk about him.

She looked at her watch: 8.30 p.m. Her wine was finished and the restaurant was getting busy now, with people shifting their weight from foot to foot at the door, side-eyeing the empty stool next to her. She called him again and listened to his phone ring out. He didn't allow for voicemails on his phone. She sighed and texted him.

Sean, I'm going to presume you're not showing up. Call me when you get this.

She stood up, grabbed her bag and walked to the bathroom. Some people beckoned to her to ask if the stools were free. She nodded and smiled, and entered the bathroom. It was cool and dark.

She sat down on the toilet and saw that her sanitary towel was filled entirely with blood. She cursed under her breath. Her period pains were crippling lately. She clicked open her handbag to find another pad, and saw her phone glowing. She hurriedly swiped across. It was TJ.

Ma can me and Timmy get a takeaway on your card? Dominos. x

She typed back.

Yes, but not more than 20 quid and no more takeaways this month.

Her son was fifteen years old and towering over her now, spending more and more time in his bedroom, and hogging the bathroom for what seemed like hours. He was sleeping and growing, like when he was a toddler, she thought; she had to buy him new clothes every few months. His feet alone went up a full size in the first six months of this year. She pictured him slouched on the sofa with his friend Timmy, guffawing at the television, his voice cracking through to a new bass tone.

She pulled herself up to look in the small mirror above the sink. She was wearing black trousers, the same ones she had bought over a decade ago for her interview for Bedwood. She had bought a soft wool polo neck from Marks and Spencer. It was the colour of moss. Her hair was tied up in a loose bun and she wore gold-plated pearl-drop earrings. She hardly ever looked in the mirror these days. Her nose was crooked. Her freckles had run into constellations so there were dark clusters of them on the bridge of her nose. Her whole face looked patchy and uneven. She had allowed herself to feel excited about a Saturday night in town, about feeling something new.

Stupid. She was stupid.

There was a soft knock on the door and she quickly exited, whispering an apology with her eyes lowered to the floor. She paid for the wine and set off, walking at a brisk pace. She walked up Dublin Road, past the cinema and the old second-hand shops. She stopped at the traffic lights and then walked across the road as they beeped into the pink dusk. A group of young men ran across the road, cackling with laughter. She stopped walking to let them run around her; a stone in a stream. She hurried across the road and made her way towards the strip of shops on Bradbury Place.

She kept walking straight, but as she passed Lavery's Bar, her legs moved a different way and she found herself pulling open the ornate glass doors underneath the 'BAR' sign. The darkness of the room was a comfort to her. The sounds of the street were muted in here, soaked up in the wood panelling and the musty air. She relaxed her shoulders and tilted her chin up to the bartender.

Vodka and orange, please.

She drank it as fast as she could, and when the drink was gone, she crunched the ice in her mouth. She pulled a wooden bar stool towards her with her foot and sat down on it. The room was perfectly full, with a steady hum of chatter and music. The woman behind the bar had a kind face and smiled at her as she said, You on your own?

Aye, said Mary, breathing in deeply. I got stood up.

Jeez, that's terrible, said the woman. Sure, just let me know what you need.

I'll have another. Please.

The woman placed her drink down in front of her on a fresh coaster and took the ten-pound note Mary had left on the counter. It occurred to her that the woman thought she was stood up by a date. She exhaled a long, low sigh. She thought of Sid. Sid who had helped her so much in understanding how to deal with Sean's addiction. Sid who had eternal empathy, who said addiction was an illness. She found it hard to excuse her brother of his illness tonight. The selfishness of him. And now she would spend the night worried sick about him until he contacted her. Maybe she should call to his house and get the wait over with? She didn't want to leave here yet. Maybe she could call Sid. Would he want to come and meet her for a drink? Was he alone? Were his bow legs crossing one another on a dance floor somewhere? She hoped he had boyfriends in his life. Someone to hold. Someone to hold him.

She felt a stab of guilt at the thought of her lack of correspondence with him. Her promises of visits blown away in the evening breeze. She had been putting off telling him her news. She didn't want to see his face when she told him she had left Bedwood two weeks ago. She had tried, of course. She tried to ignore that the other workers grumbled about her behind her back. She knew they had teased Sid and it was her turn now. She remembered the quiet deference he had commanded amongst the team. Of how he batted away the discontentment with gentle humour. She tried to train up the new guy, Alan. She thought he would be the perfect distraction from Sid. Maybe they could be friends, and she could teach him with patience and passion, as Sid had taught her. But she found that she couldn't talk like Sid.

Two months on the job and you still haven't learnt how to trim a hedge, Alan, what will we do with you!

It was meant to sound light-hearted and admonishing in a gentle way, but it came out cruel. He responded with nervous laughter and an expression of raw sadness that made her want to headbutt the shovel. It just wasn't the same. She remembered Alan finding her in the drying room at the end of that day, looking with longing at the place where Sid used to hang his coat.

Mary, are you okay? Alan had asked.

No, she wanted to say. I have a hole in my heart.

Now she worked on her own. McKee said he would put

her where she was needed and she had to be prepared to travel. And she said sure, she had her car and that was fine.

Another one?

The bar woman was pointing at her empty drink. Had she drunk all of it already? She nodded.

The volume in the room had crept up; there was a man in the corner with an electro-acoustic guitar, singing 'Dirty Old Town'. Her daddy loved 'Dirty Old Town'. It was a plodding and drink-sodden song, like him. Her eyes smarted at the first thought of him. She blinked back tears, deflecting her thoughts to TJ. She thought of what she would tell TJ tomorrow about Sean not showing up. He would be furious, of course, and smug in his suspicions of his uncle's uselessness being affirmed. He had no time for Sean any more. He got angry at her for sticking up for him. She let him rage. He didn't have a brother or sister.

She put the new drink straight to her mouth.

She'd never told TJ what his grandfather was like when she and Sean were kids. About what he did to Sean. Sean's face flashed before her eyes, ashen and dead-eyed, staring over the top of his father's coffin. She hated her father for crushing his son and then leaving him behind. Leaving her to keep him upright. She hated him for being a slave to alcohol. For allowing it to smother him, to clog him up against any sort of clarity of feeling. He allowed the memories of their mother to blur and fade, when he could have polished them and refined them and given them life. Why didn't he help them to know her? She looked down at her hands clutching her empty glass. People strained their voices to speak over the singer and suddenly it felt oppressively loud. Is this what he left them for? This feeling of being loose and unravelled? Was it worth it? Her phone pinged and she pulled it out to look. A text from Sean.

Shit Mary I totally forgot. So sorry I'll make it up to you.

Sure he will. There was a missed call from TJ. Here she was in the pub, and her son was at home wondering where she was. She should leave. She nodded at the bar lady as she stepped off the stool, and when she had both feet on the ground her body felt unfamiliar, like her legs weren't answering to her any more. She had to focus really hard on walking, balancing herself on the wall of the corridor that led her to the exit.

It was dark now, and the stars hung low in the sky above Benedicts Hotel opposite. She hailed a taxi and felt the driver's eyes on her in the rear-view mirror. She crouched as low as she could, so her face would be obscured by the passenger seat headrest. The buildings coming towards her out the window were making her dizzy, so she stared at the ripped leather of the seat in front all the way home. When the car came to a halt outside the house, she handed over ten pounds and said nothing, afraid of how her words would form and sound. She did her best to exit the car slowly and with grace. She looked at the time – 11.30 p.m. He might still be up. He shouldn't be, but he might.

The light was still on in the front room. It took her three attempts to open the front door. When she did open it, she tripped on the step and stumbled into the hall, just managing to catch herself before falling. She stood for a second holding on to the bannister of the stairs, steadying herself and blinking rapidly to try and erase the blurry film that she was seeing everything through.

Ma!

Her son was staring at her. His face had an expression of incredulity, like he was seeing something for the very first time.

Ma, are you okay?

She raised her eyebrows and held on to her handbag very tightly. She nodded, solemnly. The flower pattern on the wallpaper behind him was making her feel sick.

Have you been drinking?

There was a shuffling behind TJ, and his friend Timmy's face popped out the door, freckled and spotted and wide-eyed with curiosity. He had a slice of pizza in his hand, half-eaten, and his mouth bulged with the last bite.

Mary swallowed.

I'm off to bed. Enjoy your night.

Nodding in the vague direction of the boys, she slowly pulled herself upstairs. She stopped halfway up to unzip her boots, which were getting in the way of her ascent. She glanced down with one boot off, and saw TJ watching her with a curious look on his face. Timmy was beside him, still chewing, and giggling now. Little snorts of laughter at her. He elbowed TJ, looking for him to follow, and TJ smiled then, and shook his head. He turned to look at Timmy.

She's pissed!

Mary had her boot in her hand. It was black leather, with a small weighted heel. She threw it. Over her shoulder, straight at the boys. It landed on the wall by TJ's waist and bounced down on to the carpet. They stood in stunned silence; Timmy's eyes glinted with laughter, but her son looked pale with shock.

She turned back around and crawled up the last of the stairs on her hands and knees.

The sky was clear of clouds, and the midday sun flooded the park. Mary was dragging a strimmer out of a lean-to tucked in the corner behind the cafe. She was wearing shorts, which she hated. Her legs looked tiny and childlike in her clumpy work boots. Her face had been scrunched into a frown all morning. As she went to close the doors behind her, she paused in front of a blanket of clematis covering the green corrugated iron wall. She leaned into the delicate pink flowers and breathed in through her nose deeply. Did she get a hint of apple blossom? She sniffed again. It was hard to tell a second time. She looked down at the stem of the plant and held it in her fingers; it was dried a light white brown and looked to her to be completely dead. She followed its course with her gaze; it had climbed up and over the doors of the lean-to, given rough guidance with a few rusty nails. Some of it had run down the other side of the door, but a few adventurous stems veered north and wrapped themselves around the knobbly branch of a crab apple tree hanging over the lean-to. Sid's voice flashed up in her head.

Never presume a plant to be dead until you look inside it.

After strimming, she would get out the step ladder and set the plant back on its course.

She was over in the north of the city. The park was made up of four playing fields, an outdoor gym, a cafe and a playground, and she was doing her utmost to stay away from the relentless cacophony of shouting parents, screeching children and barking dogs. It was all so different after Bedwood. Different without the layer of death under the topsoil. Without the crowds of stones, looking on you from every angle. She'd thought she would enjoy the freedom of moving from park to park, but there was so much *life* crammed into them. So much noisiness and mess. She spent as long picking up rubbish and chasing people to pick up their dogs' poos as she did trying to tend to the beds. It was no peace, perfect peace.

She didn't mind the loudness of the strimmer, though; it blocked everything else out, like the police helicopters did when she was a girl. She had saved this job for today, knowing that the park would be busy and that people usually tended to steer clear of the roar of the motor. She walked over to the main path and reached up to her mess of hair, pulled her protective mask down from the top of her head and then pulled the trigger, side-stepping along the path. She must speak to McKee, she thought. Tell him to take her off the rota for Saturdays. After a while, lost in the roar of the motor, she looked at her watch. It was nearly lunchtime. There was nowhere for gardeners to stop and eat there, so she would sit in her car with the radio on until it was time to go back to work.

She finished along the side of the path and stopped to look back and check her line. She saw a woman with two children approaching from the direction of the cafe. She recognised the way the woman held her head. The way it bobbed from side to side on her neck as she walked. She was holding hands with a young girl of about eight years old. The girl was skipping merrily beside her, trying to keep up with her pace. On the other side there was a boy, maybe of eleven or twelve dressed in Gaelic football attire. He was saying something to the woman and she was laughing loudly and unselfconsciously, swinging the girl's hand in hers. Mary had heard this laugh on a loop in her head enough times to recognise it immediately. It was a repetitive honk that fell into breathless, raspy convulsions, and it immediately made her feel floppy with joy.

Louise.

Louise.

Mary's mouth moved into a smile under her mask. She stared at them as they walked towards her. Louise was still remarkably tall and slender, but had grown into herself more – she seemed to fit her body. There were layers and attempts at volume in her white-blonde hair. She wore navy cropped jeans with neat white trainers and a sleeveless white blouse. They were close enough then for Mary to make out the faint tinge of blusher on her cheekbones. The boy turned towards Mary and Louise followed his gaze. Mary's stomach lurched as she remembered herself then, the dirty goggled mess of her face, and she immediately began to walk away, over the grass on to the adjoining field.

Fuck, she whispered under her mask. She walked for twenty steps before realising that she had left the strimmer by the path.

Fuck, she said again as she turned around. They had stopped by the strimmer. The children were looking down at it, but Louise was staring at Mary. She called her.

Mary?

And Mary turned and ran. She ran all the way across the football pitch to the far side of park. And when she turned around again, she saw them leaving through the main gate, and she cried into the Perspex screen of her mask all the way back to the cafe.

CHAPTER 34

TJ, PRESENT

It is 9.30 p.m. and TJ is standing outside Buss Buildings. He can feel the burnt chips from earlier in his stomach and he is worried he might be sick soon as his queasiness has strengthened into a rolling nausea. He thinks of Aiden, when he had food poisoning a few weeks ago. It's rough seas down there, he'd said, pointing to his belly, his face the colour of milk.

He is comforted to have something useful to do, and equal parts terrified and assuaged by the woman's description of the roll-out for the morning. Active search parties and police at the house. He has a small lump of hash in his pocket, wrapped in tinfoil, that he intends to throw in a wheelie bin when no one is looking.

The taxi left him off at the back of the flats of Buss Buildings and he can see some large bins, lined up like animals waiting to be fed, across the ground floor of the red brick. The block is about three storeys high and is the last section in a caterpillar of council blocks, all adjoining. There are three floors of balconies looking out over the road. They are filled with satellite dishes, old plastic toys, laundry hanging on makeshift washing lines. His eyes are drawn to one balcony, right in the middle of the block. The small space between the railing and the roof is packed with pink, white and red blossom in pots and hanging baskets, cascading down over each other and the red brick all around them. It is a festival of flowers, totally obscuring any view into the balcony itself and, TJ assumes, any view out of it. He has a feeling this is Sid's place.

He takes a deep breath and walks across the road, past a drab off-licence and a newsagent, and past the wheelie bins. He lifts the lid of the one most secluded from the road and throws in his tinfoil in a nonchalant move. A dog barks loudly and startles him, and he takes a big breath and whispers to himself 'Number eighty, number eighty' as he walks around to the front, scouring the front doors for the flat numbers. There it is. A brown battered door at ground level. He walks up to it and rings on the buzzer. He can smell a faint odour of weed in the air and looks behind him into the small flower bed to see several butts of joints trampled into the soil. The flowers out here aren't as cared for as those out the back. The door opens.

Well, hello!

A small, stooped man is looking up at him. He has messy white hair, a big nose and a missing front tooth. He looks like a wizard, TJ thinks. He is wearing a waistcoat, buttoned up over a white shirt.

Hi, I'm TJ.

Sid looks at him with an instant fondness, as if he is very familiar with him. TJ is thinking that maybe he recognises Sid, too. I must have met him, he thinks. At Bedwood. Sid beckons TJ in and closes the door. TJ notices his polished brown shoes, and a flash of green from his socks underneath as he slowly pulls himself up the stairs. There is a daintiness to his steps. The frailty of the old man takes him by surprise. I could knock him out. Steal his money. Run away. Something holds him back from asking Sid if he needs help. He is talking to him now.

These stairs are a pain in the arse. I'm too proud to get a stairlift. Did you take the bus?

I took a taxi.

TJ looks around him as they walk from the small reception area up to the first floor. The walls are dark green, and the paintings are gilt and gold-framed, pictures of plump oval faces and draped cloth, of pictures of faded flowers and rolling hills. The carpet is thick and beige brown.

I should take my trainers off.

Sid carries on.

Tea? he asks, as TJ bends over to untie his laces.

Honestly, I'm fine, thanks.

He thinks of the time ticking. Of how long it would take Sid to make a cup of tea. He follows Sid's finger, which is pointing into a room on the right-hand side. It is small and cosy, rich red sofas and armchairs on a faded red carpet with an ornate pattern on it. The wallpaper is covered in thick vine leaves, with bunches of purple grapes popping up sporadically over the television and sideboard. There is a dresser just inside the door on the right that is filled with books of all shapes and sizes. On top of the dresser is a black framed photo of Sid in a pair of dark green overalls, standing beside TJ's mother. They are at Bedwood. They are both smiling at the camera, but very much still in the process of doing their jobs. Sid is leaning on a shovel and Mary is holding on to the handles of a wheelbarrow. Her body is facing away from the camera, but she has turned her head back as if someone has shouted at her to look. She looks so happy, TJ thinks. Her cheeks are shining pink. Her smile is natural, easy. He smiles looking at it and feels his eyes smart with tears.

He hears Sid walking into the room and turns around to the window and the back of the bloom-filled balcony that he had been admiring from below. From this side, it is the plastic brown pots that are most visible. There are small glimpses of the buildings and small patches of light from the streetlights, but the room is lit mainly by a corner lamp, above a red velvet armchair. It feels like a hiding place in here.

I love the flowers.

Ah, thank you, Sid says, lowering himself into the red armchair with the help of a wooden walking stick.

I like to think it brightens up some people's day. Have a seat, TJ.

He makes a wide sweeping gesture towards the sofa.

Shame you don't get to see the flowers in here.

TJ walks over to the sofa and sits down, surprised by its squishiness. He sinks right down into it. He reaches for a cushion to prop up his back as Sid is talking.

Yes, such a sacrifice! I don't see the reciprocation yet, TJ. There were about five young men smoking cannabis outside my door last night. They didn't knock on the door to offer me any at all. I had to make do with sticking my head out the window and breathing wafts of the bloody smoke that was drifting up. I have lost all my dignity.

Sid tut-tuts to himself and settles back into the chair. TJ smiles and thinks of the small tinfoil package he just disposed of.

Any news?

Sid's left eyebrow is curled up like a small furry creature on his face. His eyes are fixed on TJ.

No, TJ says, looking into the swirls on the carpet by his feet. Nothing.

Sid is still staring at him intensely.

How was she?

I'm sorry? TJ says, looking up at him.

How was your mother? The last time you saw her?

We had an argument. She made me dinner and left it for me and went to bed early. I went to sleep, and this morning she wasn't there.

Do you mind me asking what the argument was about?

271

I got in late. I stayed in bed late. She wants me to get a proper job. I'm working in a pub, trying to save up so I can leave home.

Does she know you want to leave home?

I told her during the argument. Well I didn't *tell* her, I just . . . floated the idea.

Is there a reason that you didn't tell her?

TJ sighs a big, deep sigh that lingers in the air between them. The sound of passing traffic is a low rumble. A woman shouts at her child to slow down outside the window.

I think she is sad. And I didn't want to make her sadder.

Mm, I was worried when she left Bedwood. It didn't really make sense to me, said Sid.

TJ stared at him, and after a brief pause said, Well, I think she's sad because Sean died.

Sean died? Her brother Sean?

Yes, about six months ago.

How?

Overdose.

Sid's eyes roll and he lets out a sigh, as if the news was expected: disappointing, but expected.

TJ's gaze drops down to the carpet again.

They were picked up on a cold, bright Sunday morning by a whispery man who explained all the rules. The journey felt interminably long; the hearse crawling along the slow lane as cars whizzed by, faces within them peering intently at the hearse. He wanted to punch them. He made a mental note to never stare at a hearse again. When they got there, there weren't enough people to carry the coffin, so they had to wait for it to be wheeled into the service room of the crematorium ahead of them. TJ and his mother stood side by side in silence while he searched for things to say to her, but no words felt appropriate.

The room smelt of damp that had dried out. TJ followed his mother to the front row of chairs and sat down obediently beside her. He wore a pair of black suit trousers and a grey shirt, and black shiny shoes that she had bought him especially for the day. She said he could always use them for job interviews too. He tried to wiggle his toes in his shoes, but the leather was too tight. His mother sat in a cloud of sweet, musky perfume, bolt upright, eyes fixed on the empty pulpit. Her left hand was curled around her right, holding it down on to her lap.

There were ten people in the room. Two old ladies huddled close with their coats on, like garden birds on a branch in winter. Directly opposite them was Aunt Bridget, spilling off her chair. She clutched a packet of tissues with one hand, while the other held a packet of sweets. TJ hadn't seen her in years, and he was shocked at how grey she had become, the walking stick by her feet. A younger woman, with dyed hair and big earrings, sat behind her. On the back row, there were four men; one of them was balding, and seemed to be staring at TJ, but looked away quickly to the front of the room when TJ turned towards them. TJ followed his gaze.

There was a long table, covered in floor-length purple

drapes, lying perpendicular to a large mustard-coloured curtain. Purple and mustard, Bedwood Crematorium's chosen colours of death. The coffin was on top. TJ wondered what expression Sean had on his face. He had always seemed to wear his facial expressions like garments. Like they were obligated to be there.

TJ.

He turns back to Sid, who is looking at him with an expression of concern.

How did Mary, your mother, take the death?

She was the one who found him.

Jesus Christ.

Sid's brows stick out over his eyes, leaving them in complete shadow. He picks at the material of the chair on the armrest and TJ can see that there is a small frayed patch down around where his hand is. He closes his eyes and tilts his face towards the light from the window.

TJ had come home for dinner around 6 p.m. on a Sunday and found his mother standing over the sink, crying, with her hands in the dish water. Like the water was painful.

Ma! What's wrong?!

He pulled her hands out of the water and they were wrinkly and glowing pink. He wrapped them up in a tea towel and pulled her to a chair by the kitchen table.

He said it again, Ma – *Jesus, Ma*.

He felt an unsettling fear. He had never seen her cry like this. Not even when Grandad had died.

He's dead, TJ. He's dead.

Who's dead?

My brother.

TJ had tried furiously to process this information.

What happened?

Sundays were his mother's days for visiting Sean. She was one of the only people with a key to his flat. Her face was right in front of TJ's, but she was far away, her eyes stretched wide open, a crazed look in them. She must have found him. She fucking found her brother dead. He held her then, close to him, comforting her as if he was the parent and she was the child. She stayed rigid in his arms. He couldn't bear to ask her what state Sean had been in, but he was curious. Did he choke on his own vomit? Was he foaming at the mouth? Knowing his ma, she would have tried to clean him up.

He remembered the visits to Sean's flat when he was a boy. Always with a car boot full of groceries and a trip to the cash machine on the way. The red sofa was covered with dark stains, and the smell of mould and smoke always surprised him with its strength when Sean would eventually open the door.

She stopped bringing TJ with her as he grew older. Or maybe she just gave up asking him to come. One of the last times he saw Sean was Christmas two years ago. Ma had spent two days cooking a feast like only Ma could. A big turkey with homemade stuffing, her homemade coleslaw, roast potatoes, cranberry sauce, gravy, her homemade soda bread. A choice of trifle or Christmas pudding for dessert. It was the year she bought TJ his first proper iPhone.

She was wearing her cardigan with the sequins on it and she was chirpy like a bird. Sean had arrived with no presents and a face the colour of cement. His teeth were yellow and crooked. He looked shrunken, like there was less of him. There wasn't much to say. Sean drank three Irish whiskeys before lunch, and by the time Ma was serving up the dessert, he was asleep, sitting upright at the kitchen table.

TJ remembers the priest at the funeral; the wire glasses wedged on to his face. He had directed his words at the empty space in between the rows of chairs at the back of the room.

Sean's loss will be felt by all his childhood friends from St John's and St Michael's School, his friends from his job at Atlantic Homecare, which he loved, and his subsequent job at Moore's Antique Deliveries. But most of all, he will be remembered by his loving family: his sister Mary, his nephew TJ and his Aunt Bridget. As we all know, Sean struggled with finding the happiness he deserved. It gives us comfort to know that he will finally be able to join his mother Mary, who he lost when he was just three years old, and his father Joseph, who he lost more recently in 2010. May he rest in utmost peace. With the forgiveness of Jesus and the guiding light of the Lord to show him the way.

People coughed and shuffled their feet.

And now for a song, chosen for Sean by his sister Mary. 'Sweet Thing' by Van Morrison.

There were three long seconds of awkward silence and then the sound of an acoustic guitar strumming, followed by the warm throbs of the double bass and then his voice. His ma knew Sean loved *Astral Weeks*, and she'd told TJ she thought this one was the most suitable. She had asked him to bring it on a USB stick. TJ's eyes smarted as he thought about his ma listening to this song on her own. It was the first time he had properly listened to it, and he had to concentrate hard on not crying because the music was pulling at his emotions in a way he had never experienced before.

The coffin started to slowly move away from them through the curtains, and TJ wondered whether there were wheels under those drapes, or was someone pulling it from the other side, like some sort of macabre theatre production? The song ended and the curtains closed and the priest stepped down on to ground level. His ma was still staring. She hadn't moved the whole time. He felt the slow movement of the congregation behind him and realised that it was over. It felt embarrassingly short.

Ma, are you okay?

She turned quickly, nearly a flinch. Glassy-eyed.

I'll be fine. Are you okay?

Yep, Ma, I'm grand.

TJ remembers her grabbing his hands in hers and shaking them about a little while still looking straight ahead. She turned her head then and looked at him intensely for a few seconds before drawing in a big breath and starting to stand.

Then Aunt Bridget moved in on them and awkwardly hugged them both with one arm as she clung on to her walking stick.

Mary, ach Mary!

Hello, Bridget.

Ach, he was too young to go, Mary, just too young.

His ma nodded. Her mouth pinched shut. She moved away from Bridget to walk out of the room. TJ followed, with Bridget close behind. They stepped out into the fresh air of a March morning.

While his mother was speaking to one of the older men, TJ took out a cigarette and ignored Bridget's disapproving expression as he sucked in the smoke. He turned towards the cemetery to exhale. He always loved Bedwood. He remembered his visits to see his ma in the school holidays, watching her on the mower, so adept at manoeuvring it, so confident in her movements. He used to get a tingling feeling when he watched her, that went up his spine and to his neck; it was always when she was doing something with her hands, deep in concentration. He was never able to articulate what the feeling was.

His mother was back beside them.

Bridget, are ye keeping well?

Ach, I can't complain, Mary. My back is playing up at night so it's hard to sleep, y'know? I'd be lucky if I'm getting five hours. And sure, even if I was in full health, I wouldn't get any peace as those kids in the flat above me are so loud, like a herd of galloping horses.

Ach, I'm sorry to hear that . . . Bridget, thanks for coming today. We'll see you soon?

Bridget looked put out. She fumbled about in her bag and walked herself towards the car park. TJ looked at his ma and smiled a small smile. She looked alarmingly pale in the light of the day. Her eyes looked haunted.

Who were those guys? he said, looking back over his shoulder briefly as the four men strolled away from the crematorium, blazers hiked up to make room for their hands in their pockets. The short one who had been staring at him stopped to light a cigarette and, as he inhaled, turned one last time to look back. They caught eyes again.

Come on, she said and took him by the arm, leading him into the gardens.

TJ smoked his cigarette and kept silent as they walked through the rows and rows of plots. He could sense that she was deep in thought and he only wanted to disturb it with something that felt worthy. So, he looked at the graves as they walked by, taking in the different shapes and sizes of them. He stopped beside an unusually small; white stone with a cross engraved on to it, and leaned down to read it.

Lloyd
Carol
Beloved daughter and sister.
1953–1956

Jesus, he said.

Yes, it's always the smaller graves that break your heart. That's one of six gravestones for children under the age of six in this place. And that's not including the garden of remembrance for the babies.

He remembered at that moment understanding that all those years at Bedwood had imprinted the epitaphs of hundreds of people on her brain. She was an encyclopaedia of dead bodies and their plots. She was still talking.

The birch trees are getting more and more popular these days. There's a whole new little forest of them over there, you see?

TJ turned to follow his mother's finger and nodded.

So much nicer, don't you think? To be put under a tree and mould in with the roots, rather than be in a wooden box under a big heavy stone.

Aye, that is nice, he said, to please her.

The leaves on the birches, they're small. It means the light is dappled when it shines through on to the ground.

Mm, he murmured.

She went quiet for a second and then said, It's strange to be back here.

He remembers being aware of how she took his arm and leaned her weight on him as they walked in silence the rest of the way, down the main path and past the lake. They took the smaller path along the back wall and walked under the ash tree to the headstone. They stood side by side in silence, looking down at it.

McConnell
In Loving Memory of
MARY
Beloved Wife and Mother
Died 11 February 1984
JOSEPH FRANCIS
Grandfather, Father and Brother
Died 3 May 2010

The words for his grandfather were newer on the old stone. Someone had scrubbed the stone until it shone and mown the grass around it. It was the only freshly manicured grave plot on the row.

Is this where you'll put him?

Mm . . . I don't think he'd want to be buried with them. I've reserved a birch tree for him here, but I'll take his ashes somewhere else. That's what people do. Sprinkle their loved one's ashes in the sea or on mountains or special places. I've been trying to think of his favourite place and I . . . I can't.

TJ falls out of his reverie with a start. Sid is still scratching at the armrest, shaking his head, deep in thought.

The ashes.

Sid looks up, mouth dangling open.

What ashes?

Sean's ashes. She wanted to take them somewhere. She told me at the funeral.

The silence is loaded while they both think. Sid speaks first.

Go. Go now. Please keep in touch.

CHAPTER 35

MARY, PRESENT

The tide is out. She is a dark shape, curled up on the shingle. The cold is in her bones now and the noise of her chattering teeth is drowned out by the breathy repetition of the waves in the distance, their suction and their release. She holds the urn tightly with both hands.

Sean never swam in the leisure centre, so she never did either. She never asked why. She sees him now. The bruised, pale face of him, frowning into itself, when she cut his hair before big school. The creases on his cheeks. The wide eyes searching for reassurance.

Was his whole life over when their mammy went? He told her that she died in the garden. Parents are there at the start of their child's life, so it's only right that the child should be there at the end of their parent's life. Was Mary there? Wobbling around in the grass somewhere by her mother's legs? Did she see her mother falter and stumble to the ground? Did Sean watch her fall and try and shake her awake? She wasn't there for her father's death. She sees his sickly face, swollen and twisted into confusion when they took him away in the ambulance. She sees the back of him walking away from her, down the steps and out of the gates, on her first day of primary school, and she feels the wet warm feeling on her legs before the puddle formed on the floor by her shoes. She sniffs the air around her, trying to remember the stale smoke smell of him now. Her breaths are short and she keeps them going like that, loud and exaggerated. She blinks into the black, trying to see the water line, but the darkness is impenetrable.

She sees Aunt Bridget again. The bulk of her standing hunched over the kitchen sink, eclipsing all sunlight coming through the window. Her feet puffing out of the edges of her slippers as she watched TV. Bridget taught her how to clean herself. How to clean the clothes she wore. She sees Bridget's face inches from hers now, her finger pointing between her eyes. Mary was never able to chop the onions. She cut her finger badly one time when she was eight. Bridget hated that.

You stupid girl.

She puts her hand up to her cheek, remembering the sting of it after Bridget slapped it. She hears the sound of Bridget's huffy exhalations, sees her chins wobble in compliance with the shaking of her head. She remembers their baptism, hers and Sean's, the whispering secrecy of it, Sean giggling as the water trickled down from his forehead under his shirt. She remembers the large, rough fingers of the priest sprinkling water over her, as if he was conducting a magic trick. The priest's murmurings and her aunt's methodical reciprocations. All of Bridget's lines of communication were steeped in the semiotics of Catholicism. She seemed incapable of affection. She couldn't kiss them but she could baptise them. Was it good or bad? As a girl, she had felt relief that she would be allowed into heaven. But she knew her mother didn't want her to go to heaven. Something serious must've happened to her, like Bridget said. When the argument started with Bridget and her father, Mary crouched up in a ball behind the armchair in the living room and listened.

I had them baptised. For their own sake!

You conspired with that prick Father Treacey? Fuck you, Bridget. Fuck you and your fucking meddling.

Her father punched the wall. Bridget slammed the door so hard when she left that Granny Olive's picture fell off the nail. They hardly saw her after that. Until the funerals.

They buried her father's ashes in her mother's grave. They opened it up, this dark, damp hole, like a dressed wound, and the sun shone into it for the first time in twenty-six years. The proximity of her mother's coffin made Mary dizzy. She was closer to her than she could ever be again. She wanted to jump down into the hole and dig with her hands, clawing out the soil until she reached her mother. To climb into the coffin and wriggle herself in between the bones. To lay her face next to the rotten skull, cheek to cheek. Her whole life, her whole loss in that godforsaken wooden box that was just out of reach. She sees the coffin now, in her head, the dull marl of the wood. The ornate ridges around the sides of the lid. She wonders if a coffin would float on the sea. If you gently pushed it into the waves, like a bottle with a message in it, how far would it go?

A glint of the moon is pouring through the clouds, creating a clean line of golden light bridging the sky and the surface of the sea. She stares at it for a long time and it brings her back to her shivering body.

She is in Louise's room now. All strewn with clothes and make-up. Spice Girls strutting on the walls. Louise's face is right up to hers, eyes wide and lips quivering, open, coming towards hers. She sees her face give way to laughter. Louise likes to practise her kissing on her. She would have stood in Louise's room forever, blank and silent as a mannequin, just in case she needed to practise some more. She was translucent, a slender child spectre. Her friend the ghost.

Mary starts to sing. Her voice is tiny in the darkness.

Jesus Christ, you're keeping the baby.

Jesus Christ, you're keeping the baby.

Jesus Christ, you're keeping the baby.

Jeez Louise. She sees Louise ninja-kick at the door of Arndale Road. She sees her talking silent words at her, gesticulating with curling slender fingers, pleading. Then she flinches suddenly, as if she has been punched. Danny is breathing into her. Pumping her up with himself. Every essence of him. His seed and the sour breath that has fermented in his lungs. She is smothered by him again and her face screws up in pain and she holds the urn tighter. He is walking away from her again, and blood is pouring out of him from his eyes and his ears and in big thick clots out of his mouth. She moans into the black and shakes her head violently.

The water is so far away from her now. She inches her bum towards the wet stones in front of her. The tide has to be turning soon and the water will come back to her. She will do it then. She looks up. It is all layers and textures of darkness. Cloud and sea and stone weighing down on each other like the layers of earth in a freshly dug grave. She wants to see what's left of him. She wants just enough light so she can see what she's doing.

CHAPTER 36

TJ, PRESENT

He is sweating through his shirt as he walks back up from the bus stop, phone clutched tightly to his ear. He is trying to be patient with the man from the police station.

I just know she's gone somewhere. Her brother died. She's gone somewhere to put his ashes and . . . something must have happened . . .

I don't *know* where . . .

He walks past a group of guys, young, sharp faces. Suffolk lads. He stops to let them go by and tucks his head into his chest, covering his mouth with his hand as he talks.

I think maybe, out of Belfast. Towards the sea, or the mountains. She said she thought people sprinkled the ashes in places like that.

No. No. I can't think of any, no.

He sighs with exasperation.

Just, I think, you should look out of Belfast too.

Okay, okay, thanks.

He keeps walking, closes his eyes and breathes deeply. He can see the roundabout ahead of him. He turns down the hill towards the entrance to the estate. He wants to break into a run, but he tells himself to keep walking. To stay calm.

Sid's worry about her leaving Bedwood and going to work alone never crossed his mind. Was that a big alarm bell in his face that he had missed? It was years now since she'd left. Maybe it was strange that she chose to be all on her own, moving from park to park, rather than managing a team at Bedwood. How many other alarm bells had he missed? He remembers when she scared him a few times with strange behaviour after Grandad died. How one Saturday, when he came home from an away match, he had found her in bed in his old blue room at 2 p.m. Not even reading. Just staring up at the ceiling, like she was in a trance. And then there was the night she got drunk and threw a shoe at him.

He rounds the corner on to Purves Road, focusing on her bedroom now. He is nearly sure that the urn wasn't on the mantelpiece earlier. He would have noticed it. Of course he would have! It freaked him out when he saw it first. His uncle, turned to powder, in a brass urn. It felt like something from beyond their time. Aiden had talked about being able to smoke people's ashes. Skin them up in a joint and smoke them into you. He was full of shite, of course. He didn't ask her about the urn after that day at the grave. There was no wake after the cremation.

I don't know any of his friends now. I wouldn't know who to invite, she had said, staring out the window of the hearse as it crawled down the slow lane of the dual carriageway.

Does he have any friends left? TJ said, not hiding the sceptical tone in his voice.

She just shook her head slowly and stared.

Ma, what will we do with all his stuff? And the house?

She let out a slow sigh and turned back around to him.

The council will take back the house. When, I don't know. There's so many forms to fill in. There's no way he had a will.

She looked so utterly broken then. He remembers wishing there was someone who he could call on who knew the right thing to say and do to make her feel better. Wishing for the appearance of a father figure, to come and be strong for her, for him. Later that evening, he, stood at the door of the living room in his black collared T-shirt and grey school trousers.

Ma, I'm off for my shift.

She was sitting cross-legged on the sofa, picking the skin around her fingernails. The TV was off and the room was silent. She raised her eyebrows.

Of course, she said, as if to herself. She turned to him with a sad smile.

Take care, darlin'.

I will, he said and walked into the hall. As he did so, he processed what he had just seen and popped his head back through the door. His mother was still staring at the wall ahead of her.

Ma? Are you going to do anything tonight? You should watch a movie . . .

I'll watch something for sure, love. Now go on you, don't worry about me.

So, he didn't. He went to work and lost himself in the conversations weaving their way around the downstairs bar of Devaney's. Happy to have something to do and some people to listen to. He surreptitiously downed the shots that Aiden left out for him behind the counter over the course of the evening, and the shift flew by in a blur of beer mats and bursts of laughter. At 1 a.m., when Tommy the bar manager was counting out the notes on the bar, he and Aiden were sitting on bar stools, feet dangling, rolling cigarettes and finishing their pints. Of course, he went out to the late bar. And of course, he doesn't remember getting home that night. He tries to remember what happened the next day. Was she there when he woke up? God, why can't he remember things any more?

Now he is striding towards his house, key in hand, and he is pushing open the door and running up the stairs. He is staring at the mantelpiece over the boarded-up fireplace. Staring at the gap where the urn used to stand. He feels a surge of adrenaline and moves around the room, pulling out drawers and searching the wardrobe he was sitting in earlier. He can't find it anywhere. She has it. She's got to have it. He sits on the side of her bed again, facing the fireplace. How did he miss this?

Fucking idiot, he says out loud to himself. He should have offered to come with her one day to sprinkle the ashes. He must have presumed she would have organised it and asked him to come. She never did. Did she want to have the time on her own? He knew her devotion to Sean was unending.

He was the closest thing to a father you ever had, she had said to him once, after a long and embittered tirade from TJ on how useless Sean was and how he took advantage of her kindness again and again.

Well Ma, it seems to me that you were the closest thing to a mother he ever had, and he should not take that for fucking granted.

She went quiet then, he remembers. When she's made to confront things, she always shrugs off the conversation at the first opportunity. That's why it is so strange for her to disappear; she isn't a person who likes the attention on her. Was she not worried about him? Something must have happened. He pictures her slim physique at the top of Black Mountain, the urn open in her hand, the ash falling out in grey clouds on to the heather below. Her walking down the track on her own and a man coming towards her. Then he pictures her car, dented and folded metal, shards of glass and the horn sounding in a long, unrelenting beep. A hand on the road, bloodied and grey. He must stop. He stands up and lets out a frustrated growl.

He can feel his body start to sag with tiredness. The realisation that he has to go to sleep dawns on him now. He has left the light off downstairs so as to hide all the signs of her. He spends hours alone in this house without her, he thinks. He needs to pull himself together. He needs to take control of this. He remembers the look of concern on the policewoman's face. Is this supposed to be something he can deal with? Technically, he's not a child now that he is eighteen. Should he have adult supervision?

He will go to his room. It's the only place that doesn't feel weird in the house. He goes to the bathroom first and cleans his teeth slowly, staring at himself in the mirror as he brushes. They have the same nose and mouth, people say. The same sloping eyebrows. He didn't get the redness in her hair. Or the green in her eyes. He takes off his trousers and falls into bed in the same T-shirt. His phone beeps as he is plugging it into the wall by his bed. It's Aiden again.

Going round Mickey's. If you're coming bring carry out.

He puts his phone down, turns over to face the window and curls up into himself, clinging on to his pillow. He thinks of his friend Timmy, moved down to Galway now, apprenticing as an electrician. He remembers the ache he used to feel growing up on the estate, watching Timmy with his brother and sisters, this unconscious closeness they had with each other. Timmy shared a bed with his brother. TJ thought about that a lot as a child. He used to talk to an imaginary big brother, in bed at night. He remembers having long conversations in the darkness with this boy, who taught him things. How to jump off the high wall on the green. How to do an over-the-head kick. How to kiss a girl. Sometimes he would wake up with his body curled up into a spooning shape, his arm slung across a pair of imaginary shoulders.

Timmy is probably out tonight, he thinks. Galway is supposed to be class. Everyone is out tonight, it's fucking Saturday night and Belfast is in full swing. What the fuck is happening to his life? Where the fuck is his mother? TJ weeps into the soft cotton of his pillowcase.

CHAPTER 37

MARY, PRESENT

The light is seeping in over the sea. She shivers all over and takes a step into the water. It takes a few seconds to leak into her work boots and through her socks and when it does, the shock of the cold takes her breath away. She has to keep moving. Her heartbeat is so loud in her head. She pushes her legs through the weight of the water until she is in up to her waist, facing away from the beach. Then she stops and tries to breathe slower.

Her hoodie is filling up with water and bulging out with air. Something brushes against her shin.

She can see the line of the horizon now and she focuses on it, because the ebb and flow of the waves keeps pushing her off balance. She gradually finds the rhythm of the waves, moving forwards and backwards with them, like the kelp slow-dancing on the sea bed below. The cold has stilled the pains in her head. She can't feel anything of herself any more.

She can hear the seagull, squawking lazily as it circles above her. She is clutching the urn with two hands under her chin, as if it is a cup and she will drink from it. She looks at the distorted reflection of herself in the polish of it, and then quickly down to the water below.

Her thoughts are moving so rapidly and she wants to feel this. She tries so hard to focus on listening, tuning her ears into the soft slap of the water on her hoodie, pulling herself back to now. Her hands shake violently as she holds the urn out from her face and starts to twist the lid open. It takes all of her strength to untwist it and when it is done, she holds the lid in place and looks around her. There are no cars on the road, no movement across the bay. She lifts the lid then and slowly tilts the ashes into the sea in front of her. They are gone in an instant, caught by the wind and dissolved into the water around her.

She stares at the water's surface, her mouth hanging open. She sees her brother's face when it softened around TJ. The way he bounced around the kitchen with him on his shoulder when he was a baby, gently patting his bum. She sees his face darkened by shadows and stubble on his thirty-fourth birthday, as she placed the cake with candles lit in front of him. It was hard for him to really smile in those years. She never saw it. Even when he cried, it was only the tears that moved – his face remained still. She sees his hunched shoulders in the doorway, one hand raised in goodbye, with a cigarette in his fingers. She sees his dead body in his bed.

Cold from the inside out. His nails and lips a purple-ish blue, like watercolours. His hands clasped over his chest, as if he was arranged by the undertaker. As if he had planned it and thought it would be funny, this imitation of the dead.

She remembers the overwhelming quiet of the house. The sink overflowing with dishes. The clothes dirty and scattered on the carpet. She found the spoon and the tinfoil, the empty baggie, all tossed on the bedside table in haste as he'd settled in for the slow slide into nothingness. She fussed around him for a while, even packed a bag of his things, as if they were off for a weekend away. In the end, she lay down beside him on the bed, and they waited for the sirens together.

Mary is crying now. Rasping big breaths of air in and out of her. She lets the urn and the lid fall out of her hands and splash into the water below. They said it was an overdose, but not an exaggerated amount. Just a large amount of what he would usually take. He would have passed out almost immediately. What was the last thing he thought of when he was holding the lighter under the spoon? When he was sucking up the brown liquid into the syringe? Was there a face in his head? Was it their mother's? No one comes back from the dead, he used to say to her. But Bridget said Jesus came back from the dead, so why not their mother? Why not?

Her favourite words at Bedwood are on a birch tree memorial. Gold plate on black stone. They say:

I am beside you.

She's never been sure who was beside who. Is it a message

from the person left behind to the soul of the dead? Or from the dead person while they were still alive, as a message to the person they were leaving? That is it. It's the person who is dead, it's them talking from the ground. I am beside you. Everywhere you go. When you drive in the car. When you shower, when you cry into your pillow at night. I am beside you.

She was supposed to come back. But maybe she was there all along. Her mother. Mary. Is he with you now, Mammy? Take care of him. All he ever wanted was you.

Mary lets her head fall back behind her shoulders. She can feel the soft blush of morning light on her cheeks. She thinks of a line in the song they played at Sean's funeral – it was a promise, to never grow so old again. Her brother grew old as a young man. He decayed; hardening at his edges and curling into himself, like autumn leaves. Now he is gone, in the water. Now he is free.

She drops her hands into the sea and swirls her fingers around as if to find some essence of him in there that she can still feel.

CHAPTER 38

TJ, PRESENT

TJ is woken by a loud knocking on the door. He sits up quickly, and shouts, *Coming!* as he pulls on his tracksuit bottoms. He thunders down the stairs two at a time and pulls open the door.

Parcel for Mary?

A man with a beard is holding a large cardboard box, about two feet tall. TJ takes it out of his hands and sees the arrows pointing to the top of the box and the Handle with Care stickers. He puts it down gently and rubs his eyes.

Sign here, please.

He looks at the man's face, but he is staring at the card, waiting for TJ's signature, and as soon as he has scribbled the letters of his name, the man mutters his thanks and strides off to a red van parked up on the kerb outside. He watches the van bump off the kerb and drive down the road out of sight. It's a clear morning, just a tiny bit colder than yesterday. He sees a spot of red in the corner of his eye as he's closing the door and hesitates to look. It is the first showing of a full bloom on the red plant in their front garden. TJ never remembers what it's called; all he knows is that it blossoms all the time and it means he is home. His ma calls the colour fire-engine red. He likes that description of it. He shuts the door.

Fuck. His stomach drops suddenly. Did she come home last night? He plonks the box on the carpet by the front door and runs upstairs to her bedroom. It is exactly as it was. There is the slight dent in the bedding where he lay yesterday morning. This is bad. He is crying again as he walks back to his bedroom and finds his phone on the floor by his bed, plugged into the wall. It's 7.15 a.m. How are deliveries happening at 7.15 a.m. on a Sunday? He hasn't received one new text or call. He calls her again and can't bear the ringing of it. He hangs up before it clicks into her voicemail.

Fuck fuck fuck, he says as he jogs back down the stairs and picks up the box, carrying it into the kitchen and putting it carefully on the table. It's got to be another plant, he thinks to himself as he opens the drawer to find some scissors. A minute later and there it is. The label says *Tree Peony. Plant in a sunny or lightly shaded position. Avoid frost.*

It looks pretty unremarkable to him, but no doubt she will find something precious about it. She likes to give plants to people. He wonders if it's someone's birthday, someone that he doesn't know about. The plant itself is about a foot and a half high, brown stem leading into a big bush of leaves. There are a couple of tight buds attached to the stalks. It looks lush and healthy to him, and he suddenly loves this plant. He is grateful for its presence in the kitchen. He imagines her here now, her carefully turning it around to inspect it. Her misting it with her spray and wiping the soil off the side of the pot. The tiniest of smiles, her face curious.

He has to do something. He has to find her. It's simple. He will find her. Today. He pulls on his trainers and puts his keys back in his pocket and walks out of the house. He will do whatever it takes. He walks out on to the street and immediately turns back into the front drive of Dolores's house. He rings the bell. He is kicking the front step with his trainer over and over again. He can hear the dogs and the long, slow shuffle up the hall carpet to the door. He speaks as the door is still opening, before she can open her mouth.

Dolores, she's still not home.

Dolores's face drops, her jowls flopping over the collar of her dressing gown.

Since yesterday?

Yes. She hasn't called. She wasn't at work. I went to the police last night. I have to call them now again, don't I?

Dolores is flustered. She is shaking her head in disbelief.

Dear Jesus, yes, darlin', ye have to call them.

I'm trying and trying to think, where would she go? I just don't know why she wouldn't tell me.

His voice breaks, his eyes scrunch shut in pain and his

palm hovers over them, trembling, blocking the tears from Dolores.

Get in here, she says and he lets her pull him by his hand into the kitchen and lower him on to a chair while his shoulders bounce up and down in sobs, and he can feel her hand rubbing up and down his back.

CHAPTER 39

MARY, PRESENT

The noise of the siren bends high and low and she follows it in her head, the swooping and soaring of it, as the voices above her speak soft instructions. When the siren stops quite suddenly with a staccato finale, followed straight after by the ambulance, the doors are flung open and she grimaces under her mask. One of the ambulance men jumps out and grips hold of the stretcher.

Got her?

Yep, says another male voice from behind her head. She is moving smoothly again and she sees the large red letters above the door move past her. EMERGENCY DEPARTMENT.

Take her into cubicle two, says a man's voice.

More hands — faces over hers and voices together in chorus.

One, two, three, and her body is lifted, and she is on another bed in a white room. All she can hear is a dull, incessant beep, and it is burrowing into her, focusing the pain in her head into a sharp point.

Monitor her breathing,

How long was she there for? Another voice, loud and brash.

We don't know exactly, but long enough. She drove there by car, the police are searching the reg now.

Hands fiddling with the mask on her face. The pain is stabbing her skull, over and over again, and she closes her eyes and falls into black.

She's gonna pass out, get her legs lifted, get a cannula in and get her some warm fluids.

A man's face is right over hers.

Hello. My name is Rob Johnson. I'm one of the doctors here. You are suffering from hypothermia and we are going to get you warmed up and breathing regularly. While we're doing that, I need you to help me. If you can hear me and I'm making sense, I want you to squeeze my fingers.

His words are so loud they hurt. She tries to lift her hands to push him away. She tries to speak, but the words slide around her mask in a slur. She can feel her face rolling from side to side on the pillow.

Look at me, look into my eyes.

She wants him to stop talking. His eyes are the colour of the water. She tries to move her fingers.

Good, okay, now are you in pain? If you are, can you nod?

She moves her head again.

Okay, that's great. Well done for letting me know. Where is the pain?

She stares at him, unmoving.

Is it your head?

She nods. She sees him look over at someone out of her eyeline.

Alongside the fluids, let's give her paracetamol IV – and I will write up morphine, in case she's still in pain after that.

Gotcha, whispers a soft voice.

His face is gone now, and she lets her head fall on its side. Her breathing is loud, amplified in her mask, and she is panicking because it is all too slow and the stabbing in her head is relentless, and every bone in her face is throbbing and pulsating with pain. Every beep from the machine behind her is a thrust of a sharp blade slicing her raw. She sees the nurse taking packets of fluid out of a cupboard. She is petite and scurries around the room with a hurry on her, thin-lipped and brown-eyed, like a wren.

The woman walks over to the bed.

This might sting a little, she says as she ties some rubber around Mary's arm, then lifts a cannula and, in one fluid movement, pierces her forearm with the needle point and fills tiny bottles with the blood that emerges. She gently tapes the cannula in place. Mary sees what must be her own fist, clenched tightly, and tries to release her fingers. They are swollen and doughy looking. She can't feel them: maybe they aren't her fingers. She turns her head towards the ceiling and stares into the harsh strip light above her, focusing on the rhythm of her breaths in her mask.

A dark shadow appears in the corner of her vision.

Hello, the receptionist sent me in. I think I may have an identity for her, she's been reported missing. Everything matches, but I just need a confirmation. Can I try?

Silence but for the beeps. The nurse is standing over her and reaching behind the bed, pressing some buttons. Mary feels the bed rising slowly, and a woman is in her eyeline now, clad in police uniform and standing back by the green curtain. The woman is staring at her.

Mary averts her eyes to the ceiling, trying to move her fingers, trying to feel them against her leg. She hears the policewoman clear her throat and then the nurse says, She's very delicate, so no words from her, just nodding and shaking of head.

Hello! I am Officer Wright from the PSNI and I wanted to ask you a few very quick questions, if that's okay?

The policewoman's voice hurts her head. Like the doctor's. Every word is piercing.

I have reason to believe that you are Mary McConnell. If that is your name, please can you just nod to confirm it for me?

Her eyes fall closed for a second, and when she opens them again, she sees the policewoman has turned to the nurse for help. Her face is wet with tears and she feels heavy, so heavy. She is crying hysterically now, spluttering into her mask, and the nurse is stroking her arm and whispering,

There now, don't worry now, it's going to be okay, just breathe.

CHAPTER 40

TJ, PRESENT

He is walking out of the estate – up the road to the round-about. He will hail a taxi. He is going to her now, wherever she is. He left without a coat but he is glad of the cold; it is propping him up, propelling him on. He swallows down big hauls of air as he remembers what Lydia from Northern Ireland Police had to say on the phone.

So, TJ, we have pieced it all together. Your mother's car was seen at Bedwood Cemetery on Friday night. Yesterday evening she drove to Donaghadee Beach and parked there for another night. She was found at six-thirty this morning, in the water, stood up to her waist. She was there for quite a while.

She had a smugness to her tone that made TJ want to reach his hand down the phone and flick her in the forehead like he used to do to Timmy in school.

What was she doing? he had asked.

We don't know that yet, TJ.

Who found her?

He needed to know.

It was a local man walking his dog. He stayed with her until the ambulance came. She's at the Ulster Hospital now. She identified herself, so they'll have her name there when you ask at reception. Okay?

A sing-song finale, as if she was teaching the fucking ABC.

And now he is bending over by the main road because he is about to be sick, and yes, he is vomiting on to the footpath, but there's nothing in his stomach, so it's just retching, and he keeps walking and retching and walking and retching, and he hails a black taxi and sits in the back trying not to retch. He sees the driver weighing up whether he should ask what's happening. He wills him not to speak and stares out the window. He has been down this road a million times, but when he squints his eyes now, there is an iridescent edge to all the shapes he sees, as if he is winding down from a night on pills. As if everything has been different all along, and only now can he see it.

She was in the water. Stood in the fucking sea up to her waist. He feels a rush of emotion, as they drive from the Andersonstown Road on to Glen Road, and focuses on the buildings falling away outside, concentrating hard on stopping the tears gathering in the back of his eyes. He can't stop seeing the shape of her at the chopping board. The slope of her shoulders. And he sees them in the water now, and imagines her crying into the sea and how alone she must've felt and how out of her mind she must have been to *do* something like that. He wonders will anything be the same again now. Will she know him?

They drive under the bypass, past the stone arched entrance of Milltown Cemetery, past the Falls Road Library and the Royal Victoria Hospital. Where he was born. She said she did it on her own, it was just her and him. No father, no support. She never expressed any desire to have it any other way. She was eighteen years old. The same age as he is right now. He tries to imagine how it would feel to be a parent now. The absolute implausibility of it. They move down the Grosvenor Road into Belfast city centre, past the police station, wrapped in wire and brick.

He imagines the reunion in his head, her taking him in her arms, telling him it's going to be okay, telling him how sorry she is. Him forgiving her. He looks at his phone and finds the number for Sid and texts him.

They found her. Going to see her now. xxx

CHAPTER 41

MARY, PRESENT

Mary is waking up and her vision is adjusting to the light burning on the right side of her face from the two walls of wide windows in the room. She hears some shuffling and sees a woman stand up and draw a curtain across the front of her bed berth so that her face is shaded. The woman is staring at her, squinting even, as if Mary is blurred in her vision, too, or as if she knows her from somewhere and is trying to figure out where.

Mary sees the woman sit back down and shuffle herself to a comfortable position in her chair. A nurse walks past the end of the bed and starts talking softly to the patient in the next bed. They are behind a curtain. Everything is bright and gleaming and painfully white. There is a feeling of nausea creeping up her body. It is in her head now and she can hear the dull throb of her heart beating loudly in her ears. She swallows and feels her bottom lip begin to tremble.

Mary, breathe with me.

The woman's eyes are still on Mary; they are pulled wide, eyebrows raised in suggestion.

Copy me: through the nose and out of the mouth, like this.

The woman sticks her chest out, arches her back a little and inhales, inclining her chin upwards as if the air is elevating her, and then slowly blows out her breath through her lips, shaped in a circle and now, widening into a smile.

And again?

Mary is not trying to join in, but her eyes are fixed on the woman's face. They move down to her chest, and watch it swell and cave in rhythmically. She has a burst of noise in her head, the sound of the waves and the feeling of the water pulling and pushing her legs under the surface. She feels a surge of nausea then, and the woman can see it, because she quickly reaches for a silver tin bowl by the bed. Mary vomits into it. She is able to prop herself up on her elbow to do it, and when she is finished, she realises that the woman has been holding her hair and is now gently laying her ponytail on the pillow and taking the weight of her shoulders as they fall back down on the sheet.

She knows the woman is still watching her. She can hear the sound of breaths, loud and gasping, and it dawns on her that the sound is coming from her own mouth. She focuses on slowing her inhalations down, and stares up at the chrome circles patterned across the ceiling and the faint light they give out. The woman is talking to her.

Hello there, my name is Sarah Taylor. I am the consultant who will be looking after you on this ward.

Mary is counting the lights, trying to see if there is an even number. There needs to be an even number. She can't see over the curtain to see the other side of the ceiling.

Mary.

She turns her head to Sarah Taylor, who is smiling gently at her.

Do you feel okay? Can I get you anything?

Mary stares.

Why am I here?

Hearing the sound of her own voice, timid and cracked, startles her. She looks down at her hands. They are grotesque. Swollen, white and puffed, covered in wrinkles. She moves her fingers slowly to make sure they are hers.

When you arrived you had hypothermia. We managed to warm you back up and stabilise things. You were quite confused when you got here and I just want to check how you are doing now.

Mary is staring at the small mountain made out of bed sheet, held up by her toes.

My job is to try and help you with what's in your head, Sarah Taylor says. I am sorry if some of these questions seem silly. Can you tell me your full name?

Mary feels the tears come in a slow, steady, wet stream on her cheeks. She says nothing. She turns her head back to the spotlights.

How about I tell you what I think it is and you can just nod? I think it is . . . Mary McConnell. Is that correct?

She closes her eyes and winces, then gives a small nod.

Great! You are thirty-seven years old?

Mary's stomach rumbles loudly. She remembers her birthday four months earlier. Coming home from work and closing the curtains of her bedroom to the world. Lying on her bed in her overalls until the gold clock softly chimed for midnight.

She nods.

And am I right in saying you have a son?

Mary freezes. His face is huge in her head. She can smell him suddenly. Her eyes dart around the room. Where is her son?

Anthony is his name? Or TJ to those who know him?

The lady is delicate when she utters the letters. Like she could drop them and smash them. She watches Mary's face intently.

Mary pulls herself up to a sitting position, tugging at her hospital gown and looking around the bed for her clothes.

Heeeey, Mary! Just slow down a little.

Mary looks down at the cannula mark in her arm and rubs it with her hand, as if trying to rub it away. She lowers her feet on to the ground. As soon as her soles are flat on the floor, her legs buckle underneath her. The doctor holds her in a hugging position and shouts.

Nurse!

Mary is fighting her, pushing her with what little strength she has. The doctor has her arms locked to her body, so she pushes the weight of her head into the doctor's chest and tries to use her legs to bolster her.

She collapses in the firm grip of the nurse and allows herself to be lifted back on to the bed. Dr Taylor is talking to her.

Mary, TJ is safe. He is well. He is coming to see you very soon. You do not have to go to him now. He is coming to you.

Dr Taylor nods at the nurse to dismiss her.

Mary can still see him in her head. His big frame bumbling around the kitchen. His hand with the scar on his thumb.

She is being watched again. She is back lying down, out of breath, one hand holding the other and rubbing her finger. She turns her head towards the woman and this time, takes her in. The woman senses that she has Mary's full attention.

Mary, why did you go to the sea this morning?

I wanted to empty my brother's ashes.

Okay. When did your brother pass away?

Mary pulls her lips together and swallows.

About six months ago. He was a drug addict.

I'm so sorry, Mary. Was he your only sibling?

She nods.

And do you have any parents?

They are both dead.

When did they pass, if you don't mind me asking?

My mother when I was almost two. My father about eight years ago.

Do you have any other family? Or support?

I manage. I have always managed.

I'm sure you have. Tell me, Mary, have you ever been to therapy before or had professional help?

No.

Dr Taylor looks at Mary for a long time and then down at her notes.

It's just that I have here that you were admitted to hospital for symptoms of post-partum psychosis after your son was born.

Mary starts now. She feels uneasy and speaks hesitantly.

Yes. The health visitor made me go.

She was worried for you?

I wasn't myself. It was the sleep deprivation.

Lack of sleep is the most dangerous thing for any human being, especially after they have just had a baby and are incredibly vulnerable emotionally. It was the right thing to do.

They let me bring him with me to the hospital. They put me on pills.

And after this time in the hospital, you weren't referred to a therapist?

I was. I – I didn't go. I didn't want to leave TJ.

Okay. And Mary, can you remember how you felt when you were on the beach last night?

I . . . I just felt. Black. And like I wasn't really there. Like I was in my dreams.

She is crying again now. She feels melted. She is a thin gruel puddle of tears and bone on the floor. She lifts her fingers up to feel her face and wipes the tears away with her palms. The skin of her fingers repulses her.

How long was I there for?

On the beach, all night. In the sea, we don't know that for sure, but it really doesn't take long to deteriorate in cold water.

I don't know what happened. Where I went. TJ! He must be worried sick.

He'll be here soon. He'll be so happy that you are here, and you are safe and well.

How am I well, when I could do something like that?

She stares imploringly at the doctor.

Tell me, were you close to your brother?

Mary looks back down to her hands.

Not so much recently, but yes. All my life.

And did you ever get any help after he died?

I was going to ask TJ to go over to the house and help me, but I just couldn't face it.

No, I mean for you. For your grief.

Mary is still. The light from the window is glaring into her eyes. She frowns.

No. I haven't.

She looks back at Dr Taylor to see her writing notes on her clipboard.

Okay, Mary.

She looks up from her notes.

I want to keep you in for a few days, just to monitor you and get you better.

Mary slumps back on to the bed.

Will this happen to me again?

That's what I'm here for. To try and make sure it doesn't.

Mary sighs and closes her eyes, and sees her son. The worried look his face can catch when he doesn't know anyone is watching him. The slight inward turn of his right foot when he walks. She sees him walking, searching wards and rooms, looking utterly lost.

When she opens her eyes again, the doctor is gone.

CHAPTER 42

TJ, PRESENT

The curtains are pulled around both sides of her bed. He swallows and breathes out as he pulls the curtain aside. As soon as he lays eyes on her, he breaks down into sobs and quickly tries to cover his mouth with his hands. She is tiny in the bed. Her face is collapsed into sleep and is turned sideways on the pillow, towards him. Her mouth hangs open and her breathing is loud and laboured. He stands, still holding the curtain, and stares. She looks so fragile and utterly breakable.

He has an overwhelming urge to close her mouth for her. Can I touch her? he thinks. He sticks his head out of the curtains and scans the room for staff, but the ward is silent. He closes the curtains again, sits down on the plastic chair by the bed and leans forward to study his mother. Her hands are flat on the bed by her side, and from the fingers to the forearms, the skin is white and wrinkled and swollen-looking. Her hair looks very dirty and matted. He can smell

317

the faint mildew smell of the sea on her. Have they not washed her? he thinks. There are a few millimetres visible of the whites of her eyes where her lids havn't closed all the way. He didn't know her eyes did that when she slept. He looks around the bed to see if there are any clues as to what medication she's on. There's nothing. He should have got flowers. A card? Something.

His stomach groans loudly. He clutches it, as if remembering it's there. He forgot to eat, of course. He will go to the hospital canteen after this. Maybe he could get some flowers from outside then, too. He has to be there for her when she wakes up. There is a slight rustle from the bed and he turns back. Her eyes are half open now, staring to the side, and he squeezes the side of his chair with his hands and opens his mouth to speak.

He waits for her, watching her close her eyes and open them again and stare at the curtain some more, and he lets out a tiny cough, just the slightest clearing of his throat, and he's sure he sees something happen in her eyes. He knows she's heard him. He tries again.

Ma.

He is surprised by the fear in his voice. By the weakness of it. She moves her eyes to him now and they immediately fill with tears. She doesn't move to wipe them away. He is waiting for her to start explaining herself. He is starting to feel frustrated. Why is she just lying there and leaking like this, like an inanimate object?

Ma, are you okay?

She is licking her lips now, trying to make them move. Her fingers have started to tremble and she lifts her hands to him. He moves to her and takes her hands in his. They feel waxy and cold. He wants to pull away but he doesn't. He moves his face into the crook of her neck and he feels her hands on his back pulling him closer. He starts to sob again, his shoulders bouncing up and down. He kisses her cheek and pulls away to look at her.

Ma.

This time it's desperate.

Ma, talk to me.

She coughs – and slowly shakes her head.

Son. Are you okay?

She is holding his face now in her swollen hands, and his tears fall on to her face, joining in with hers.

He snorts and nods, pulls back and wipes his nose with his hand.

Yeah. I was so worried.

She doesn't answer.

I thought . . . I thought something had happened to you.

He is crying again now, his mouth pulled wide into a grimace. She reaches for his hand and squeezes it. There is hair across her face and she doesn't seem to notice. He exhales a long, wavering sigh, looks down at her and moves the strand of hair from her cheek.

Did you – was it the ashes? Did you go to spread Sean's ashes?

She squints her eyes at him, pulls her lips closed and swallows.

Yes. But I – I lost myself.

He sees her eyes flicker and lose focus. She is somewhere else again.

I looked everywhere. I even went to Sid's flat last night.

She looks at him now, her eyebrows raised, her face softening with the mention of Sid's name.

Ach. Sid. I've worried everyone.

Well.

Silence.

You're all right now, Ma.

He looks down at her wrinkled hands.

Are you sore?

I just feel . . . just . . . wiped out.

Her eyes are heavy, like it is an effort to keep them open. She lets go of his hand and her eyes close again almost immediately.

He stands over her. Is she on shitloads of drugs? Like, sedatives? He doesn't want the conversation to end. Of course, she's going to be exhausted, he tells himself. But every part of him wants to shake her awake. He flops back down on to the chair and slowly shakes his head, eyes fixed on her. After a few minutes, as her breathing becomes slow and heavy again, he takes out his phone and takes a photo of her in the bed. Her head is tiny in the frame. He holds the phone between his legs, and stares at the photo.

Half an hour later, there is a tap on TJ's shoulder that makes him jump.

Sorry!

It's a smiling older lady, in normal clothes.

Hello, you must be TJ!

He lowers the volume of his voice to match hers.

Yes, hello.

I'm Dr Taylor. Can I borrow you for a few minutes, please?

TJ looks back at his mum. I don't want to leave her. She might wake up again.

In which case, do you mind if I join you here?

I guess.

She draws the curtain back and pulls a chair over beside him. He watches as she pulls a pen and notepad out of her pocket and sits down, carefully crossing her legs.

TJ, am I right in saying that you are Mary's next of kin?

He looks blankly at her.

You are her closest relative?

Aye.

What is your date of birth?

20 February 2000.

She jots it down in her notepad and looks up at him.

So, TJ, I just wanted to let you know about your mum. I'm a consultant psychiatrist on the ward, and my job is to assess your mum and make sure she is okay and safe before discharging her home.

Okay. When can she leave?

Well, I'd like to keep her in for a couple of days, to monitor her and make sure we can get her back on track.

He pushes his words out through a rising feeling of unease.

Ehm . . . what's . . . wrong with her?

Dr Taylor's voice has a whispery urgency to it. She speaks like her sentences are chasing to keep up with her thoughts.

I spoke with her earlier. And I spoke to the ambulance people who picked her up. She had a mental-health crisis – something you might think of as a nervous breakdown, though we don't use that term anymore.

The lady watches TJ's face. He is trying to process those words. Nervous breakdown. He is trying to keep his face from changing. Break. Down.

TJ.

Dr Taylor turns around to face him and leans in.

Mental-health crises can come in many variations. In Mary's . . . your mum's case, she lost touch with reality. She spent the night in Bedwood Cemetery.

Yeah, I know. That's where she worked, TJ interrupts, feeling the need to assert himself.

Is it where her family is buried?

He hesitates.

Aye. My grandad, I mean, her dad and her mum are both buried there. In the same grave.

I understand, says Dr Taylor, writing in her notepad again.

Why is the skin on her hands all white?

It's from the water. It's like being in the bath for too long.

It'll gradually get back to normal. She was also very cold when she arrived in hospital, which is called hypothermia. We had to help to warm her back up.

Has she still got it?

No, I'm happy to say her temperature is back to normal now, TJ.

Have you got her on drugs? She was seriously spaced out earlier.

They both turn to look at Mary now.

She's been on mild painkillers for a headache. We did also have to give something to help her stay calm as she regains clarity. That will still be in her system now, but hopefully we won't need to give her any more. I can imagine that it was very frightening for her to lose control of herself like that.

Dr Taylor sits back in her chair. TJ notices a small ladder in the side of her tights.

It's my job to make sure she is medically stable and safe. I want her to stay here until I feel confident that she's stabilised. Then I will be referring her to a psychologist. She needs support going forward. There's a lot of grief that needs to be processed.

TJ is silent. His mind is racing.

Dr Taylor is looking at him now.

TJ, we will help her in every way we can. She will need your support, too. I would like to see her reach a point where she would like to help herself.

He answers sharply. My mum never does anything for herself.

Well, Dr Taylor says, with a gentle smile, let's see if we can help her to help herself.

TJ sighs.

She was worried about you when I was talking to her, Dr Taylor continues. I assured her you were on your way and told her you have been really helpful to everyone involved in finding her.

TJ blushes.

I realised about the ashes last night.

Yes. You did well. Has everything been all right at home?

He looks at her suspiciously. What is she getting at?

It's been fine. It's all very . . . out of the blue.

Dr Taylor pulls her lips together and nods. TJ continues.

If she doesn't wake up again, can I stay longer?

Anytime up to six p.m. But she will be sleeping a lot today. She needs to rest. You can come back anytime from nine a.m. tomorrow. The visiting hours are written on the board just outside the door.

TJ finds he doesn't want Dr Taylor to leave. The low vibrato of her voice is comforting and gives him a tiny tingle on the back of his neck. She seems to know everything about his mother, more than he has known in a lifetime. She straightens her skirt and goes to stand up.

So. What, like, what can I do, for her?

She hesitates.

Please tell me what to fucking do, he thinks, and tries to shape his mouth into a smile.

She needs someone who can help her unravel all these suppressed emotions, to help her feel them and figure them out in a safe space, and she can get this in her therapy sessions. I think from her son, she needs love and patience and support. It will take time for her to get better and she needs someone to keep a close eye on her. But you also need to look after yourself, as she needs you to be well and fighting fit, so you can be a support to her.

He nods, staring down at his hands; he can feel his cheeks burning. He knows they will be red, that it will be moving to his neck, like a rash.

I shouldn't leave her, should I?

Were you planning to?

Before he speaks, he looks back at his mother to check she is asleep. Then he locks eyes with Dr Taylor.

I've been seriously thinking about it. But if I do, she has no one left.

Dr Taylor straightens her skirt again.

I think it would be best to get her settled back into the normal routine of her life and into a good support system. Then maybe you could revisit it.

Okay, he says, nodding.

I must head off now, TJ. I will need to ask you some more questions over the next day or two, but why don't we leave it at that for today.

Righto. Thanks.

TJ watches her as she moves away silently. Does everyone have cotton wool on the soles of their shoes or something? He turns back to the bed, letting out a long, slow sigh. It's clear that he is not going to speak to his mother again this morning. A man on the other side of the ward starts crying. TJ cranes his neck to see where it is coming from. It is a long, low keen, a distressing sound that makes him shift his weight in his chair and look around for a nurse to come and see to this man. The whole ward is so quiet. He feels an urge to shout at someone. He can't bear the small outline of his ma, surrounded by all this stark white. This white sheet in this white room full of dulled pain. He allows the tears to fall down his cheeks as he stays staring at his ma, one leg crossed over the other, resting his elbow on his thigh and his chin on his hand.

CHAPTER 43

They walk in silence along the corridor of the hospital towards the light of the exit. TJ is a good foot taller than his mother. They share the same gait, both of them slightly hunched in and leaning into their steps. TJ has a boyish bounce to his strides. Mary takes nearly two steps to every one of his. Once they are outside, the taxi pulls up as if it is waiting just for them.

It is ten-thirty on Tuesday morning, and the roads are quiet after the morning rush to the city centre. The sky is bubblegum blue and stretches out ahead of them invitingly. They sit side by side in the back seat. Mary is enjoying the warmth of the sun on her face as she looks out on the buildings falling away behind them. Her hands are neatly folded on her lap. She is wearing jeans and a jumper and fresh socks that TJ brought for her this morning. He had stood over her underwear drawer, wondering whether he should bring her underpants and a bra, but it felt too intimate a gesture. She never asked him for them, and he didn't want to do anything to make her feel uncomfortable. He is watching her, slyly, trying to get a sense of how she is feeling.

You stay on this road for ages now, he says, as they turn on to the dual carriageway.

Mary looks at him sideways. Her face is scrubbed clean. He can see fresh lines around her eyes. She speaks softly.

I guess you know this journey well by now.

I only got a taxi the first time. But the new Glider is class, so it is; it goes right from the hospital up to the roundabout. Honestly, you'll love it.

He looks back at her, catching her nod and smile. He looks back out the window of the cab. He thinks of the trip to Donaghadee the day before, with Aiden, to pick up the car. Sitting on the train, with the envelope in his pocket with her car keys in it. Of how he asked Aiden to wait on the road while he walked down to the beach and took it all in. The tide was way out and the sand stank of dead fish. There was a pile of crushed cans of beer and an empty box of Marlboro Lights washed into the rushes. When he tiptoed through the wet sand so as not to dirty his trainers, and swept his fingers through the shallows, the coldness of the water stung his flesh. He had to move quickly after that, so as not to get upset. He was happy for Aiden's chatter all the way home. He thinks of the house now. Of how clean it all is. How he hoovered and dusted and put flowers by her bed. He speaks again.

I'm just happy to be bringing you home.

God, me too. I don't think I've ever been so idle in my life.

Well Ma, guess what, everything has survived without you. Your plants are still alive.

Did you water them?

She looks at him again, in surprise.

I did. Not a lot, but just a little – enough to not die, I guess?

That's enough, she says.

Mary and TJ are in the kitchen on a grey, drizzle-soaked morning. TJ has been present in the kitchen every morning since his mother's return three weeks ago. He sits, naked from the waist up, leaning over the table, scrolling through his phone; a roll of stomach flesh folded over the elasticated waistband of his tracksuit bottoms. The peony tree is on the windowsill and its leaves point upwards towards the ceiling, glossy and full. Mary has been spraying and wiping the surfaces and is halfway through emptying and cleaning the contents of the baking cupboard. Suddenly she turns to face him.

TJ. I need to speak with you.

He looks up from his phone immediately. She is leaning against the kitchen counter. Her hands grip the sideboard and she is leaning back into it, bouncing her body off her hands. Her face is imploring.

Course, Ma. What's up? He looks concerned.

I need to tell you something.

She takes a deep breath.

All my life, I wanted to know my mother. I asked my father

a few times, but he never wanted to talk about her. Asking him about her felt dangerous, as if I could really upset him, and I didn't want to do that. I was so angry with him after he died. So angry.

TJ is staring at her intensely. He leans forward over the kitchen table, pushing his phone and breakfast cereal bowl out of the way. Mary swallows and continues.

At Sean's funeral, your . . . The man who I had you with. He came to it. Totally out of the blue. It's the first time I'd seen him since . . . since before you were born.

TJ is furiously trying to think.

But . . . I thought he didn't want to know us? He's in America?

TJ. I didn't know where he was. I said he was in America because I thought it would be too hard for you if you knew he lived in the same city.

He lives in Belfast? TJ says softly.

I don't know. I don't know where he lives. He lived here when I knew him. But that was so long ago. And then he just arrived at the funeral.

Was he one of the four men?

Yes. He was the shorter man who lit up a cigarette when they were walking away.

Her voice is just a fraction louder than a whisper.

TJ lays his palms flat on the table top, eyes stretched wide. He sees the man again, short and stocky, holding his cigarette like a dart. He blinks slowly towards the tabletop.

Why didn't you tell me?

Because I had to get my head around seeing him. You see, me and him, we never loved each other. I never even knew him to love him. We only ever slept together the once.

And he fucked off? And left you?

Well, yes, he did. But something happened that changed things between us.

So, what happened?

Sean. You see, he was Sean's friend. Sean was raging when I told him that I got pregnant with his friend. He went out and found him and . . . and beat him.

A lone tear is rolling down her face. She is looking at the floor.

TJ is trying to imagine his Uncle Sean beating someone up. His blank face, the indentation of his backside on his sofa.

He beat him up very badly, TJ.

She sniffs and breathes in deeply.

I saw him once after that. He was on crutches, in the city centre. We never spoke. He walked away from me.

TJ is staring at his mother.

So, Uncle Sean beat up my father for getting you pregnant? Yes.

And weren't you mad at him?

I didn't want to believe it. That he could do something like that. I did believe it in the end, and I buried it. I was so focused on you and making sure you were okay. I just put all my energy into that.

And you never thought about finding him again?

No. I didn't bring it up with Sean.

What's it to do with Sean?

Mary looks at her son. He is sitting bolt upright. She can see faint tan lines on his arms and around his collar.

Why'd you have to let him rule you like that? Why didn't you ring the police?

There is a long pause. Her voice wavers.

He was my big brother. I just accepted that it had to be that way, and Danny never tried to get in contact again . . .

Danny?

The kitchen is silent, apart from the low rumble of the dishwasher. TJ is staring at her.

Is that his name?

Yes. She is whispering again.

His name is Danny Donnelly.

TJ sits back into his chair. His face is white. He is shaking his head.

Ma. How. The. Fuck. Have you never told me this?

I'm sorry. That's all I can say, TJ. I'm sorry.

Why did he come to the funeral?

Mary squeezes her eyes shut and releases a stream of tears down her face. She knew as soon as she saw him from a distance, walking into the crematorium. She knew those thick legs, that swagger. She was aware of his eyes on her and TJ's back the whole way through the service. Afterwards, she told herself that she would be mature, she would remain calm. She made sure they were a safe distance from TJ. Danny wore an ill-fitted grey suit that had a subtle shine to the cloth. It did not complement his complexion. His head was completely bald and shining with sweat. He walked up to her and shook her hand, like they had just become acquainted.

It took all her strength to not turn and sprint away over the stones. She kept seeing his face right over hers, sweating and panting. As she put her hand in his to shake, she felt the pain of him again. It was such a visceral reaction that she looked down at her groin. She had to hold it together. She didn't want him to see her frightened. She turned away from him and saw her son lighting a cigarette, hands cupped over his face to shelter the cigarette from the wind. Danny was looking at him too, with a ferocious intensity.

I'm glad he didn't get the short gene, he said, squinting into the sunlight.

She couldn't speak.

She could smell the faint musk of an aftershave. He was talking at her.

Mary.

Her lips would not move. She felt flimsy and aerated, like she might be caught in a breeze and dragged along the gravel like the fluffy duck feathers by the lake. She tried to concentrate on her weight on her feet; the solid form of herself pushing down on to the ground. Danny cleared his throat.

I'm here because your brother has meant a lot to my life. Both before and after he attacked me. Before, because I believed him to be my friend; and after, because I was in fear of him. I have spent the last eighteen years looking over my shoulder. I have been in years of physiotherapy for my leg and my hip, and years of therapy because of my PTSD.

You must be relieved, she said.

I would like to know my son. He was staring at her then, and she noticed that he was trembling ever so slightly.

She dropped her head and closed her eyes. What about me, she wanted to scream. What about me?

I haven't even buried my brother yet.

Of course. You've a lot to get through. Could I take a number for you, so I can contact you down the line?

He was taking his phone out of the breast pocket of his blazer. She watched him type in the letters of her name into his contacts and hand the phone to her. She remembered the birthday card, his shaky handwritten letters.

She had to concentrate on keeping her fingers from trembling as she typed her number in.

She looks up at her son now. TJ is looking at her with such a frightened expression that she wants to curl up in bed with him like she did when he was a toddler. To stroke his nose until his eyelids fall shut.

He came to the funeral, to find me, I guess. So that he could find you. He took my phone number.

She thinks of that missed call on that Friday night. Of her son holding her phone, coming so close to speaking to his father. How Danny called again an hour later, and she sat on her bed watching her phone screen light up with his number, the last four digits, seven-four-seven-eight, and then go dark again. How he rang back nearly immediately, as if to say, I'm going to give you another chance here, Mary. Don't do this again. She thinks of how many missed calls she had in her phone next to his number. Six months of missed calls, from Sean's funeral to the Friday night she left the house, each one another brick in the wall of terror building up around her. She turned the phone off and lay on her bed for hours, with her heart thumping through her chest. She held a pillow over her face and pushed it down as hard as she could until she saw stars swirling in the black. When she went to pick up the urn, her hands were so wet with sweat that it slid around in her palms. When she ran out of the house, she thought about driving up to the top of Black Mountain and driving off the edge of it. But her arms steered her down the hill, past the golf course and on to the main road towards Bedwood.

She takes a deep breath and blows it out slowly. Then focuses her eyes on TJ again.

He rang me. That Friday night. He rang me and I just, I wasn't ready to talk to him. But I will. I will for you. If you want.

TJ's mouth is hanging open.

I would like to meet my father.

She breaks down into sobs then, her hands still clinging to the sideboard behind her. TJ covers his face with his hands and his shoulders twitch as he weeps.

I'm so sorry, love.

You lied to me, all my fucking life.

She goes to him, hands outstretched towards him, but he stands up quickly and pushes past her.

TJ.

She calls to him as he walks out of the room.

CHAPTER 44

Mary curses herself for not wearing her warm coat as she pulls the door shut behind her. Her jaw is tense, her cheeks tracked with dried tears.

Today's session was draining. Her outpatient psychologist is called Katie. She is an older woman, in her fifties, with drooping skin around her eyes and cropped silver hair. She is comfortable with silence, unbothered by tears, and Mary is learning to be okay with both of these things. When she arrived for her first session, she stood in the reception area and noticed a large framed poster of the sea, with a wave cresting and catching the light of the sun before it crashed on to the water below. At first she thought it was a bad omen, but now she sees it as a symbol of her journey. She was trying to soak herself clean.

Be kind to yourself today, Katie said to Mary before she closed the door behind her. Mary has discovered a pattern in her behaviour after these sessions. First, her thoughts always drift to the old folks' home where Freddie, Dolores's husband, stayed until he died. She remembers sitting with Dolores through these visits, in that strangely muted room, with the smell of cleaning chemicals and potpourri. Freddie only ever spoke about the first few decades of his life; his youth in its most raw form. It was memories of meals that his mother made, the animals on his father's farm, childhood games. He existed exclusively in his own personal showreel of sun-kissed memories. It was pragmatic in a way. He found the parts of his life that weren't painful and tried to experience them again and again. Freddie didn't want to be reminded of the ugliness of now.

Mary realises that she is going through this in reverse. She wants to charge forwards all the time, away from her childhood, but Katie is urging her to stop and turn around, to excavate her past, without the luxury of selective memories. She must confront the ugliness of *then*. She is digging things up from deep inside her consciousness and dusting them off and looking at them from every angle. Things that are rough to the touch. Things that can tear her open. She has found that after her sessions with Katie, she has an overwhelming need to hide from the noises and interruptions of the world, somewhere quiet and warm. Somewhere safe.

She exhales and reaches up to tuck her hair behind her ears. It is shorter now, stopping at her shoulders, after a tentative visit to the hairdresser two weeks ago. *Be kind to yourself.* She is off to meet Sid this evening, for fish and chips at Buss

Buildings. But what now? If she was her father, she would go straight to the pub. Maybe she could go for a nice coffee. She looks to the end of the street, to the back entrance of CastleCourt Shopping Centre. She stretches out her arms over her head and takes a big deep breath through her nose, catching the faint fruity smell of shampoo from her hair after her shower at the gym this morning.

Driving home from the gym, she'd had a sudden notion that she would take TJ to the Botanic Gardens. She had picked him up from the house, promising a stop for food and coffee on the way. They walked down the main path, sunbeams cutting through the branches above.

Well, the leaves are well and truly down, Mary muttered.

They looked up at the threadbare branches and then their heads moved in perfect sync down to the ground. It was covered in a brown blanket of leaves, pulled into textured mounds by the wind.

Are you dying to go and pick them up, Ma? TJ said, smiling down at her.

Ha, ha, she replied. But she had felt an urge to fill her hands with the wet density of the leaves. She would ring McKee soon. There would be no reference to her absence, just a gruff greeting and a new assignment, and that suited her.

They paused to sit on her old bench. TJ busied himself taking food out of a plastic bag while Mary blinked behind her sunglasses.

I used to come here when I was your age, TJ. This was my bench.

On your own? he said, unwrapping a sandwich from a packet and handing it to her.

Yes. After school. I hated going home. It was lonelier there.

He took a bite of his sandwich and looked towards the square of grass before them, chewing and thinking. He swallowed his mouthful and turned to her.

Ma. Danny. What was he like? Like, when you did know him?

She was deep in thought.

I really didn't know him well, love. He looked up to Sean a lot. He was small and I think he wished he was taller. He seemed nice enough.

And when you spoke to him at the funeral?

He seemed angry and nervous. He said he has been in therapy all his life for what Sean did to him.

Jesus, TJ said, staring down at his trainers.

She closed her eyes under her sunglasses and put her hand out to TJ's thigh, squeezing it.

Can you tell him to call me? I'm ready to speak to him.

She looked at him then, taking him all in. Her son, who couldn't look at her for days after she told him about her lie. Who, when he slowly began to talk to her again, was desperate to feel out the idea of having a father he could touch, a father he could know. She noticed the little cluster of whiteheads tucked into the corner of his nose, his freshly shaven chin, his big heavy eyebrows frowning over half-closed eyes from the brightness of the sun.

Okay, love. I'll do that tonight.

And she will. Katie has helped her figure out what she wants to say and how to say it. There will be a new family for her son; aunts and uncles and cousins and grandparents and maybe even half-siblings. On his mother's side, there is only his mother. But she can be enough. She pulls her bag tight across her shoulder and walks down the road.

As she approaches the pedestrian crossing, a woman is walking out of the car park across the road, towards her. Mary knows this person. She is swinging a biker jacket over her shoulders and pushing her arms into the sleeves. When both arms are in, she straightens herself up and stops at the other side of the pedestrian crossing. Her head moves left to right, checking for cars, until her eyes catch on Mary, who is standing still now, directly opposite her, staring.

Mary watches Louise's expression change as they lock eyes. The tiniest flash of shock, then pain. Then a quick reset into polite surprise. Mary can't say anything at all. Time seems to expand and contract; her childhood memories are raw and exposed in her head after therapy and she can see young Louise vividly in them, her overbite and her skinny legs, her honking laugh, radiating heat and joy. These memories wash over her and she knows that this woman standing across the road, this Louise, whoever she is now, was always the light in the darkness of them.

They stare at each other. A woman in a car that has been waiting for them to cross gives up, and drives between them to turn into the car park. They stare until Louise's eyebrows drop and her face breaks into an enormous smile. Mary feels the force of it sweep through her like a slow rush. She steps off the pavement towards her.

ACKNOWLEDGEMENTS

To the warm and generous people of Belfast who helped this forgetful Dubliner to remember the city I love so much.

Gil Stewart – thank you for stopping in your van for a chat that day at the cemetery. You were such an inspiration in this whole process.

Caitriona Lambe, for giving me so much of your time, all of the time, and sharing your extensive historical knowledge with me. You are an oracle!

Maeve Hughes and Claire Boyle, thank you for your generosity in sharing your stories, and Mary Boyle, for your tea and your scones!

Tiernan Boyle, for your very valued perspective and your honesty. I so appreciate it.

Susanna Hislop – your wisdom, fairness and encouragement allowed this book to exist. My times with you never felt long enough.

Ben Dunn, thank you for your enthusiasm. You helped me to believe that my mess of words could be a saleable book. You made me so happy that I cried in a city bar!

Kate Stephenson, you took a punt on my writing when no one else would. I hope I don't let you down.

Ella Gordon, thank you for your continued help and encouragement in editing this book and for being a constant source of calm around my whirlwinds of panic.

To my first readers, Ben Dunn, Rosetta Macmanus, Janet and Douglas Bell, thank you for your criticism.

Becky Walker, my beautiful friend, thank you for your unwavering enthusiasm and encouragement from the first draft and throughout this whole process.

To Mary Ni Lochlainn – you went above and beyond, as always. Thanks for lending me your medical expertise.

Andrew Antonio, thank you for your inspiring conversations!

Oliver Sasse and Lucy Coates, for your guidance, and Megan Carver, for being the overseer!

To my husband Tom, thank you for allowing me all those hours of family time to go away and write – and, most importantly, thank you for not asking any questions.